THE MASKS WE WEAR

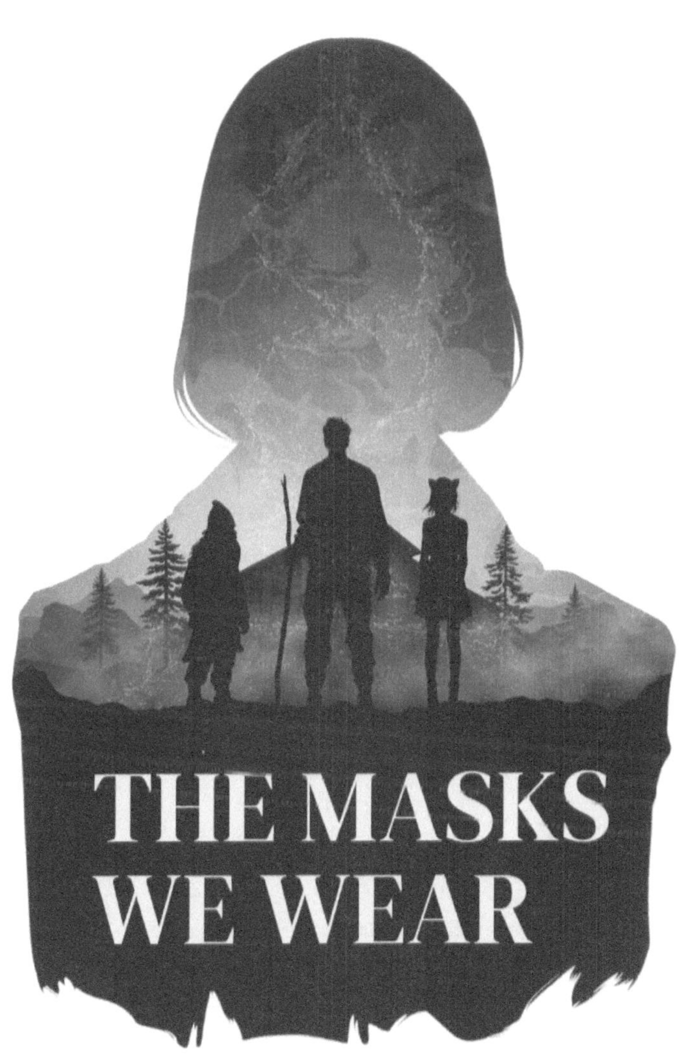

THE MASKS WE WEAR

B.D. CARPENTER

First paperback edition April 2024

Book edited by Devon Atwood
Book design by Rubre Art

ISBN 979-8-9899363-0-4 (paperback)
ISBN 979-8-9899363-1-1 (ebook)

Trigger Warning

Welcome readers,

Within these pages, you will find a world that looks like our own and a cast of characters that, for the most part, feel like us. We are all flawed in some ways and have our strengths in others, just like them.

You will find **curse words** and topics of **bullying, stalking, parental verbal/mental abuse, medical trauma, mention of sexually explicit materials,** and **sexual language**. None of the topics are intended to be graphic or triggering, but each individual has their own level of resilience and are on their own path of healing. Remember to practice good self-care.

To my loving husband and best friend,

Your creativity shines brighter and is deeper than any ley line. You made this entire magic system without the use of a Gnome-hold. If that's not some kind of false-Kin ability, I'm not sure what is.

Love,

B

CONTENTS

PART
ONE

CHAPTER ONE

NOT THAT KIND OF BARISTA

Concealment and Discretion: Maintaining a low profile is crucial to avoid drawing unnecessary attention and potential discrimination.

MEEP

You know the saying, "Fake it 'til you make it?" Sometimes, I thought I had pretended to be a human for so long I had become one. They also say, "You are what you eat." They say a lot of things; I never ate a human, though, and that might be my problem. That said, if anyone found out I was a Lynx, if they saw what I really was, they'd probably burn me alive. "Humans tend to set fire to things they don't understand." That was a line drilled into me every day growing up.

"Don't be too flashy."

"Don't be too capable."

"Don't stand out."

Live a boring life.

So, there I was, at Clair's Eclairs, slinging coffee to college kids. Clair—whom I'd never met, and after three years, was not sure was even a real person—had wisely decided to open the town's only twenty-four-hour coffee house to better serve the sleep-deprived college population. Usually, it was quiet here, with no rush or urgency in the air. Working here wasn't *un*pleasant, for a food service job, but it wasn't exactly my long-term goal. I was good at it; I knew the business inside and out and had been given the creative freedom to create weekly specials. The hardest part of working here, working anywhere really, was to pretend to be something I was not: Clumsy. Humans were *not* so graceful.

As I cleaned the counter, I thought of the second hardest part of working here—the societal expectations of being a young woman, just barely an adult. Be demure. Be small. Be weak. Be subservient. *Fuck that.* Has society ever *met* a woman? Because no woman I knew would be content with that life. Sure, I'd seen stories online suggesting maybe some ladies liked to live that way. If that was how one really chose to live and that made her happy— yay—but that couldn't ever be me. I wanted something more in my life that would spark my interest and keep me engaged. But "excitement" was exactly the kind of career path I was supposed to avoid. I slammed the towel into the cleaning bucket with a bit more force than necessary. *Great, I irritated myself.*

My mood soured even more as I heard the shuffling gait of my least favorite customer outside. He wasn't a bad person. Not like a permanently pissed-off asshole, or an entitled elitist, but he was awkward. Cringingly uncomfortable. He missed the mark of being suave and charming by a wide margin, but that didn't stop him from trying.

The bell tinkled over the door, and Jeremy sauntered in, greasy black hair pulled low over one eye. Cowlicks left craters in the back of his head, screaming to the world that this was not how he usually wore his hair. Who was he trying to impress? Hopefully, not me. I liked men who showered.

But I plastered on a smile in my best impersonation of a customer service automaton. "Good morning. What are you having today?"

"Well, hey there, Meep-Meep. What's a beautiful girl like you doing in a place like this?"

My smile didn't falter, yet I inwardly flinched at his body odor as the sharp stench of rotten broccoli hit my sensitive nose. He had used this line at least once a week, and I hated it when he called me "Meep-Meep." It reminded me of the old cartoons where I was the bird to be chased, and he was the hapless coyote who could never catch up. Yet, he sure kept trying. "What can I get for you this morning, Jeremy?" I asked, trying to keep the exasperation out of my voice.

"I will have whatever you had this morning to make you so *fine.*"

This was another line he had used on nearly a daily basis for the past two years. I thought about giving him a book of one hundred and one pickup lines just to hear something new occasionally, however, giving him *anything* might send the wrong message.

At first, he was more overt with me, asking for my number, when to pick me up, and even what I liked in bed. I put a stop to it with a threat, a well-practiced *look,* and enough physical force to scare him into a semblance of respect. I would've smiled at the thought of it, but he would've thought it was for him.

"Okay, one mocha snot iced coffee with vanilla boogies, coming up," I said.

Jeremy frowned as I turned towards the coffee machine, intentionally bumping into the edge of the counter with my hip as I remembered to move more like a human and less like myself.

He always feigned being adventurous, but then ordered the same thing every day anyway, and we both knew it—one large white chocolate Americano with amaretto, whipped cream, and a dash of cinnamon to make it pretty. I tried it once while he wasn't here to see me, and I had to admit it was tasty. It just seemed like I shouldn't drink it on principle.

After Jeremy slunk away, back to classes, or his cave, or whatever, my morning proceeded as normal. Boring and snail-paced. Disgustingly plain. Just a steady stream of bleary-eyed people hoping that a hit of espresso would change their outlook on life. I would have been happier if I'd had a coworker, someone I could talk to, bitch at, or collaborate with. But no.

In a fantastic turn of events, my best friend, Jessie, arrived to keep me company. She was the opposite of me in many ways. Long blonde hair to my short, dark pixie-cut, and her piercing crystal blue eyes contrasted with my deep amber ones. She wore her usual ripped and loose-fitted jeans, and a tight tank top with the TARDIS still visible despite the cracked and faded vinyl. While pouring her a black coffee, I concentrated on adding a subtle tremor to my hand in order to maintain the illusion of being just as human as she was.

I sat next to her at the countertop bar.

"So..." Jessie placed both hands on the countertop, palms down. "You broke up with... who's his name? James, was it? That's like the third guy in less than two months."

I sighed. "His name was Brian. And yeah. Last night... he said he wanted kids one day."

"Meep. I love you like a sister, and I would never want you to stay in an unsafe situation, but you can't break up with everyone for being nice to you. This is a small town. You are going to run out of guys to date."

I shrugged. "I guess I'll date girls then."

"We've already heard about how you treat the boys. Why would we want to date you?" she asked with mock severity.

"I don't care who I date, or even *if* I date. I am not even twenty yet. Do you think I want to settle down and start having babies already? Like my mom? No, thank you. I want to *do* something with my life. To *be* someone. At least something more than an extra paycheck to keep the house afloat."

Jessie sipped her coffee, pinky out. "Why, Meep, I'm shocked. You don't normally talk this much."

My face heated. "I guess I'm in a mood today."

She placed her mug on the counter. I noticed it was empty, so I reached for the pitcher of strong, black coffee I kept on standby, mostly for her and a few of the elderly people who came in. When I finished filling her mug, she said, "What I don't understand is, if you want to be someone, why do you seem to work so hard at being nobody at all?"

I froze halfway into settling back onto my stool.

She continued. "You have a great family, a great support system, and so much talent. I have seen you do some amazing things when you think no one is looking, like—"

"So, what's your point?" I topped off my own coffee for something to do after cutting her off. I didn't want her to continue that line of thought. Jessie had spent the most amount of time with me, basically every day, so she was bound to have seen something at some point. Had she seen me leap a ten-foot tree to rescue Old Man Mark's favorite cat? I hadn't thought she'd been looking, but she might have been. Or had she seen me walk that tightrope without any apparent training that year a circus band set up outside of town? Or was she simply talking about my gymnastics routines being good?

Jessie was still speaking. "... you can do incredible things, and yet you can't take being in a healthy relationship."

Oh. Of course, that's what this was about. I sighed.

"Anyway, you have been in gymnastics your whole life, and you haven't even won one competition? I've seen you practice. I'm no official judge or anything, but it looks damn near flawless to me. Why do you keep fumbling competitions? If you want to be someone, why not be the person you were meant to be and be an Olympian or something?"

Damn. There it was. Today was the day I had to lie to my one and only friend.

The truth was that some of those humans at the Olympics I could not be completely sure they *weren't* Lynxes. But wouldn't it be tantamount to cheating if I even thought about going to the Olympics? Knowing what I was, it wouldn't be fair to the humans who had worked so hard to get there on their own.

Gymnastics allowed me to use my gifts without drawing unnecessary attention to my abilities. Foot placement was never a concern because my instincts guided me effortlessly; the concept of falling was foreign to me, and I had never even sprained an ankle. It was a perfect cover for a Lynx child because it allowed me to avoid all sorts of awkward questions like, *where did she learn how to do that?* or, *why shouldn't I light her on fire for being different?*

But I couldn't even tell her that. I couldn't be honest with my friend. This was what I had feared. This was why I had kept every-one at arm's length. But humans—and cats—are social creatures. I needed at least one friend... but I had hoped this day would never come. The day I had to flat out lie to her.

She wasn't a Lynx, but her aura exuded a wildness that was

both captivating and mysterious, and I indulged in a fantasy that maybe she wasn't too different from me. That was a fruitless line of thought, though. I knew better. Goblins, vampires, fairies, and any other fantastical creatures were figments of the imagination. There was only Lynx, and Not Lynx. Only *us*, and not *us*.

My mother had prepared me for this. Prepared me for the lie I would have to tell people when they started asking questions. Step one: Change the subject. Step two: Remove yourself from the situation.

I stood to get back to work and glanced at Jessie, still sitting on the bar stool. "I am satisfied with just being with myself. That's all that's supposed to matter, right?" I gave her a smile, hoping she would not see how weak it was.

Jessie shook her head sadly. "Meep, I love you. Never stop being you."

I rounded the counter and said, "I love you too. I couldn't live without you." I knew she hated compliments like that, and I *loathed* myself for tapping into that insecurity. She deserved so much better.

Even though she often told me she loved me, when I returned the sentiment, she always clammed up for a while. For some reason, she seemed to think she could love me, but somehow, felt undeserving of the same love in return.

My mom had told me that because Jessie grew up in foster care, she might have felt this way sometimes, and to give her time and space. Mom was pretty great that way. She had always treated Jessie with love and always welcomed her into our home. I used to argue with Mom when I was little about wanting to officially make Jessie another sister and adopt her, but Mom always said Jessie wasn't a Lynx, so adopting her would be too awkward. It was many resentful years before I realized Mom was probably right. She never used the excuse of having too many kids though, which I later appreciated.

Jessie sat in silence for a long time, and I cleaned machines. Eventually, she relaxed, and we discussed some of the hot celebrity gossip spreading like wildfire around social media. "Oh, also did you hear about the argument between Pete and Linda? I bet the whole town knows by now. Right in the street, she screamed at him for screwing her cousin at their uncle's funeral!"

I loved how Jessie talked and talked. I only needed to smile and laugh in the appropriate spots. She carried on the whole conversation all by herself. It was so peaceful; I didn't have to invent a thing.

Hours after Jessie had left, a small gray-haired man appeared, standing behind a woman who had just received her order. I leaned over the counter, trying to glimpse his face beneath the rounded top of his hat, one of those pilot-type hats with floppy ear flaps on the sides. His wire-rimmed glasses constantly shifted, magnifying his eyes, and then drawing back until his pupils were tiny dots. The way each eye zoomed in and back out at different rates gave him a disconcerting, otherworldly appearance.

"I require hydration. What do the locals drink?" he asked instead of any introduction while tapping on his tablet.

I blinked. I had never seen anyone like this man before. Why was he talking like he was from *Star Trek*? Maybe he's foreign. Maybe English was not his first language, and his tablet was a poor translating device? He smelled odd, though. Like ozone, sort of metallic and clean. And those curled-up boots...

"Uh, the Sunrise Class is popular," I said in a voice I hoped hid my confusion. "It has caramel and oat milk in it."

The small man said absolutely nothing else, with no sign he

wanted the drink or even that he had said anything to me in the first place. He stared at me with those unnerving eyes enlarging and shrinking until it became very, very uncomfortable. With an effort, I turned away to make the drink, which was the most unsettling feeling I had ever had. If I'd had fur, it would have stood on end.

I kept my ears on him; my ability to hear things others could not was like my second sight. I did not hear him move. No footsteps scraping against the linoleum. No rustling of cloth. Not even the slight sound of his breathing. My muscles worked by memory, pouring caramel, mixing flavoring into the steaming coffee, and stirring. This guy had shaken me, and I didn't know why. He was only some foreign dude with weird clothes and a faulty translator, right?

But somewhere in the back of my head, I thought of how humans normally smelled. Everyone smelled slightly awful, to be honest, a byproduct of the pollution around them coming from cars and capitalism. Even in this small mountain town, the pollution scent was everywhere and on everything. Yet, this guy smelled wholly clean, like he had never been around any pollution his entire life.

When I turned to hand him the finished drink—figuring if he didn't want it, I could evidently use it myself because I must have been dreaming—I jumped backwards, startled to discover him at the other end of the counter, five feet away. There was no way he hadn't made even the *slightest* sound without me hearing it. He had made so much noise when he'd come in that the silence now was doubly unnerving.

I swallowed hard and approached him cautiously, glad the counter separated us, and extended the coffee towards him, refusing to let my hands tremble with fear. I locked my eyes on his and calmly said, "It's $5.75."

He gave me a crisp hundred-dollar bill, took the cup with both hands, and then finally asked my name.

"Meep." My voice was shakier than I wanted it to be, and I cursed myself. *Damnit, stay in control.*

"What is your sex?"

"Female." My eyes shifted around. *Yup, I'm alone.* At that moment, I would even have been grateful to have Jeremy there. For now, at least I had a longer reach than him. "Is this for a class?"

"What is your age?"

I considered leaping for the exit and abandoning this café. Whomever Clair was, I was sure she'd understand. "Eighteen."

"What is your allegiance?"

What the fuck? "Sir, I feel uncomfortable." I pushed his change towards him, or rather, by the top of his head. "I would appreciate it if you left now."

"What is your allegiance?" he repeated in the same flat tone as he had been using for all the other questions. He had raised his arm and tapped at a bulky watch.

"Earth." I edged closer toward the end of the counter, where my purse and cell phone were.

"How many people are in your household?"

"Excuse me?"

"How many people are in your household? Your cooperation is required."

"Yeah? Who is it required *for*, though?" I pulled my phone out of my bag and held it to my ear. "I am asking you to leave or I will call the cops."

I pressed the emergency button on the home screen and my phone started dialing. He stared back at me, completely unfazed. I blinked, and...

He was gone.

He had taken the coffee, leaving the change on the counter.

My mind spun with possibilities. Who was that guy? What did he want? Would I ever see him again? I suppressed a shudder. *I will be prepared for him next time.*

What was with this $94 tip? Had he left it intentionally? He had to have. Ninety-four dollars was much too large for a tip. Even for one of those lucky, bikini-wearing baristas who made gobs of money in campy drive-through coffee stands. *Maybe I should give Jeremy the heads up that those things exist. No. Never mind. Those girls do* not *deserve that.*

The way I saw it, if the weird guy really wasn't from America, and he hadn't understood American currency, then this had all been a big misunderstanding. Or this large tip was bribe money to buy my silence for him to be intentionally creepy. Either way, I didn't want to take it. If it was the former reason, then taking the money seemed dishonest, like taking advantage of him. And if it was the latter reason, then it was gross, and I had principles.

Many things defined me, and at times, a drunken farmer might have calibrated my moral compass, but I had never accepted bribes to condone misbehavior. A girl's got to set her boundaries.

CHAPTER TWO

DUDE, WHERE'S MY HAT?

Human Appearance: Adopt a human appearance as much as possible. Pay attention to hairstyles, clothing choices, and overall grooming to match human fashion trends.

BEAU

"Where's my hat?" I asked my roommate, Kyle, as I dug through piles of dirty clothes and scattered notebooks. It wasn't a mess. I knew where everything was. Well, I should have known where everything was.

"How should I know? You never take the thing off," Kyle replied, lounging on top of his neatly made bed. His nose, as always, was in a book.

"It must have fallen off while I was asleep or something." I rummaged through a pile of aluminum plates and wires, though it clearly wasn't under them.

"You are going to be late. Can't you look for it later?" Kyle reluctantly looked up from his book, clearly annoyed that I was interrupting him.

"I mean... I guess." I couldn't articulate why I needed my hat. There was just something right about a good hat. I felt naked without it. I couldn't expect a *human* to understand. I pulled at my beard in frustration.

I quickly glanced at Kyle's side of the room, which made it clear my hat wasn't over there. Books lined his shelves, organized alphabetically, and everything else was tucked neatly away. Nope, definitely not over there.

A large shadow fell over the open door. "What's the matter, nerd? Lose somethin'?" Chud asked with his Texas twang as he loomed in the doorway. His body language oozed confidence as he taunted me with a smirk. I tilted my head to meet his gaze. His massive frame seemed to be twice the size it should be.

I groaned in exasperation. "What did you do with it, Chud?"

"Me? Nothing. I'm just a concerned rubbernecker. Why would you think I was involved, Beauregard?" I hated the way he sneered my name like it was a dirty curse. Like his name was any better. *Chuuud.* It sounded like something a cow would do.

I *preferred* Beau; I knew my full name was a mouthful, and the diminutive form was far more efficient. Chud, though, seemed to have mistaken my preference for brevity for a dislike. I liked my name. I could see it on a plaque labeling my statue, standing in front of the engineering firm I will have founded: Beauregard Artemis Reginald Cornelius. It was a name deserving of awe and respect, befitting a man who would change the world. That was, if

I could manage to pass my lame math classes.

"Maybe ya wouldn't lose stuff if ya kept your eyes to ya'self and off *my* girl," Chud said.

Ah. He had noticed me looking at "his girl," even though we both knew he and Samantha weren't officially a couple. He thought I would back off if he put on some pressure? By stealing my hat? My hat was like my child. How low could you go? This guy gave a bad name to humans. I hated bullies. Gnomes didn't bully other people... Well, at least my family didn't. I'd never met any other Gnomes, actually.

They say a bully wants a reaction from you, so ignoring them will make them go away. Maybe. But in my personal experience with bullies, ignoring them simply never worked. *It tells them to escalate to get a reaction out of you.* A dangerous game. No, bullies prey on those they perceive to be weak. Best to disabuse them of that notion posthaste.

I had to figure out how to deal with this. Fighting was clearly not an option. He was over twice my size. Yet, letting him get away with bullying me would just encourage more of this in the future. Alright, step one was to rob him of his victory. Step two, get to class... I could worry about step three later.

"Oh well, it's not important. Now I can get a new hat." I let excitement color my voice and Chud's cocky grin wavered, clearly not expecting indifference.

I grabbed the nearest gadget, an automatic shirt folder I made last week, and thrust it at Chud's chest. He shifted his balance as he used both arms to cradle the object like he would a football. I squeezed past him into the hallway. "Bring this to Samantha," I said, patting his biceps like a good dog before hurrying away.

I dashed down the hall and hoped Kyle was paying enough attention when I left to describe the look on Chud's face after I bested him in our little stand-off. Outside, I clipped my helmet on, glad to have something on my head again, and took off on my electric scooter at full speed. A glance at my watch confirmed I was already late, but I still stopped briefly to pet the stray dog and dig out a packet of crackers I snagged from the dining hall. "Good boy."

The teacher was writing on the whiteboard as I entered, and I slid into my customary seat in the back, unnoticed by anyone other than Jeremy.

"There you are. Why are you late? And why are you still wearing your helmet?" he hissed at me.

"Chud stole my hat," I whispered back.

Jeremy was only a little taller than myself, and much more overweight than I was. He also had greasy black hair, a neck beard, and let's not start on his smell. I turned my attention to the board. Equations filled it, and I sighed internally. I hated math. This surprised people because I had a reputation for being a complete nerd. Except math just made no sense to me. Oh sure, I could solve an equation as well as the next guy, but ugh... it took so long. There were so many steps. It was so pointless.

Yet, engineers had to do the math... *apparently*. Kyle was the mathematician, not me. Why couldn't we just leave the calculations to him while I made things that worked?

I noted the equations while the professor discussed how to calculate the load weight of various materials for construction.

See? Pointless. Just make it strong enough. Period. Why did we need these equations to show our work for something so obvious? Was it to showboat? To prove, theoretically, our design was worth something? Just build it and let whoever test it with their own hands. Simple.

But I needed to do the math to pass the class. And I needed the class to get a degree. And I needed the degree to be an engineer—it made humans feel better or something. Becoming an engineer was the first step toward my mission of changing the world. And I needed to change the world to get the statue.

So many hoops. Just like math. It was aggravating.

I left the building, walking alongside Jeremy. The cool fall air was normally refreshing, but without my hat, it was just uncomfortable.

"Chud stole your hat? Really?" Jeremy sounded skeptical as he continued our conversation. Chud was his roommate, and although they were not friends, he clearly didn't think theft was in Chud's wheelhouse. "I didn't even think he was smart enough to pull off a heist."

"I'm not sure how he did it. It was on my head when I went to sleep."

"He broke into your dorm room at night? Creepy."

"Disturbing is more like it. I'll have to set up some safeguards." I stopped in my tracks and tilted my head.

A man ahead of us was talking to a couple of other students while tapping away on a tablet. He was a three-foot-tall figure with a hooked nose and a gray, pointed beard wearing a patterned yellow and orange outfit with curly-toed boots, and to top it off, something like an aviator hat on his diminutive head.

Now, this was certainly an unusual enough sight, yet I was staring for an entirely different reason. An old saying my mom used to say came back to me. "Gnome knows Gnome." Well, this guy screamed Gnome.

Every subtle detail I knew to look for was present to a grossly exaggerated degree. I expected Gnomes to be short, usually about five feet tall, like me. But this guy seemed to be more like three feet. There were some distinctive facial features if you knew what to look for, but his face was like a caricature. We often had a quirky fashion sense, but this guy's tastes seemed outlandish with his bright orange coat and silver boots with curled toes, like elf shoes. It was like a parody of Gnomes. Every detail that might identify him to others of his species was exaggerated and on obvious display.

The strange man finished his conversation and then noticed us staring. He approached with a brisk, purposeful walk, his curly-toed boots jingling like bells.

"What is your name?" he asked. His voice was high and nasally with a strange accent. Up close, I saw that he wore a strange pair of goggles that appeared to refocus as his gaze moved around. It made his eyes appear to be dilating at different times.

"Uh, I'm Beau."

"Jeremy."

"Full names." He sounded slightly exasperated, yet distracted.

"Beauregard Artemis Reginald Cornelius," I answered, confused.

"Jeremy Vimes."

"What is your sex?" he asked, tapping away at his tablet.

"Yes please," Jeremy replied eagerly.

"Hold on, you didn't give us your name," I countered, trying to ignore Jeremy's witless remarks.

"That's unnecessary. Please answer the questions. What is your sex?"

"Unnecessary? Look, I don't know who you think you are. You can't just go up to people and ask a ton of questions and offer nothing in return. Like, who you are? Where are you from? Why should we answer your questions? Is this for a class?"

"This is an official audit. Your compliance is required," he said, as if our cooperation was assumed.

"What the hell is that supposed to mean?" I wanted answers, dammit. He couldn't just show up here looking more Gnomish than all the Gnomes and not tell me anything.

"Dude, just play along. This guy's funny. I want to see where it goes," Jeremy said. The Auditor narrowed his eyes at Jeremy. "Male," Jeremy said in response to his previous question.

"Fine," I sighed. I might find out more by playing along. "Male."

"*Askerbin*," the Auditor muttered under his breath, "What is your age?" he asked with more tapping on the tablet before he raised a bulky watch to us, then frowned at it.

"Twenty-one," I said.

"Twenty," said Jeremy.

"What is your allegiance?"

Allegiance? What the hell was he talking about? And what did *askerbin* mean? It could be Gnomish, I supposed, which would just be the cherry on top of all this weirdness. I had never paid much attention to the old language. My sister did, though.

"Boobs," Jeremy replied.

"I pledge allegiance... to the flag... of the United States of America?" I offered.

The Auditor gave a displeased grunt and continued tapping away. "How many people are in your household?"

"Currently, I suppose it's just me and my roommate" I said.

"Same," Jeremy agreed.

Tap tap tap. "What is your household income?"

"Whoa, you're getting pretty personal, don't you think?" I asked.

"Your compliance is required," he repeated.

"Come on, this is getting good," Jeremy said.

"I guess about forty-thousand a year," I admitted.

Jeremy whipped his head around to stare at me, doing a fair imitation of the Auditor's eyes in his glasses. "Where did you get so much money? I'm only getting ten a year working at the convenience store."

"I make a bit of cash selling some gadgets, and I've invested some of it." I tried to show with my tone and eye movement that we should get back on track.

"If you already make that kind of money on the side, why do you even want this degree? Just work full-time instead."

"Can we not have this conversation in front of present company?" I emphasized the last two words with a jerk of my head.

"What crimes have you been accused of?" the weirdo asked.

I pulled a face. "What? None! This is getting ridiculous."

"Only being too good-looking." Jeremy ran a hand through his hair and struck a pose. I rolled my eyes at his unjustified confidence.

Tap tap. "Are you a member of the military?"

"No. I'm a student."

"The army of *love*." Jeremy traced an hourglass shape in the air with his hands.

"Have you found any glowing crystals recently?" The Auditor's eyes locked on mine as if he found this question to be significant to me.

Jeremy stared back for a quiet moment. "No," he said simply, all humor gone from his face and tone.

"No?" My voice lilted up with confusion at this bizarre conversation.

"Do you have any unusual abilities?" His eyes locked with mine again. I had the sense that he knew. And why wouldn't he? "Gnome knows Gnome," after all. Still, Jeremy was right there, so I couldn't exactly confess. What did he want from me?

"No. No special abilities," I said slowly.

"No. Of course not. What do you mean by special abilities? People don't have special abilities," Jeremy said abruptly. I shot him a piercing look. Why would that question fluster him?

"Mmm hmm. Does anyone you know possess any unusual abilities?"

"No."

"Nope," Jeremy said a bit too quickly. Was he hiding something?

The Auditor tapped a few last things on his tablet and turned to leave.

"Hold on, I want some answers from you." I reached out to grab the small Gnome, but he *stepped* away. It wasn't a normal step. Instead of moving him about nine inches, he rapidly receded, rushing away in a moment and leaving me grasping at air.

"Woah," Jeremy exclaimed.

"What the hell?"

"So awesome."

I couldn't agree. I was confused, and my world was upended. What the hell was he? How did he do those things? What did all of those questions mean? This dude made me question everything.

Chapter Three

An Embarrassing Friendship

Communication Skills: Develop effective communication skills to express yourself clearly and confidently. This will aid in building relationships, resolving conflicts, and promoting understanding between yourself and humans.

Beau

If he was a Gnome, then what was I? That was the single thought that plagued my mind the rest of the day. I thought I knew what it meant to be a Gnome. It meant being close to your family and having specialized Gnome-holds in your brain. It meant having an amazing memory and a tendency to obsess over your interests. It meant secrecy and a nagging fear that *they* would catch you.

Jeremy and I walked through the small local mall that smelled of mold and neglect. Whatever else was going on, I needed a new hat. Distracted hat shopping wasn't ideal, but I *needed* a hat. Not just any hat; it had to be perfect. Most of the hats I saw were awful, cheap, and plastic, with no elegance.

Jeremy pulled me into several anime and gamer stores along the way. He picked up three new anime figurines, a replica dagger from his favorite Windrunner series, and about a dozen sets of dice. I picked up a little bumble bee ABC sticker for my sister, Jo.

"Dude, what's that?" Jeremy asked, peering into my little bag.

"It's for my sister. I thought she might think it was cute," I said.

"I'm pretty sure that is for, like, actually small children. Didn't you say she was only a little younger than you?" he asked.

I frowned down at my bag. "But she does spelling bee championships." I pulled the sticker from the bag to look at it again. The holographic glitter reflected the lights around me onto the stylized letters that served as a backdrop to a fuzzy bumblebee perched on a pink flower. "Because, get it... It's a spelling bee."

Jeremy grinned and shook his head. "Buddy, you are incurable."

As I continued my silent crisis, he enthusiastically explained the merits of each set of dice he had just bought. I smiled, happy for his enthusiasm. I had one set of dice and considered them to be tried and true. Besides, the rigorous testing I put them through to ensure balance would be a pain to repeat for each new set. *Meh, we don't have to share every interest.*

I was about to give up when I saw a hat with potential through the window of a small, locally owned boutique. I took a closer look at the bright red beanie and found that it was made of wool and solidly built. "It's perfect."

Jeremy followed my gaze. "Dude, it's a hat."

"It's a *good* hat. Never underestimate the value of a quality hat."

I made my purchase and swapped out the helmet I was still wearing for the new red beanie. The pressure felt comforting, like a warm hug, and some of the tension I'd been carrying melted away. I put my palms to my cheeks, feeling my coarse beard beneath my hands, and took a moment to appreciate the hat.

"You are so weird," Jeremy chided, sticking his tongue at me.

"Says the man with two figurines of Felicia from Darkstalkers in your bag," I shot back.

"What can I say? I'm a man of taste and culture. I know what I like."

"Scantily clad cat-girls?"

"Scantily clad cat-girls, indeed," he smiled.

"Come on, I still need some things from MediaHutt."

We meandered towards the shop, and Jeremy picked up three monster trading cards along the way. Now that I had a new hat on my head, my mind felt free to fret even more about that Gnome. Was he inbred or something? My parents had never mentioned anyone like him. We were Gnomes, and that was that. I froze in my tracks as I glanced down at the level below.

There she was. Samantha James. I loved the long, hazelnut hair flowing over her shoulders, perfectly wavy and shiny, and I took a second to appreciate her shapely, muscular legs and cute halter top.

"You're staring," Jeremy said.

"What? No, I'm not."

"Dude, learn some subtlety. You stand there gawking, and girls will think you're a creep. Ask me how I know."

"I don't make a habit of gawking at girls," I protested.

"No, just that one."

"Is it obvious?"

"Talk to her. Make a move. She can't say yes if you never ask," he offered.

I sighed. "She can't say no, either."

"Seriously, she is right there. Go introduce yourself." Jeremy gestured at Samantha in frustration.

"Now? No way! I need a plan. I'd need the right outfit, a good pickup line, a way to approach her, and the right scene... Oh, and I'd need to figure out where to take her if she says yes. I need to look up reviews for restaurants in town, check their menus for date-appropriate fare—"

"You are way overthinking this. Allow me to demonstrate." Jeremy spat in his hand and ran it through his greasy hair, which did little to improve it, and turned towards the staircase.

"Wait!" I hissed, reaching for his shoulder. He shrugged off my attempt to stop him and slid away.

I watched in horror as he went downstairs and approached one of Samantha's friends on the left. I didn't even know her name. I knew none of their names, nor did I care. I hadn't even noticed she was with anyone until now, I was so focused on her. Jeremy struck a pose in front of them, and, I assumed, said some words. I watched as the girls exchanged disgusted and horrified looks, as if a porta-potty had just exploded in front of them. The lead girl, the one he apparently spoke to, pulled a small object from her bag and held it out in front of her like a shield, and urged her group to back away from him. Was that mace? I flinched for him; glad I was unable to hear the words being said. I noticed a few onlookers tracking him with their eyes as he turned around and rode the escalator to the second floor.

Jeremy returned, looking unphased from the spectacle he had made moments before.

"Yeah, I should definitely take romantic advice from *you*," I said, rolling my eyes.

He shrugged. "At least I tried."

"That isn't always a virtue. It's embarrassing to be your friend sometimes."

"Oh, come on—"

"I don't know what you said to her, but if they pulled mace on you, it was inappropriate." I pulled at my beard in frustration.

"Alright, fine. I may have been slightly out of bounds. I'm sorry." His tone wasn't entirely convincing. And I was pretty sure it was not me he should apologize to.

Remembering Chud, a plan began to take shape in my head. Payback was a bitch... or was that karma? "Come on, I still have some things to get before we go home."

At MediaHutt, I looked for the supplies I wanted. I already had ideas stewing in my mind and picked up an assortment of servos, pneumatics, wires, and gears. Everything else I needed was back at my dorm. I smiled to myself; this prank was going to be awesome.

CHAPTER FOUR

SPARE CASH

Cultural Understanding: Familiarize yourself with human customs, traditions, and social norms. Understanding the culture of the human society in which you intend to integrate will help you navigate social situations more smoothly.

MEEP

I absent-mindedly twitched the yarn back and forth as Rays batted it. She was my older sister, dark-skinned like me, but more bronze to my brass, with the same deep amber eyes. She had never spoken and tended to act more like a human-shaped house cat than my big sister. We weren't sure why, but it wasn't like we could take her to a doctor; she was a Lynx like me. Mom said she had visited various doctors when Rays was young, trying to get answers to why her baby was developing "slowly," but none of the specialists she had found were Lynxes, so any diagnoses they made had no relevance for her specific case. In other words, it was all a big waste of time and cash.

Other Lynxes were rare, and I'd never even met one besides my immediate family. My mom had traveled a lot more in her younger days, and she had sniffed out the occasional Lynx, but I was stuck in Hemmons. My house was the only little pocket of Lynxes in the Pacific Northwest, for all I knew. Mom said other Lynxes were overrated, and not to worry about finding one. After all, my kids would be a Lynx regardless. Not that I was thinking about such things, yet. In fact, I actively avoided thinking about such things, like immediately ditching a guy who made even a whispered wish for a child. I had enough to deal with trying to raise Kip. Sure, she was only my sister, but I felt sort of responsible for her anyway. *I'd do anything for her, and for Rays... and my mom.*

The truth was, I was getting so tired of only dealing with humans. I had so many things I wanted to talk about, and I couldn't tell anyone, not even Jessie, because they were humans. I'd asked Mom how to find more Lynxes, and she said I'd know them when I met them. *Helpful.*

Kip ran into the room and threw herself into the armchair, landing on her back with her head dangling upside down. "Mom told me to tell you that the cheerleading fees are due."

I stood, and Rays, now lacking a playmate, sat back in a crouch and started licking her hand and running it through her hair. I'm wasn't sure what this accomplished for her, and it wasn't like we owned a pet cat for her to mimic, but this behavior must have come from somewhere. "Alright, I'll take care of it."

I followed the scent of fresh cotton and found Mom in

the kitchen doing laundry. She was still in her work uniform of white and teal scrubs. I had to assume that when her uniform was intended for cleaning, it only made sense to keep it on for her own chores. I didn't know how she stood wearing it for longer than she had to. I always got out of my Clair's outfit the first chance I got. "How much does she need?"

"A lot." Mom sighed. "She needs a new cheer outfit again. She's outgrowing her current one." Mom held up the outfit in question to demonstrate. It still looked like new thanks to her laundry skills. Also, we hadn't even bought it that long ago.

"Damn, she's growing fast."

"She's seven. You grew a lot at that age, too." Mom smiled fondly.

"So, another $450 for the uniform and practice wear?" I asked incredulously. "Can we at least sell the old stuff to an incoming girl?"

"We might be able to sell it, though cheerleaders are strange with the concept of 'hand-me-downs.' But unfortunately, the fees, too, will be $300. Prices went up this year," she sighed again.

I went to my room and pulled out my not-so-secret stash, an ornate green and cream teapot decorated with roses. After counting $750 to cover the fees and the new uniform, there was only a couple hundred left. I hoped we didn't run into any emergencies with the house. I sighed as I folded the money and pushed my teapot back onto my shelf. This was why I stayed at Clair's. This was why I had worked so hard to graduate high school early. And this was why I was struggling with what I wanted to do with my life. I brought the money downstairs and handed it over to my mom.

"Thanks, hon. Kip really appreciates it." Every time I gave her money, I saw her eyes crinkle at the corners. I heard the slightest hitch in her voice, and I smelled the dull spice of regret on her skin. But I didn't mind helping my family. I loved my family. All we had was each other in this hostile world we lived in, and only they could truly understand me, no matter how well Jessie fit in. *Even though I want her to.*

I sat down across from Mom as she returned to her mountain of laundry, like a dragon from legend sitting atop a hoard of clean clothes. "Mom, why do you work as a maid? Surely, with your abilities, you can find something else and get paid more for it?"

"I make enough; I'm not complaining," she said sweetly. Enough for us to survive, perhaps.

"That isn't what I asked. I know you think it's wrong to compete with humans, but—"

"It certainly is. I won't take money for beating a baby at a foot-race."

"Fine. But working isn't competing. It's just using your skills in the market," I said, picking up some jeans to fold as I talked.

Mom finished a shirt and set it on the pile. "I used to think like you. It's stressful. You want to be good enough to perform well, just not so good that people notice. But, why should I let being a Lynx define who I am? I can do what I want, not just what being a Lynx makes me good at."

"So, you decided to be a maid?" I raised my eyebrow.

"It's relaxing. Routine. As I work, I can get lost in thought, and there's something satisfying about putting things in order."

Sounded like a snooze fest. Being a barista didn't pay any better, nor was it more interesting, but what else was I supposed to do in this town at my age? "I feel like I am meant for something more," I admitted to her as I matched a pair of Kip's socks.

"You can do whatever you want. Don't let me stop you."

Before I could respond, Rays sprinted through the room with Kip hot on her heels, and a moment later, they came back through in the other direction.

"No zoomies in the house!" Mom roared. "Outside! Now."

They dashed through the back door so quickly they barely had time to open it first.

Mom stood, balancing a pile of clothes in one hand. "You can be anything. Don't let being a Lynx limit you." She took the clothes into the bedroom, and I took a walk to clear my head.

As I meandered through the downtown main street, kicking rocks, I thought about what I wanted to do with my life. I enjoyed using my athleticism by being a gymnast. There was a deep satisfaction in pushing my body to its limits. Nothing else compared or even came close, and I had a hard time imagining being at all satisfied with sitting at a desk all day or performing some boring routine day in and day out. What I really wanted was to be looked up to, to help people. Maybe put on a cape and name myself Karma and seek justice with my fists and a smartass word or two.

My introspection stopped abruptly when I noticed the short stature and the outlandishly bright clothing of the figure ahead of me; it was the little creep who had come into the shop the other day.

He was talking to a group of college students, and they looked uncomfortable as he tapped away on his tablet. I had to know what he was doing. This guy set off all my alarm bells, and it would probably be in my best interest to just leave him alone and go on with my life. Curiosity killed the cat, right? But as I crept forward, I finished the saying—satisfaction brought her back. My footfalls were silent as I kept behind his field of view. I stopped, pretending to window shop as my keen ears picked up their conversation.

"Do you have any unusual abilities?" his nasally voice asked them.

"What? No, man, you got us all wrong."

Another one chimed in, "Yeah. What kind of dumb question is that?" They turned and left.

I continued trailing after him as he went from group to group, running down the same list of questions. It was really a matter of how far down the list he got before his interviewee gave up and left.

Eventually, he tried a new tactic. "I'll give you this money paper if you answer my questions," he said, holding out twenty dollars.

This seemed to work at first; the young lady he was questioning answered everything dutifully, until he reached the strange, "Do you have any powers?" question.

"Eww, cringe," she huffed.

He left her then.

"Hey, what about my money?"

"You did not truthfully answer all the questions."

"The hell I didn't. Get back here!" She stormed after him and swung her handbag at his head. The purse curved, deflected by an unseen force. The unnatural arc threw the woman off balance. I gaped. *What the hell just happened? I'm pretty sure that's not how physics works.*

"Oh, fine then, take it." He tossed the bill at her, and she snatched it and sprinted off.

Offering cash for his strange questionnaire seemed to be serving him better. He was getting to the end of the questions much more consistently, and even stopped trying to withhold the cash after the second man threatened to punch him in the face and one kid waved his phone around, loudly proclaiming he was streaming this on social media.

I couldn't tell what he was getting out of this. He didn't react in the way I'd expected a normal person to.

It was late enough that the light was dimming around me, the small groups of people in the streets petered out, and I had to stick to the shadows to avoid his attention. My Lynx eyes were able to track him easily in the gloom. I was dying to know what he was going to do next. Was he staying in a hotel? Did he have a space-ship? Was he going to crawl into the sewers?

I had braced myself for any possibility when he did something so random, it still managed to surprise me. He walked parallel to a wall next to the local credit union where an ATM had been inset into the brick. He surreptitiously looked around, and I slunk low behind a blue postal box to avoid his eyes.

He fished out a long rod from his jacket, wider and flatter than a wire hanger, like a thin and flexible crowbar, and fed it into the cash return slot on the ATM. He twisted it around, worked it back and forth, and finally leaned on it as bills started flying out of the machine. He hastily shoved as much as he could into his pockets as the machine kept spewing twenty-dollar bills. He was sloppy, with lots of bills falling to the ground in the process, and he glanced around again before he removed the bar, then casually walked away.

I'd just witnessed a robbery. The strangest robbery I'd ever heard of. As I sat there, still crouched behind the postal box, I realized there was still a lot of cash on the ground. After ensuring I was alone, I gathered the bills before fleeing into the encroaching shadows. I hoped he had somehow disabled the security cameras because I thought I also just committed a bank robbery. An accomplice?

I counted the bills by feel and determined I'd managed to grab several hundred dollars, which wasn't exactly life-changing money. My mind filled with thoughts of Kip, and I smiled. The little man was gone, though. I had no clue where he had gone. With more questions than answers, and a bit of spare cash, I decided it was time to head home.

CHAPTER FIVE

REVENGE SERVED HOT

Legal Compliance: Familiarize yourself with local laws and regulations. Adhere to these laws to avoid legal complications or discrimination.

BEAU

I burst into my dorm, dumped my new supplies on my desk, plucked my drill off the pegboard above, and then snatched a piece of aluminum from a pile under the bed. I paused only to push a pair of safety glasses onto my face before clamping the aluminum into a vice and drilling holes. The drill whined against the metal, and shavings went flying. My movements were quick and precise, and my creation began to take form. The vision of what I was making was clear in my mind.

It wasn't like the idea came to me fully formed; I still had to put in all of the work of designing it. Then I could hold the mental image precisely, including specific details and nuances. I had the ability to visualize how everything worked together and even saw problems with the design. In turn, I could easily eyeball my construction and make it to spec without needing to measure. I could judge the distance perfectly well from one point to another, yet to put exact numbers on it I would need to use a ruler like everyone else.

I had been mulling over this plan for hours, so I knew exactly what I wanted to do. The aluminum plates formed a frame, a wide base for stability, with actuated legs for mobility. On the ends of the legs, I built rubber grippers controlled by servos and pneumatics, and then I attached batteries to power it. Next, I worked on the wiring harness, neat and orderly, with every wire the right length running along the body in tidy channels.

Satisfied with the basic construction, I switched my attention to making the brain. Conventionally, this would be computerized nowadays, with a specialized program written for it. But coding just doesn't click for me the way machinery did. I supposed I wasn't much worse at it than the other students, but to make matters worse, control codes tended to be math-heavy. There was no way I could pull off something that complex in the short time frame I had given myself.

Fortunately, I had an alternative. Clockwork machinery did make sense to me, and it was capable of intricate motion. For this kind of fine detail work, I got out my special goggles with a built-in magnifier, and I utilized a set of tweezers to manipulate all the various bits and bobbles. I was reminded of the goggles that Gnome wore, if they were the same then his was much more intricate than mine. I set that thought aside to examine later.

I slipped the last gear into place and snapped a cover over the gearbox as a little alarm clock buzzed quietly at me. Kyle had put a little clock here to try to remind me to go to sleep, too, but I normally ignored it, mostly by accident. It was touching that he had tried, though. *Why don't I hang out with him more?*

Apart from the work light illuminating my bench, the room was dark. A heavy curtain had been drawn around Kyle's bunk, and the sound of regular breathing and the synthetic imitation of rain pattering on a tin roof coming from within told me he was asleep. I often worked on projects throughout the night, and adding curtains and a white noise machine had been necessary adaptations to keep his sleep cycle intact. Outside the window, the world had turned a pale gray.

How late is it? 5:00 am. I really lost track of time. Come to think of it, my eyes were heavy, and my stomach was hollow. *When did I last eat? Did I remember to eat at all today?* Or technically yesterday. It was too late to try to get some sleep anyways, because I had a revenge crow to serve.

I went to the bathroom, took a quick shower to freshen up, and then returned to my room to change into a fresh set of clothes. I put on a pair of rugged jeans with large pockets for a few basic tools I always carried with me, a loose, long-sleeved shirt, a pair of leather work boots, and, of course, my new beanie.

I passed the mail room on the way out of the building and dropped the envelope containing the sticker for my sister in the outgoing mail slot. Then, deciding to check my own box, I saw a cardboard package. I scanned the address noticing it was from home: 636 Fairgrove Ave, Lingsburg, MN.

Dear Beauregard,

I hope college is going well. Josephina won her spelling bee last week, and Mortimer finished the quilt he had been working on. Your father even made us a new kitchen table. We all miss you and can't wait till you come down for winter break. Your Grandmother promised to make your favorite mincemeat pie.

I know you must be missing my home cooking, so I sent you some goodies to enjoy. Eat up.

We are so proud of you,

Mother

By the time I finished reading, my smile was as wide as could be, and I was filled with warm memories of home. Inside the box was a jar of homemade blackberry jam and a batch of biscuits. My stomach growled at the sight of them. Still, I restrained myself and closed the package, tucking it under my arm as I headed to my scooter. I needed the right atmosphere to properly enjoy the taste and texture of my home cooked treats.

I buzzed down the sidewalk, leaving campus and heading into town. Large evergreens lined the road, and a light misting of rain carried the fresh scent of early morning. The dull sun was just starting to peek over the gray horizon, its golden rays shining through the clouds to shimmer off the glistening road. Early mornings in the Pacific Northwest were always peaceful, albeit damp.

Hemmons was a small town, with most of its economy fueled by the college. I passed a closed hardware store and bookshop before arriving at Clair's Eclairs. Their outside food policy was pretty liberal—as long as you ordered something, they wouldn't be miffed if you brought your own snack. I went to the counter and found one of their normal night baristas, Bella, standing at the counter.

"Welcome to Clair's Eclairs, what can I get you?" she recited in a bored voice. I recognized her, of course; the goth-emo look was not common around here.

"Hot chocolate with a double shot of Espresso and extra whipped cream." After paying and stuffing a tip into the glass jar, I seated myself at a table and dug out a biscuit and the heating plate I carried in my backpack. In moments, the bread was warm and the scent of it greeted my nose like a long-lost friend. My stomach garbled again, and I applied the home-canned blackberry jam while Bella brought me my drink.

"Thank you," I said pleasantly. She rolled her eyes and walked away.

As I bit into the soft, pillowy biscuit, the seeds added a delightful crunch to the texture, and I closed my eyes while I savored the sweet and savory combination.

They say hunger is the best spice, and while hunger was very much present, nothing could compare to home cooking for a homesick gnome. A little package of Mother's love. I took a deep swig of the hot chocolate, warm and sweet, which paired beautifully with my biscuits and jam.

After savoring my breakfast, I headed back to the dorm. The sun was fully up and illuminated the red brickwork of the college buildings nestled in amongst the dark green of the forest. I breathed deeply, enjoying the scent of pine and rain. *There is a reason people try to make air fresheners with this scent.*

Oh, right. I needed to find some fresh flowers. And I knew just where to go—the little arboretum the botany department uses.

On my way to get my scooter, I thought about Jeremy's reaction when I made my request to him to help me. All I needed was for him to plant something embarrassing in Chud's bag and to sabotage it in such a way that it would fall out at the right time. I *was* involving Jeremy against his roommate, which was normally a no-no. However, if all went well, his role in this should pass unnoticed. Besides, it wasn't like there wasn't already friction. Chud didn't get along with Jeremy and found him to be a convenient target to bully.

I should have gotten some flowers from a shop while I was out, but I hadn't ironed out this aspect of the plan yet. I pulled out my skeleton key and unlocked the gate. The gate opened, and I slipped inside to find gorgeous plants filling the area in every direction. I didn't want to damage anything, so I decided to minimize my impact, keeping to the stone walkway meandering through the building, and I made my way from plant to plant, taking a single flower from each.

An orange and red tulip, a crimson anthurium, a brilliant bird of paradise, an amethyst hyacinth, an amaryllis and a lily, and another pink and blue watercolor bloom I could not identify. When I had gathered enough, I retreated out the gate, locking it behind me.

I tied the stems together with a segment of red ribbon to form a bouquet. I chuckled to myself, thinking, *it's a Beau-quet because I made it. Well, I think I am hilarious.*

I wrote a note.

Samantha,

I am enthralled by your beauty and left speechless by your voice. Please accept these flowers as a token of my affection, pale as they may be to your own radiance. If you would do me the honor, I would love the opportunity to show you my feelings in person. Please meet me by the great tree outside Allistar Hall at 9:00 am.

Your Admirer,

Chud

I cut the note into a cute heart shape for good measure and spent a moment twirling the thin plastic ribbon into some spirals.

Satisfied, I rode my scooter to sorority row, their white fronts and columns almost eerie in their repetition. I approached the one I knew Samantha lived in and left the bouquet on the steps. I rang the doorbell and quickly hid behind a nearby bush. *Like the coward I am.* The door opened with a groan of heavy wood and old hinges, and then someone rustled the flowers, gasped, and sang, "Oh Samantha, there is something for you!"

After a moment, a second voice sang, "What is it? Oh God, don't tell me those are for me."

Her voice. Beautiful. Musical. Lovely. I itched to peek my head over the bush to glimpse her. Did she have a messy bed-head? Was she still wearing pajamas? Had she done her makeup yet? I longed to see her, but I fought the urge.

"Looks like you've got an admirer," the first girl said, her voice soggy with sentiment.

"From Chud? Ooh. I think he's cute, and those arms... We've flirted a bit, but this? I didn't know he was so elegant with his speech."

The girls were joined by a third voice, and they continued talking as they closed the door. I frowned. I was hoping she wouldn't be *that* into him. Well, it just meant this plot was even more important. She couldn't fall for me if she was already falling for Chud.

I zipped over to Allistar Hall on my scooter to find a good vantage point for the action, and then I waited. This was going to be epic.

At the top of the hour, groggy students filed out of various lecture halls as classes let out, and before long, they clogged the area. I noticed Samantha was in place, hair and make-up done, leaning against the large oak tree.

Chud appeared, lumbering down the steps like the great ox he resembled.

"Chud," Samantha sang loudly, giving a flirty wave.

"Samantha! What'cha doin' here?" His big face spread into the dumbest grin, and I readied my video.

I recorded with one hand, and with the other, I pulled out my contraption, which was about the size of my palm. Eyeing the distance to Chud, I twisted a few dials before flipping the power switch and setting it on the ground. It stretched its spider-like legs, calibrating itself, and then scampered forward, weaving between the feet of various passersby, until it arrived at its destination: Chud's shoes.

"Well, you certainly gave me a reason to come." She twirled her hair around her finger.

"What'd I do?" He scratched his head, the perfect image of a brainless jock.

The drone deployed its front claws and gripped Chud's shoelaces. With a quick tug, they came loose, and with a flurry of movements, they were knotted together. Shoelace-bot was a success, and the dumb oaf didn't even notice. Perfect.

"You don't need to play secret admirer, Chud. You even signed your name. I have to get to swim practice, but afterward, you can get me coffee." Samantha winked and turned to leave.

Chud stood like a boulder for a few moments. "Wait, hold on." Chud shook himself out of his stunned daze and reached out to her, taking a step forward... or at least, he tried to.

He tripped, sprawling to the ground. His bookbag swung forward, sending its contents spilling out: anatomy and taxonomy textbooks, various notebooks—mostly black and red—some loose sheets of paper with scribbled writing and doodles—my hat! — and several pages of... cartoon pony porn. I palmed my forehead. The pages were surprisingly detailed and graphic. Jeremy had really outdone himself.

Samantha knelt down to pick up some of the fallen items. "Oh, are you okay... Wait. What the hell is this?" She dropped the magazine she had picked up like a live scorpion.

I tried to keep my hands steady as I zoomed in on Chud's face. "Gross, you fricking *pervert!* Stay the hell away from me." Samantha recoiled and jogged away. Everyone nearby had picked up on what was happening, and laughter erupted around Chud as people pulled out their phones to record.

Chud looked utterly confused until he glanced down and saw what had spilled from his bag. His face turned bright red.

"This isn't mine!" he yelled in protest, real panic in his voice as he waved the offending magazines above his head. He tried to scoop up his things and run, however, with his shoes still tied to each other, he face-planted yet again.

Instead of taking his shoes off and darting after her, he seemed to give up on running and lay on the grass in defeat, curled into a fetal ball of shame and confusion.

Eventually, the crowd dispersed, either needing to get to class or losing interest. I slipped Shoelace-Bot back into my bag and turned off my phone. Then I strolled casually up to Chud, looking down at him.

"Chud," I said, and he peered up from behind his tree-trunk thick arms. I leaned down close, putting my face inches from his. "Perhaps these things would be less likely to happen if you didn't break into my room and steal my stuff."

CHAPTER SIX

KARMA

Establish Trustworthy Connections: Cultivate relationships with trustworthy humans who can serve as both allies and alibis.

BEAU

After leaving Chud, I took the time to walk slowly back to the dorm. I had class soon, but I felt wrung out like a used rag at a car wash. I thought I would have felt elated after getting my revenge so spectacularly, but all I felt was shame and bitter regret. Why would I feel bad for what I had done? He was a bully. But what does that make me, now?

"Hey, check out the rack on this one," a familiar voice said as a matte illustration of a voluptuous woman was shoved in my face. I pushed it away, knocking the manga to the ground.

"I'm not the creep, Jeremy, *you* are the creep!"

"What? I thought you appreciated Hunter Mega Z." Jeremy knelt down to retrieve his comic.

I took a deep breath. "Sorry, you caught me at a bad time."

"Well, get over yourself. Chud came back and hid under his blankets like a baby. What did you do to him?" I pulled out my phone and started the recording of Chud so Jeremy could watch the humiliation. "Damn, dude, I figured you were going to embarrass him, but that was brutal."

"I didn't expect it to be pony porn," I snapped, slipping my phone back into my pocket.

"And I didn't expect it to be in front of the whole school," he said, dryly.

I flinched. "You think it was too much?"

"Hell no. He had it coming. Jerks deserve what they get."

"People think *you* are a jerk," I said sardonically.

He shrugged. "Yeah, but I'm a good-natured jerk. Chud's just mean."

I was still beating myself up when I got back to my dorm. Jeremy had made some noise about the food hall and left me to my moody ruminations. Distracted, I walked in without knocking, which was a clear violation of our roommate agreement.

Kyle's thin legs were folded beneath him as he sat on top of a small circular rug with various knick-knacks scattered around him. I noted only it was the most cluttered I had ever seen his side of the room before he shouted at me, "Dude! Learn to knock!" He had a book open in his lap, and with a glare, he snapped it closed before shoving everything in a backpack.

Without giving his odd behavior much more thought, I morosely said, "Lock the door... for whatever you're doing."

"Why are you here?" Kyle rolled up his rug to stuff things into the bag.

I groaned, "Got any advice about women?"

Kyle snorted as he shoved his bag under his bed, "Do I *look* like I have advice about women?"

"No. I guess not." I flopped into my bed, defeated.

"Are you alright?"

"I've probably blown my chance with Samantha." I vaguely knew my mind was jumping to the worst-case scenario. *What was the word? Oh. Catastrophizing.*

Kyle pushed his thick black glasses up his nose. "Look, sorry for glibly deflecting your question. I didn't realize it was important to you. I thought you just wanted advice for getting laid." He chuckled. "And I can't really help you with that."

"There's a difference?"

"Of course. If you're trying to get laid, then most of the effort is finding a girl who is willing. You don't need to worry about things like long-term compatibility."

"So, you know all about getting laid?"

"No. I mean, I have a theoretical understanding of the process, but no, I wouldn't be good at giving advice about it. My point is, a *serious* romantic pursuit *is* something I might help with."

"I've never even seen you talk to a girl, much less go on a date."

He shrugged, "Look man, you asked me."

"Alright then, lay some advice on me."

"Learn how to be yourself."

"Really? That's all you've got?" I yawned.

"I'm serious. Think it through. What's your goal?"

"To get a date with Samantha."

"*Bzzzzzt.* Wrong."

"Dating her *is* my goal." I was so tired, my mind, which usually moved fast, felt like it was slogging through a thick swamp.

"No. Your goal is to form a romantic relationship. And a key part is finding someone who likes *you*. Not some persona you put on to attract people, not the person you want to be, but *you*, as you are now."

"What if she doesn't like me for me?"

"Then she is the wrong person, and you move on. Samantha may be the person who caught your interest, but that doesn't mean she is actually the right person for you."

"Hmm, makes sense, I suppose," I grumbled.

"And the best part is, being yourself is the easiest thing for you to do."

Yeah, just be me. I'm pretty awesome, if I say so myself. I just need to show her. Ideas flooded through my brain, even keeping in mind that I couldn't show her I was a Gnome. A memory of the weird little auditor Gnome flashed through my mind. Was I even a Gnome?

"I'm going to take a nap," I said.

Kyle looked at his watch. "Don't you have class in ten minutes?"

"Bah." I didn't feel like dealing with class. My eyes tried to shut off of their own volition, and my head sank into my pillow. Kicking off my shoes, I tugged the covers over myself and let sleep take me.

I generally found that naps were a fantastic way of clearing doom and gloom out of my head like a lighter clears old cobwebs. Instead of seeing problems, now I saw solutions. I hopped out of bed, landing in a relatively clear spot on my side of the room.

"Your mom called," Kyle said, not even looking up from his book. Was that the same book he had stuffed into his sack earlier?

Was he trying to divert attention from what I saw before? *Perhaps.* I sometimes didn't answer my phone, or I lost it for days at a time. So, Mom had insisted on having my roommate's phone number. Kyle, at least, seemed to understand.

I checked the time, and when I realized it was 9:00 pm, I felt a pang of guilt for skipping class. But it was quickly chased away by the excitement of a new idea.

"Thanks," I said mechanically, and pulled out my phone to call home.

"Beauregard. So good to hear from you," said the soothing voice of my mother.

"Hi. I'm glad you called." I was comforted to hear her voice. It made me feel safe.

"Did you get my care package, honey?"

"I did. The biscuits were wonderful, as usual. And tell Jo congrats on the spelling bee. I am proud of her."

"Of course, dear. And how have things been going for you?" I thought about my latest hijinks and decided maybe she didn't need to know I humiliated a boy with pony porn. I also cringed at the idea of explaining the concept of what ponies were doing in pornography. There were, however, some things I did want to talk to her about. I glanced over at Kyle and decided I needed more privacy. Keeping the phone to my ear, I struggled to get my socks and shoes on, trying to keep the conversation light—and normal—until I had the privacy to bring up what was really on my mind.

"There is this girl—"

"Oh, how sweet! Tell me all about her! Is she Gnomish?"

I glanced around nervously. Kyle was not close enough to overhear the other side of the line. But I still decided to slip my sneakers on and head outside. "No, I don't think so. I haven't really gotten to talk to her much. That's part of what I needed advice on."

"You know if she is not a Gnome, your children won't be either," she said softly. Was that… disappointment?

My face heated. "I know, but I'm not talking about marrying her, just dating." I got outside and rode off on my e-scooter toward the woods.

"Dating leads to marriage. You cannot start thinking about these things too soon."

I rolled my eyes as I navigated between groups of people on the sidewalk. "I don't even know how to find someone like me when we have to keep our existence secret from the entire world."

"Gnome knows Gnome, dear. When you meet one, you will know. Even if you are not sure at first, date a woman you think *might* be a Gnome, and figure it out in time. Besides, dating someone who is *not* a Gnome means they will never know the real you. You will always have to be on guard and hide who you are. You know what happens when humans find out they are not alone."

My family had passed down stories of what perfectly normal humans did to people like us if they ever found out who we were. These stories were the nightmares of my childhood. "Frankly, being in any relationship sounds exhausting," I muttered darkly, remembering Kyle's advice earlier.

"It would be a lot easier if you hadn't moved. We have connections with other Gnomish households here, and I could have introduced you to some lovely young Gnome girls."

"That's not the life I want for myself, Mom. Besides, she'll be the first girl I've ever dated. It's unlikely I'd end up marrying her."

"I do not see why not. Your father and I were each other's first loves, and we have worked out wonderfully."

"You got lucky."

"No, we had a family who knew what we needed," she countered.

"I don't want an arranged marriage."

"It was *not* an arranged marriage. Matchmaking is not about *arranging* a marriage or being *forced* to marry someone you dislike.

It is simply giving love an advantage by finding a good fit to start."

"I think they use computers and apps for that nowadays." Reaching the woods, I folded my scooter and carried it with me as I ventured down the path, the darkness providing a sense of secrecy.

"Such a stubborn Gnome. You cannot beat a mother's intuition."

I rolled my eyes. "I just wanted to ask you how to ask a girl out."

"Easy. Just give me her parent's information, and I will talk to them about arranging a meeting."

"No, Mother." I sighed. This wasn't helpful. "Never mind."

I continued walking down the forest path, a small clip-on flashlight leading me deeper into the trees with a soft pool of light at my feet. The darkness suddenly felt isolating. Rather than a veil of secrecy, it became a blanket of loneliness. Still, I had enough privacy to talk about what I really wanted to.

I dropped my voice, hoping to impart the seriousness to my tone. "I ran into someone strange. The most Gnomish Gnome I've ever seen." I quickly recounted what I had experienced with the Auditor. "Any idea what he was about? Is there some secret Gnome sect full of pure blood Gnomes or something?"

"No. I have no idea. We are Gnomes. I do not know what a 'more Gnomish Gnome' would be. Maybe he was just a dwarf Gnome."

"I don't know. That doesn't really explain much. It was more like... Sure, he *looked* a little bit weird, but... he *acted* even weirder. Does that make sense, Mom?"

"I am sorry, dear. I am out of ideas."

I sighed in frustration. Not at her necessarily, but at the general lack of answers to this mystery. "One more question. Do you know what *'askerbin'* means?"

"It sounds Gnomish—maybe ask your sister?"

"Good idea, can you put her on?"

I heard rustling and her muffled voice call, "Josephina!"

After a moment, and more rustling, a fresh voice sounded on the phone, young and soft. "Hello?"

I couldn't help but smile. "Jo*sis*phina! How are you doing?"

"I'm doing great, *Bro*regard. I won my spelling bee."

"I heard. I'm proud of you. Listen, you've been studying old Gnomish, right?"

"Yeah."

"Does '*askerbin*' mean anything in Gnomish?"

"Yeah. It means, 'finally.'"

"Finally?" *So, it was Gnomish.* He muttered, 'finally,' to himself when I had started answering his questions. What kind of person would use Gnomish as an interjection that way? Gnomes I knew thought about it as a historic language of interest, like Latin. Not something anyone would use in a casual conversation. Even Jo wouldn't drop it in a sentence surrounded by non-Gnomes, and she dropped in many foreign words for no good reason.

"Of course. Give me a harder one. I bet I know it."

"Sorry, Jo, that's all I've got for you."

"Aw, come on," she whined. "You never call, and that's all you've got for me?" I felt a pang of guilt. I really should call more.

I decided to level with her. "Maybe you can help me solve a mystery."

"A mystery? Now we are talking."

I explained the Auditor to her the same way I had described him to Mom. "... And he spoke Gnomish to himself. Super weird, right?"

"*Mega* weird. That guy sounds *insanis*. Maybe check if someone escaped from an asylum?"

Wait, *insanis*? Was that Latin? I started to doubt my assessment; maybe if he was like Jo, then he really would use Gnomish words randomly. "He was peculiar, for sure. I don't think we can just write it off as him being crazy."

"You should follow him," she said brightly.

"What?"

"If you want to learn more about him, see what he is up to, where he goes, what he does."

I thought back to how he had disappeared when I reached for him. That would be hard to deal with. Maybe it had only happened because he had felt threatened? If I could follow him without being noticed, perhaps it wouldn't be an issue. Ideas started percolating in my head.

"That's a great idea, Jo. Thanks. I gotta go. Love you."

She hesitated, taken aback by my quick change of tone. "Love you, too, Beau."

I hung up and retraced my steps back to my room, images flooding my mind. Maybe a robot? Something small enough to evade notice. I could reuse the drivetrain from the Shoelace-bot. I let autopilot have me until I felt the hard wood of my workbench beneath my fingers.

"Umm, before you get too comfy there, I'd really appreciate it if you didn't stay up all night again." Kyle said. "My curtain helps, and I don't want to interrupt you when you are in the middle of one of your projects, but—"

"Ah, yes. No problem. Just let me grab some things, and I'll get out of your hair." I didn't find his request rude or unreasonable at all. Sure, this was my room too, but I did *try* not to be a dick. I grabbed some supplies, the now useless Shoelace-bot, and my mobile toolkit. Clair's was a convenient place to work at night since it remained open, warm, and well lit.

I needed to show Samantha who I was—I was someone who came up with plans and schemes—and I needed to make a robot to follow the Auditor. I had an idea of how I could work towards both goals at once.

Chapter Seven

First Impressions

Community Support: Seek out communities or families that can offer guidance and assistance during times of need. These communities can provide valuable resources, share experiences, and offer advice on navigating the challenges of living in a human-dominated society.

Meep

When I arrived for my morning shift at Clair's, I was given a report from Bella, the night-shift worker, about one of our customers. She said a weird guy in a beanie had been sitting in the lobby all night, not drinking or eating a thing, but also not causing a disturbance, so she let him stay. At first, I thought it might have been the ATM-robbing psycho, but it turned out to be a younger guy.

After Bella left, the customer continued to mumble under his breath about not *Chudding* himself. Since when was Chud a verb? What was a Chud? I knew a guy named Chud, a football player at the college.

At around 9:00, I ventured over to the beanie guy's table with a cup of water, because apparently, he had not eaten or drunk anything for like twelve hours and I was not trying to call 911 because a customer keeled over on me. I set the cup on the table, careful not to disturb any of his items, and noted that he smelled like warm butterscotch and machine oil. Up close, I identified various sizes of gears, metal bits, screwdrivers, screws, and something resembling a tiny hand saw arrayed before him—but a lack of notes, blueprints, or even measuring tape is what drew my attention the most. *Is he building all of this by memory?*

The guy didn't seem to notice my approach, presence, or even the new addition of water on his table. After I cleared my throat to get his attention, he drank the water but still did not even acknowledge my presence. He was completely absorbed in whatever he was doing, which appeared to be some kind of clockwork spider camera drone thing. It looked pretty cool. What kind of class was he building it for?

"Hey," I said after he set the now empty cup down. After several more moments, he still didn't look up, so I reached out to touch his shoulder. He jumped as if I had scared him.

"Oh, sorry, I didn't notice you." He seemed flustered and apologetic. How had he not noticed me? He stared at me, eyes red and puffy.

"I just thought you might need some water after an all-nighter. You must be dehydrated. I haven't seen you even get up for the bathroom."

"Yeah, I can get carried away sometimes. Thanks." He looked down at the empty glass of water. "Oh. Thanks for the water, I mean. My name's Beau."

"I'm Meep." I gestured at the debris. "So, what are you doing, anyway?"

"Oh, umm, there's this girl I want to impress, see, so I'm working on making a big surprise for her. I need some gadgets to help, so..." He rambled on about different things he wanted to do. I stopped paying attention at some point. It sounded elaborate, including fireworks and megaphones. "... but I need to find a spot to set it up, so I'm building this drone to record her movements. Then I can find a place I know she will be passing," he finished excitedly.

"Ummm." I sat at the edge of the seat across from him. "Look, you seem pretty sincere, and like a nice guy, but dude, you're building a *spy* robot... That's *really* creepy. If you want some advice, all you'll do is succeed in making her think you're *definitely* a Chud."

Beau looked stunned for a second. "How did you—"

"You mutter."

"Oh. But no, this is *different*. This will be stealthy. She won't even know."

I stared at him in disbelief. *Is this a crime? Should I report this? Maybe not?* If he truly had nefarious intentions, he wouldn't be happily explaining this to a stranger. "Right... Well, again, this is a *really* bad idea, dude. But I should get back to work."

"Oh, just give me a moment to wrap up. I'm almost done with this part, then I'll need to get more supplies, anyway. Thanks for the water."

The door chimed a greeting, and the odor of broccoli alerted me to Jeremy's presence. He ordered his usual and spotted the dude in the red beanie packing his bag.

Jeremy waved. "Hey, bud, what in the hell are you doing here?"

"Giving Kyle some space."

"You missed class yesterday. You okay?" Jeremy clapped him on the shoulder.

I rolled my eyes. Wow, it figured that a creep in the making was friends with Jeremy.

The guy with the beanie left quickly, leaving Jeremy behind to look after him curiously and then he proceeded with his normal lame attempts to flirt with me and his feigned indecision about his morning coffee.

BEAU

I had skipped class yesterday—and the day before—so I forced myself to go, even though what I wanted most was a pillow. I got to class early and slumped into my seat in the back before laying my head down on my arms.

I immediately sat back up. Resting my head was a *bad* idea. I'd just fall asleep. I got a whiff of Jeremy before he sat at the desk beside me. "Dude, you stormed out of Clair's so fast I was sure you were going to skip this class too."

Thankfully, Jeremy was in many of the same classes I was in, especially these early year, basic ones. A civil engineer needs just as much math and physics as a mechanical engineer.

"I haven't been sleeping. I have so much running through my mind. I need something to keep me awake. I've been too busy to watch the latest episode, so what happened on *Battlespear: Hijinx*?"

Jeremy smiled widely. "Oh, it was awesome! Remember back in season four when the Mistress of Darkness unveiled her plot to take over the Castle of Righteousness?"

I nodded, yawning and trying to blink the blurriness out of my eyes. "Of course. The reveal that she had mind controlled some of the Knights, but we didn't know which ones. It created so much intrigue. We started second-guessing everyone."

"I know! It was so good. Well, it turns out that it wasn't the Mistress's idea at all. She was a pawn of Capricious. And *Capricious* had mind-controlled someone *else*, so even after they stopped the Mistress, someone was still controlled."

"*What*!? No way!" This got my heart pumping, sparking the alertness back into my body.

"I know, right? Mind blown. We have to start questioning *everything* again." Jeremy sat back in his chair looking triumphant.

"Can we rule out the Knights that we knew were mind controlled before?" Other students started filling the classroom.

He harrumphed. "It's tempting, but I don't think so. What if they were mind controlled by Capricious back then, and only pretended to be freed when they took out the Mistress of Darkness?"

"Ooh, that would be sneaky," I said, and the professor entered the room and cleared his throat loudly.

"Today, we are going to discuss fatigue," he said, wasting no time. *Well, that's fitting.*

He continued, turning his back to scrawl on the whiteboard. "When you put a cyclic load on a material, it can start to develop small fractures. These slowly grow bigger over time until the stress intensity factor of the crack exceeds the fracture toughness of the material. This will typically result in a sudden propagation of the crack, breaking the object."

That sounded useful to know and wasn't something I normally considered. I built things to work, but their longevity was never a concern. Unfortunately, as he continued to drone on about how to calculate this, the different properties various materials had in regards to it, how to perform stress testing, and I wasn't even sure what else he was rambling about, his voice turned into a dull buzzing sound to my ears. My ability to focus on the lecture was shot. I fuzzed in and out for the rest of class, struggling to stay awake, much less retain the information.

"Dude, class is over," Jeremy said, looking at me.

"Huh?" I looked around and noticed the room was empty. "This is not working. I need a nap, and my room is so far away. I have a couple of hours until my next class. I'm heading to the library."

I shuffled my way to the library with heavy feet. Barely registering any details of my surroundings, I found a lounging chair near the back amongst the lesser referenced books. I blurrily set an alarm on my watch and collapsed into sleep.

I jolted awake as my alarm went off, fumbling for my watch to silence it before I yawned, stretched, and stood up. I still felt tired, but at least I wasn't struggling to keep my eyes open now.

I half-napped, half-rode my electric scooter down to class, lazily dodging around other students walking through campus. My brain felt fried, and even the crisp air did little to invigorate me. This was dumb. I wasn't even going to remember anything the professor said while I was like this.

I slumped into my seat and started massaging my forehead with one hand.

"Dude, you look like hell." Jeremy plopped himself in the seat next to me. Unlike me, he actually had another class right before this one.

"Something, something, you're one to talk," I mumbled at him, not able to focus enough for a proper comeback.

"No, I'm serious. Those are some major bags under your eyes.

What's going on?"

Great, even Jeremy is concerned. I really must look like shit. "Just, stuff—"

"Did you get carried away with one of your builds again?" he asked.

"Yeah..." I admitted, but I trailed off, not able to think of more words. *Is this what humans feel like? Like their brain is wading through mashed potatoes for every thought?*

"What did you make this time?" Jeremy asked.

"Something to impress Samantha. There is no way she will be able to resist."

"You made a mind control device! Awesome!"

"What?" I frowned. "No. That's messed up, Jeremy."

"Oh, you said she won't be able to resist..."

"I'm going to woo her, Jeremy, not *assault* her. What is wrong with you?"

"Woah, I didn't say anything about assaulting anyone. What do you take me for?" Jeremy asked, affronted.

"You said mind control..."

"Yeah, mind control isn't assault! It makes them willing participants."

"That's... You can't consent when you don't have control over your mind." I slumped my head onto the desk. I was too tired to debate the nuances of consent right now, though this really should have been obvious to anyone.

"Beau... I know. I was just being silly. Don't mind control anyone to like you. Nerd shit taught me *something*. That never ends well. That's how you make a whole ass dark lord."

I needed something to keep me awake, so I discussed the finer points of our favorite anime. We geeked out until the professor swept into the room, and I tried to turn my attention to the lesson. *More math.*

CHAPTER EIGHT

ROBOTS AND PEARLS

Education and Professional Skills: Acquire education and develop skills that align with human society. Obtain formal education or training in fields such as medicine, law, or teaching. Avoid professions that may result in the discovery of your specific talents in order to maintain the safety and secrecy of the entire species.

BEAU

After class, I had gone back to my dorm to crash for a few more hours until Kyle came back from his own classes. He actually liked math, and was in far more advanced classes than I was—I would probably have to take those classes eventually, though. I walked into town, choosing not to ride my scooter because I probably needed the exercise and fresh air. However, I did carry it folded up in my backpack.

My first stop was Luann's Crafts for paints, rope, tacks, and a bolt of cloth. To transport everything, I had to resort to my scooter after all. Further down the street, I found Here To Party and got balloons, streamers, fireworks, and smoke bombs. Next, I went back to the electronics store for speakers, a microphone, audio cables, and an old-school boombox. This was making quite the dent in my bank account, but it was for love, damn it, and no cost was too great.

Finally, I got to the gym in time for the swim team to let out. Samantha exited the building surrounded by her swim mates. With each perky step Samantha took, the frills on her dress danced as she flounced. Her body moved in a sensual rhythm, and her hazelnut curls bounced playfully along her high cheekbones, accentuating the single dimple on her right cheek.

I realized I was staring and snapped myself back to task. I pulled out the spider drone I had spent all night on at Clair's. Then I pointed the camera at her and activated its tracking mode. A quick check told me its logs were outputting correctly, and I let it go. It scampered off, darting from cover to cover while tracking after Samantha. I'd be able to collect it later and see her movement patterns from class to class so I could pick the perfect spot.

I was more interested in tracking the Gnome with it, but it could use some field testing first, and I needed to know where to set up my surprise for her.

Kyle was out, so I had the dorm to myself when I got back. I spread out my haul and set to making a slew of gadgets to enact my vision. I crafted holders and launchers for the fireworks and banners, set up timed triggers and cascading effects, and even a couple of small flying drones. After putting the final touches on my preparations, I slumped in my seat, letting the mental image I'd been holding collapse. There was no urgency for all of this stuff to be ready so quickly. I couldn't pick a location and set up until my tracker was finished. I just needed it done so I could stop thinking about it.

I opened up a couple of spare tote crates and shoved my preparations inside, then pushed it all under my desk. Working like this was exhausting. I had been up all night, and with my mind finally free from demanding plans and schemes, I collapsed into the bed and let fatigue take me to oblivion.

I arrived outside the gymnasium a few days later, trying to remain unnoticed while I waited. I had on aviator sunglasses, a baseball cap pulled low, and a hoodie with the hood shading my face. *I feel like a spy on a covert mission.* I pretended to read *A Brief History of Time* to conceal my beard, and as my heart slowly constricted like a vice, I couldn't help but feel that time was anything but brief as I waited to retrieve my drone.

As I faced my certain death, Samantha walked up the sidewalk with a gym bag slung over her shoulder. The sound of her footsteps echoed in my ears like a drum beat, and I watched her from the corner of my eye as I buried my face deeper in the book.

After she disappeared through the double doors, I got up, leaving the book, and rushed towards the door as it closed. My spy drone shot out of a bush and made a beeline for the crack of the door as soon as I got there. Just in time, I grabbed it, switched it off, and quickly stashed it in my bag.

Striding towards my dorm, I adjusted my appearance, discarding my hood and sunglasses and exchanging the baseball cap for my cozy, red beanie. The retrieval couldn't have gone better. Now, I just needed to comb through the drone's logs to find what I was looking for.

Upon entering the dorm, I made eye contact with Kyle and gave him a quick nod; it was kind of weird to find him sitting cross-legged on the floor with books and rocks scattered around him. *Whatever.*

I pulled out my laptop and extracted the SD card from the drone.

We had started by the gym, so I mentally tagged the location and hit play, fast-forwarding the playback—there was a lot to get through. I traced her path on my mental map as she progressed: up the foot trail, down Alabaster Ave., cut through the quad, and lunch at the dining hall. It followed her through her biology class, then ecology and geology. *Interesting,* I didn't know she was in those types of classes. In fact, I was not sure what program I thought she was in. *All swimming classes, I guess?* I put the thought away as I kept watching.

Next, she met with some friends, and the drone almost lost her, but it managed to latch onto her friend's car before they drove off. I swelled with pride. *This drone is performing admirably, so it should do great tracking the Gnomiest Gnome.*

They walked around the mall, looking at a lot of clothes and accessories, not trying anything on nor buying them. This wasn't helpful. I was about to skip forward when I saw something strange. I slowed down the playback speed and rewound.

She gestured to some jewelry, apparently making some comment on it to her friends, who seemed to laugh. I filed the thought away to include an audio recorder next time. She held something to show off what it would look like against her skin, then, as she set it down, she palmed a pearl necklace and slipped it into her pocket.

Oh, Samantha. No. I had never imagined you to be a thief. Maybe she had a good reason for it? *Must be.* Maybe I could ask her about it on our date. *No, how would I ask her without revealing I had been tracking her?* I decided to ponder it more later.

I skipped ahead and resumed the sped-up playback. They went to Fancy Chick, one of the local chicken joints, and got dinner before heading back to her sorority house.

She entered the room, and my drone followed closely behind, capturing the sight of her setting her book bag down beside her desk. She began to lift her shirt, revealing a tattoo of a bird on her rib cage—

Face turning red, I slammed the laptop shut in a panic. *Nope, not what I was trying to do.* I felt my cheeks burning, though my beard probably masked it from others. Kyle looked up from his book and stared at me. He had cleared away the stuff from the floor and now sat on his bed with his ginger hair smashed against the wall.

"Sorry, I, um..." I floundered, trying to come up with an excuse.

"I'm trying to study," Kyle said. He was still giving me a strange look, obviously curious about what I was doing.

I looked back at the laptop. Opening it felt dangerous, like messing with a viper. The video was still playing, but stopped when I closed the lid. It would resume when I opened it again. *Do I have what I need?*

Possibly. I took stock of what I had learned so far.

I knew some of her classes now, and I had an example of how she moved between buildings. I should be able to proceed with my plan, assuming she would behave predictably the same day every week this term. I wouldn't have minded more data points just to be sure, but I had other jobs for this little guy.

I unplugged the SD card. This prevented the video from resuming, and in fact, crashed the entire video player. I sighed in relief.

I pulled up the Hemmons College student portal and went to the student directory. Judging by the buildings I saw her enter and the times she had been there, I was able to utilize the student portal to identify which classes she was in and the full weekly schedule. Two of her classes had a Tuesday, Thursday, Friday, schedule, which meant the path she had taken between them in the recording would be the one she would likely take again next week.

Satisfied, I plugged the SD card back in and deleted everything—I was no Peeping Tom—and put the card back into the camera. Now I just needed to find the Auditor.

I rode around campus on my scooter and tried to rely on the Auditor standing out. It didn't seem like a brilliant strategy to run around and hope to find him, yet I had nothing better. Hopefully, my reconnaissance would reveal something more useful for tracking him down in the future. And I hoped I didn't have to watch him take his clothes off in the process.

If he wanted to talk to people—audit people? What did he even mean by that? —the campus seemed like a good way to meet a lot of people. Though, it was possible he was going door-to-door in the neighborhoods. And he might even go inside to talk to people, which meant I'd miss him entirely.

I decided I would have a better chance of finding him by sticking to the little bit of his behavior I'd seen.

Having a plan in theory didn't always translate to getting excellent results. My scooter ran out of charge halfway through my search pattern, and I had to resort to scootering around with leg power. With manual scooting, the hills became a mixed blessing.

I could coast down them easily, building up a lot of speed. However, getting up the hills was awful. It was easier to dismount the scooter and just hike to the top. Still, *easier* wasn't easy, and my legs started to burn. I couldn't bear the thought of not solving the enigma, even though giving up seemed easier.

I was about to throw in the towel when I finally spotted him in the distance. He had engaged a group of students outside the physics hall. Unable to hear the conversation, I rode around behind him and pulled out my drone. Laughter floated to my ears. The students were laughing *at* him. I felt sorry for him. When I wasn't focused on how overwhelmingly Gnomish he seemed, he did look utterly goofy. That must have been a common reaction for him to get, and had to grate on someone as self-important as he was. Or maybe the pompous act was a coping mechanism against the ridicule? Why was he putting himself in this position in the first place?

I needed answers, not more questions. As I had with Samantha, I pointed the spy drone at him and activated it.

CHAPTER NINE

WHY IS YOUR BUTT FLUFFY?

Voluntary Service: Engage in volunteer work within the human community. This not only demonstrates your willingness to contribute positively, but also allows you to meet a diverse range of humans and forge meaningful connections based on shared interests and common goals.

MEEP

Sometimes I dreamed. Horrible dreams I couldn't escape from no matter how loud I screamed for someone to wake me up. I knew it was a dream. I knew I was in bed. I knew I was home. And I knew I was safe. If I could have only made some kind of noise, someone would come to wake me and pull me out of this nightmare. And yet, no matter how much I screamed internally, nobody heard me in the physical world, even with my family's remarkable hearing. I was alone. I was trapped in this nightmare, and I couldn't get out.

That short man and his stupid boots were in my nightmare. He kept lighting things on fire: trees, people, buildings, cars, and even a fire hydrant. I ran around trying to put out the flames, screaming for my mom, my sisters, Jessie, and bizarrely, Jeremy. I had to protect them. It was up to me. And I was *failing* them. I watched, frozen in horror as the short man lit Jessie on fire and I had to watch, paralyzed in horror, as she burned. If only I was able to scream. *Please wake me up.*

Like a God-send, Jessie shook me awake. "Hey, are you okay?"

I woke with a start. "Nightmare," I panted, glad she was staying over tonight.

She nodded, needing no more explanation, and squinted at her watch. "Well, it's 6:30. I don't think I can go back to sleep. Do you want to talk about it? Or go back to bed?"

I snuggled deeper into my over-large bean bag. Jessie thought I was so weird, choosing to sleep like this. I preferred the feel of its embrace as the material molded itself to my body unlike a flat, boring mattress. Traditional beds were cold and aloof. They didn't hold me when I felt alone or lost. This was comforting.

"Jessie?" I asked in the dark. "How do you know what to do all the time?"

She snorted in amusement. "I don't. Are you kidding? I'm confused most of the time."

I let the silence stretch like taffy as I stared at the ceiling, considering. "I guess that's why you're such a good actress. You always seem so confident to me."

Jessie commonly got leading roles in most of the plays hosted by the college. She would excel at any role given to her. The way she could mold herself into another person was purely magical.

I heard Jessie roll onto her side in her sleeping bag to face me. "Yeah? I guess I'm so good, I can even fool myself. My foster mom always tells me to 'fake it till you make it, kid.' So, I do. I do such a good job that sometimes I think my entire life is fake. Where is this coming from?"

I sighed again, wishing for perhaps the first time I was not curled into a ball. I felt so vulnerable as I admitted, "I am always unsure of myself lately. I want something more, but I don't know what it is."

"Well, you're really good at, 'fake it till you make it,' too, then. Because you had me fooled."

"No, I don't think so. It's more than that. Did you know my mom wants me to drop out of gymnastics? What about my scholarship? I can't afford tuition just on my Clair's salary, and it's not like Mom can pay for it, either. I spend most of my paychecks trying to help her pay bills as it is. If I lose my identity as a gymnast *and* a student, then who am I? Shouldn't girls my age be more focused on dating and romantic interests? But my love life is at the bottom of my list of priorities—right under having my teeth whitened and just above giving a crap about that weird dude in the beanie. So, what's left? A barista? Am I going to be at Clair's for the rest of my life, hiding from healthy relationships?" I wanted to pace while having this existential crisis.

She got to her knees and moved closer.

"Hey." She reached out to hold my chin, directing my gaze back to hers. "It's okay. Look at who you are talking to here. Every time I moved to a new foster home, I've had this same crisis of self. Who am I? What should I do? Who will I become? And you know what? I never *know* any of those answers, but I always evolve. Even if you are no longer a gymnast, so what? You still have the abilities, and those won't go away no matter what your title is."

She placed a light finger over my lips to stop my interruption. "Millions of poor kids from poor families go to college without a scholarship or cash to pay tuition. There are grants and loans and all kinds of financial aid and other scholarships you can apply for. So what if you don't keep a boyfriend for more than two weeks? You graduated from high school two years early *with* an associate's degree." Her hands flew in wild gestures as she spoke. "You go to college and work over thirty hours a week. Hell, you started working when you were fourteen. And all to help your mother pay rent and bills instead of buying drugs and partying like normal kids."

I tried to stop her monologue, but she shushed me again. "I have seen you make coffee for the homeless group downtown on cold mornings. Useless people *don't* do that. You're a freaking saint." Jessie took a deep breath because I didn't think she breathed at all during her monologue.

Must be the actress training to use long speeches in one breath. I smiled. "Thank you. You are like a sister to me, you know that?"

Jessie tossed her long golden hair off her shoulders. "No offense, but I don't *want* to be your sister. My name might be something crazy like Jiph, Jip, or something worse. Jessica Isabel Harris-Parker, or something. What is it with those names, anyway?"

I sat up on my bean bag and shrugged. "It's a family tradition."

"I could not imagine anyone daring to call you Mary."

I giggled. "Right? Can you imagine?" I held out my hand to her as if to shake. "Hello, my name is Mary Elise Elizabell Parker. It's a pleasure."

Jessie solemnly took my hand in hers and gave it a firm shake. "Oh, how droll, my darling, that's not a mouthful at all," she said in a thickly wilting accent.

A thud from downstairs made us jump. "Oh, it's just Rays. No worries, she likes the time in the morning when no one else is up."

"Speaking of your family's naming traditions, what is with your sister anyway? Why doesn't her name end in a P? Like Meep and Kip?"

"She had a different dad, but he died," I shrugged. "Changing her name would just be... unfortunate."

"Oh. Was her father's death hard on your mom?"

"Maybe. She had a couple of boyfriends to help her get past the grief. You can ask her. She's pretty open about it."

"A couple?"

"Open relationships are pretty normal for us. It seems even my grandparents and great-grandparents thought that way, too." Noticing the look of confusion that furrowed her eyebrows, I hurried on. "We believe it's the best way for a relationship to work."

Jessie threw her pillow at me. "That explains a lot."

Half an hour later, I sat with Jessie and Kip at the kitchen table while my mom bustled around making pancakes, her nose stuck in her most recent paranormal romance smut obsession. Jessie and I sipped on black coffee while Kip tried her best to imitate us by blowing on a mug of hot cocoa.

"Mom, Jessie was asking about Rays' father. What was his name?" I asked.

She set her book down on the counter with a wistful smile. "Ron. Oh, he was a sweet one. Best friends with your father, Meep. Sadly, he had a stroke right before you were born."

Kip piped in, "Hey, Meep? Why's your butt fluffy?"

Jessie and I turned as one to stare at her. "What?" we asked in tandem. She erupted into a fit of giggles as Jessie and I shared a look that seemed to say, "Seven-year-olds, man."

Mom sighed. "She learned a new idiom to misuse."

I nodded, finally catching on. "Oh, she must mean, 'What has fluffed your tail?'"

Jessie looked baffled. "That's no idiom I have ever heard. But I think I like her version better." She laughed and gave Kip a fist bump.

After breakfast, Jessie and I walked out the door and were greeted by dark gray clouds and random, wet drops discoloring the sidewalk. Another day, another chance of rain in the Pacific Northwest.

"Is it summer yet? I miss the sun," Jessie sighed. "What kind of mischief can we get up to today?"

"Well, there is a big career fair on campus in the gym. It's not an epic adventure, but at least it's free, inside, dry, and not at home."

The gym on our campus looked like any other; the floor was a pine-colored wood, waxed and shined, and then painted to be a forever basketball court. The bleachers were pushed against the wall, and the floor was filled with tables, each sporting a different colored tablecloth proclaiming their parent company. Representatives tended each table with a smile that showed way too many teeth. I sighed; the smell of capitalism made my nose twitch.

I did not know what I wanted to be when I grew up. All I knew was that it needed to be something exciting. Up to this point, I had taken classes in criminal justice, art, humanities, sociology, archaeology, psychology, human resources, business and marketing, nursing, and pre-med. It all made me queasy because I was conscious of how much tuition cost, even with my full scholarship.

My counselor had said I was supposed to be taking a wide variety of classes to get a fully rounded education. Pick a major? You mean, pick a shackle? No, thank you. I'd rather major in an ideal, like excitement, adrenaline, or justice, not consign myself to these boring options like business, education, or engineering.

I shook myself out of my internal ranting and back to the present. Jessie was talking to me, but I missed what she said. With hearing as good as mine, there was an adjustment phase when I entered situations with so much going on. It was easier to retreat into myself than to handle the full brunt of noise from so many voices assaulting my ears at once.

Jessie was gesturing to a map of the job fair in her hand, and when I looked down, I realized I was holding one too; she must have been talking about where we should visit.

"... and I wonder if there is a representative for a talent agency somewhere. I mean, all these places can't be looking for just models, right? What are you going to look at?"

I scanned the map in my hand. "Nothing seems interesting."

"What? There is some of everything here! There are law firms, banks, the police department, big tech companies... Do you want to be a model?" she asked in mock surprise.

"I don't know. I know what I don't want. I don't want to be stuck at a desk, or have to do paperwork, or have any type of routine. I don't want to be bored."

Jessie's eyes scanned the table in front of us, and she frowned. "So, what do you want?"

"I want to be needed, to protect people, to fight against injustice," I said.

"Yeah, I don't think they have a table for wannabe superheroes."

I scanned the map in my hand again and pointed to the hot dog stand by the emergency exits. "Hey, let's go here first."

Jessie frowned. "We literally just ate breakfast."

"Holding food is a great excuse for people-watching or not responding when someone asks you a question."

Jessie shrugged, and we wove through the foot traffic to reach the corner of the gym. The line for hot dogs was, unsurprisingly, longer than the lines for any of the other tables.

As we waited in line, Jessie scoffed and pointed at the five guys surrounding a nearby table. It had a bright blue tablecloth proclaiming "Nebula" in large neon yellow letters. Each of the guys was in various stages of pulling on a brand-new Nebula hoodie.

Even though Jessie was planning on entering the entertainment industry, she had often argued loudly about the lack of female professionals in STEM fields. She wanted to see more female representation in medicine, science, and engineering, even though she acknowledged her own hypocrisy. She had told me once that it didn't matter that she did not want to be in a STEM field, because that wasn't the point. Women in general needed those fields to be accessible if that was where they wanted to be, and she'd fight for that.

As we continued waiting, a small Korean girl approached the representative and tried to strike up a conversation. It sounded like she wanted more information about the type of engineers needed, the projected job growth, and the programming languages needed in the next four years.

"Ooh," Jessie said. "I know that girl. Miya programs all the light work for all our shows. She's brilliant and absolutely stunning."

"Have you talked to her?"

"What? No. I couldn't possibly. I don't think she's into girls," Jessie sighed. "No. I will just admire her from afar and respect her space."

"But what if she is doing the same thing?" I asked.

Jessie leveled a pointed look my way. "That, Meep, is why I find dating girls to be so hard."

As we continued waiting in line, we overheard Miya's conversation with the Nebula rep. Despite the intelligent questions she asked, the representative gave her short, one-word answers, then turned away from her to wave over a boy who was walking by. To her credit, Miya did not back down from the blatant dismissal. Instead, she asked the rep how long he had been working for Nebula himself.

After the boy continued to pass the table without engaging, the rep spun on her and loudly laughed. "I know what this is. You just want one of my hoodies. Look, sweetie, you don't have to pretend to be interested. I am not going to give you one. Do you think I just hand these out to anyone? No. These are for serious inquiries only." By the time he had finished railing on her, everyone in the hot dog line, and most of the people at nearby tables, had turned to stare at them. Miya flushed a deep coral and slunk away.

Jessie's jaw hung slack, and her blue eyes opened wide. With shaky hands, Jessie pointed to the group of guys wearing the hoodies. "Those morons are all jocks. The tall one, Chud the Pony Boy, if he has any interest in computers, I'll eat my shoes, and yours, and his for good measure."

"Chud, the what?" I asked.

"Oh, you haven't heard? I'll have to tell you later. Hold my spot." Jessie ducked out of line and pulled the baseball cap off of a passing student. She must have known him because after she gave him a quick, apologetic smile, he shrugged and continued on his way.

Jessie tucked her blonde hair under the cap and secured it on her head. The faded hoodie and baggy jeans she wore hid her conventional feminine figure already. She adjusted her stance so she appeared taller and turned her elbows outward to look more bulky. Then she set her jaw in a certain way to make her face more square. Her usually pouty expression relaxed and was replaced by casual indifference, like she was sneering at everything she looked at. Finally, her swaying hips took on a stiff and straight gait. With a few slight changes to posture, Jessie the boy stood in front of me. *Hmm, must be an actress trick.*

As a male, she strode up to the Nebula rep and spoke in a deep voice—not an overtly fake, deep voice from a female, either. She really put her all into this. "Hey man, let me get one of those hoodies."

The rep handed her a hoodie without comment or question.

"Give me two more for my brothers. They love nerd shit."

The rep gestured at the boxes of hoodies behind his table. "Sure! We love encouraging budding talent in our youth. What sizes?"

Jessie now stood holding three hoodies, and the rep continued to try to engage her in conversation. As they talked about some out-of-state sports team, Jessie reversed her transformation. She reset her jaw and smoothed her facial features back to their original set. She increased the pitch of her voice gradually, so it returned to normal, and finally, she took off the cap and shook her long blonde hair out.

The rep paused mid-sentence and gaped at her, "But... but..." he stammered, looking around, confused. He must have thought that he was talking to a guy this whole time. He had never broken eye contact, and despite that, there was an obvious woman standing defiantly in front of him with three of his hoodies.

"Did you not know you were a bigoted ass-hat? Or was it on purpose?" Jessie sauntered past, hips swaying to the fullest as she walked away, leaving him gaping in pure bafflement.

As she walked past me, she tossed me a hoodie and said, "I am going to find Miya. Hope she didn't get too far away." Jessie picked through the milling crowd in the direction we saw Miya heading earlier.

After a few minutes, I picked Jessie out of the crowd to find her handing the shirt to Miya. Miya smiled gratefully, then the smile froze and became strained. She took a few steps backwards before gesturing vaguely behind herself and turning away. *Ooh, that didn't look like it went well.* Jessie trudged back over to me, hands deep in her pockets.

"At least you tried," I said, offering a grin and a shrug.

"Girls are stupid. I should stick to boys."

CHAPTER TEN

SPYING CAN BE UNHEALTHY

Personal Safety: Take necessary precautions to ensure personal safety. Be mindful of your surroundings, avoid dangerous situations, and maintain a network of trusted contacts who can assist you in times of need.

MEEP

The evening shift was slower than usual, and the time dragged by like the honey attached to the spoon as you pull it away, the thread stretching seemingly into infinity. Finally, the night shift arrived to take my place. We normally had an hour that overlapped, so we had time to collaborate on whatever we needed when trading shifts.

"Hello, Bella," I sang brightly.

She grunted, "Hey," in her trademark deadpan tone, and stalked behind the counter.

Bella was a few years older than me, and we had both started working here at about the same time three years ago. The cheery tone was grating to her, but I got a twisted kind of pleasure out of getting on her nerves.

Most would have called Bella's look goth; her skin was a ghostly white and her hair deep black with blood-red tips, and her eyes were surrounded by smokey black makeup. I knew her to be the sweetest person I'd ever met, but she would never freely admit it. *She* had a certain reputation for aloofness and badassery to protect.

"Are you still dating Justin?" she asked. "A record, isn't it?" She was just trying to get me back from annoying her.

I blinked, caught off guard. "Uh, his name was Brian, and we broke up like a week ago."

Bella snickered. "What did this one do?" She pulled the till from the drawer and rolled her large blue eyes. "I swear Meep, you eat up boys like I eat up eyeliner."

A noise drifted in from outside, filling the diner with a familiar jangling sound. With a start, I recognized it as a certain pair of curly-toed boots. I stopped what I was doing, hand frozen mid-wipe.

I invented a random excuse to leave to follow the mysterious guy, curious about where he spent his nights.

"Whatever," was all I got in reply.

I was out the door in a moment and followed the jingling steps to the edge of town. I followed him along a parallel path, letting my ears guide me and being careful to remain out of eyesight. *He can't see me if I'm not there to be seen.*

When we reached the end of the row of buildings, he headed

into the forest. It would be hard to pass myself off as a random pedestrian if he saw me here, but he was in the thick foliage, which was my playground. Confidence swelled as I bounded into a tree, leaping off the trunk to land silently on a large branch. I followed in this way, like a squirrel on a mission, careful to keep to the thickest branches and not make any undue noise.

At the tree line, I watched him head down a large, mostly featureless hill towards a collection of warehouses. A large spider darted out from a bush below me and followed him. No, not a spider, a multi-legged robot. Hadn't the guy in the red beanie been building that in the cafe the other day? What was it doing here? I thought he had been creeping on some girl with it.

The man spotted the small drone, and he reached into his clothing to pull out something I couldn't make out at this distance. He pointed it at the robot, and the spider thing immediately burst into flames, briefly spasming before lying still.

Hoooly shiiiiiit. Was that a laser? A freakin' ray gun? My heart raced, excitement trickling into danger. This wasn't just some quirky guy; this was someone with lethal weaponry.

The tiny man approached the mangled wreckage of the drone and picked it up by a leg. It dangled limply, still smoldering, and he carried it into a warehouse.

Running forward, I leapt onto a stack of crates near a wall and flipped onto the roof. Then, creeping to a skylight, I looked down. The glass was mostly opaque, but I could just make out the silhouette of the man inside and the shape of various strange machines strewn about. He tossed the ruins of the device onto a workbench and examined it.

Okay, this is far weirder than I expected. He had ray guns and who knew what else down there. An alien? What else could he be? It would explain how weird he was. Why would an alien be *here* of all places, a sleepy little college town?

I continued watching as the sky darkened. Eventually, he stood and stretched his three-foot frame. He put his overcoat on a hook, slipped off his boots, and lay down in a hammock. In seconds, snoring drifted through the air. I didn't know aliens snored.

I carefully opened the skylight and lowered myself, dropping noiselessly onto a spacious shelf. I watched the alien for any signs of alertness, but he still seemed to be asleep.

I approached some machines cautiously, but I couldn't make sense of them, and they were certainly far too big to move. Unable to see anything useful, I moved to the workbench. The tools were arranged in an orderly fashion, but I couldn't recognize most of them. In the center sat what looked like a complicated smart watch, and next to it were the now cooled remains of the spider drone.

I picked up the watch and turned it over, noting the many dials and switches. I resisted the urge to fiddle and slipped it into my pocket and picked up the drone. A hole had gone through it, big enough to fit my fist.

"Ahem." The alien stood a few feet away, pointing what I assumed was his ray gun at me. My heart thudded. "That is mine, Meep. Put it down and walk away unharmed."

"How do you know my name?" I asked conversationally, instinctively trying to keep him talking.

"I interviewed you, did I not?"

"Yeah, but you interviewed a ton of people. Why would you remember me?" I cast around for an escape route.

"I remember everyone interviewed."

"If you remember everything, why do you use your tablet to record the results?" I prodded.

"Recording my— Oh, I see. What a quaint idea." The Auditor huffed.

"If you aren't recording what people say, what are you doing?"

"Do not change the subject, Meep. I want my property back."

"Alright! Yeah. Just let me set this down." I slowly lowered the drone to the ground, then swung it upwards, twisting my body to the side. It collided with his hand, pushing it upwards as the air near me suddenly erupted in heat. I quickly rolled into a crouch, and I saw the alien with his hand outstretched and empty. His weapon was on the ground, and I dashed for the door.

"Get back here, you *lokorn*!" he roared. He pulled out something with his other hand and gestured towards the shelf, and his weapon flew to him.

Oh shit.

I dove to the side behind some crates, and a hole appeared in the wall in front of where I'd been. Without being close enough to make it to the door, I was forced to run deeper into a maze of shelves, machinery, and boxes, relying on my natural agility to keep my footfalls light and silent.

"I'm not here to hurt you, though I will if you do not give my property back," he called after me.

His voice only spurred me faster. I kept to the middle of the warehouse where the supplies gave me the most cover and considered my options for escape.

A silvery sphere shot up overhead, and I watched it with apprehension as it doubled back towards me. As it slowed, I could see a black spot on its surface, like a metallic pupil. I wasn't sure what that thing did, but I didn't want to be in its line of sight. I leapt up, achieving a vertical clearance no human could have managed, and then swung the broken drone spider into it. It connected, and the orb was sent careening backward, spinning wildly.

Time wasn't working in my favor. There was so much stuff in that warehouse; what else did he have at his disposal to throw at me? Jumping onto the tallest shelf near me to get near the skylights, I threw the drone against the pane to shatter the glass. Then I jumped into the night, throwing myself sideways the moment I touched the solid surface. Moments later, I was bathed in heat as the roof directly in front of me vaporized into a cloud of fire and ash. The molten remnants of the asphalt shingles framed an irate little alien-man, who was pointing his laser gun at me from below. I ran in an erratic pattern across the roof, zig-zagging and dodging holes that opened randomly around me.

I jumped off the edge, tumbling in midair, before righting myself and landing gracefully on the ground below. I fought the urge to pose after sticking a fabulous landing. Not everything they drilled into me in gymnastics was applicable to running for my life.

I sprinted towards the forest, nearly making it to the trees, when an explosion made me risk a glance back. The alien was floating out of a new hole in the warehouse's wall, hovering in midair and covered in some sort of mechanical suit.

Shit, shit, shit, shit.

As he raised his gun, I threw myself sideways. The tree behind me burst into flames, but I made it into the forest and hoped to lose myself in the foliage. To avoid leaving a trail, I climbed a tree and used its branches to retreat, a much less confident squirrel than before.

CHAPTER ELEVEN

THE WATCH

Problem-Solving and Innovation: Leverage your inherent Gnome traits of resourcefulness and problem-solving abilities to contribute to human society. Use your abilities to develop innovative solutions for urban challenges, such as sustainable energy, transportation, or urban planning. This positions you as a valuable contributor and asset to the human community.

BEAU

I sat on my beanbag, reflecting on my life and using my open door as a cover for socialization. I wasn't interested in talking to anyone, but at least with it open, I didn't look like a total recluse.

I could hear other students walking through the hall, chatting loudly with others. That was enough, right? I had deeper thoughts to occupy myself with while I waited for the drone. *What does it mean to be a Gnome? Do Gnomes look like the Auditor? Am I even a real Gnome?*

"Hey, pervert."

Shock ran through me when I noticed the girl from the cafe standing at my door. What was her name again? Something with an M? Margaret? *No, it was short and didn't seem like a name. Mup? Moop? Ah, Meep.*

She strode in and dropped something at my feet. "I found your toy."

My drone. Well, what was left of my drone. "Hell. What happened to it? Why do *you* even have it?"

She crouched down in front of me, locking her eyes on mine with an appraising glance. "I think I underestimated you. You were investigating the strange little man too, weren't you?"

"Too? Why would you do that?" I was shocked. What did she mean? *Is he so obviously a Gnome that she suspected him? Do I need to do something about this? Do I need to defend him? What the heck am I going to do? Build some elaborate suit of armor and throw a trinket at her?*

She shrugged, "I think he is someone who needs investigating. Unfortunately, your robot here didn't get the job done. The creepy little guy vaporized it with a ray gun."

"Seriously? A *ray gun*? Like a little green man?" I asked.

"Exactly. Except for the green part. He has to be an alien, right?"

I shook my head. "Not an alien."

"What else could he be?"

"I can't say." I couldn't tell her I thought he was a Gnome, much less *why*.

"Don't want to share? Fine, I won't tell you what I found in his lair, then." She stood up and walked around my room, eyeing the line of detritus marking my half from Kyle's.

"He has a *lair*?" I clarified.

"Yup, and if you want to know what I found, spill it," she said stubbornly.

Well, it tempted me. My surveillance drone hadn't gotten the job done, and judging by what the "ray gun" did to it, I wasn't certain I wanted to do it myself. Jesus, I didn't expect him to be *armed*.

And yet, I would never be satisfied if I left it now. This wasn't just some strange man I was curious about. He raised existential questions about my entire identity. *If he is a Gnome, then what am I?*

I walked to the open door and checked both ways down the hall before I closed it. "This is going to sound weird."

"Honestly, I'd expect nothing else. Of whatever possible explanations exist for him, I'm already on *alien*. So how much weirder could it get?"

I shifted my weight and eyed the faded carpet. *Could I go through with this? Could I really tell her?* I had never told another person about myself, not even my own family. I mean, why would I? My upper lip itched, indicating beads of sweat were popping up under my mustache. With one last breath, I decided I *had* to trust someone. I needed help, and I could not hope to solve this by myself. "He is a Gnome."

To my surprise, she laughed. "What? Like the little round guys in pointy hats people stick in their gardens?" She mimed a triangle on her head with both arms.

My eyes popped. To me, Gnomes were as real as humans, and she had laughed? *Okay, in hindsight, maybe I can see where she is coming from, like telling her cows can talk and aliens are great at playing Canasta.* "Yes... No... We don't talk about garden gnomes."

She perched herself on my workbench, pointedly waiting for me to continue. "Garden gnomes are a cultural phenomenon that evolved over time. You can trace the roots back to stories about real Gnomes, though."

"Yeah, old folklore stories. But I mean... a Gnome? Are you going to tell me Unicorns are real, too?"

"Don't be silly. Unicorns aren't real." *I think.*

"But Gnomes are?" Her lips pressed together to form a straight line. I thought that was just an emoji, but here she sat, making the exact facial expression.

I sighed. "For the sake of this conversation, can you just *assume* they are?"

"Why should I believe in Gnomes over all the other fairy tale crap?"

"Because you've *seen* one?" I pulled at my beard. This was not going how I planned. I thought I was going to tell her the Auditor was a Gnome and she would gasp and say, *oh, jeez, that makes so much sense. Thanks, Beau.* Talking to people was hard, and I considered ways to backtrack this entire interaction. Why had I considered that telling her was a good idea?

"Only because you say so." She folded her arms over her chest.

I gave up and threw my hands into the air, fingers fluttering. "Well, I gave you my information. If you don't believe me, that's your problem."

"Fine. Let's say he is a Gnome. You're still not telling me every-thing. I can tell."

"That's all I *can* say." I lowered my eyes to the floor. "I shouldn't even have said that much."

She stared at me, and not backing down, I stared back and was surprised she looked away first. "Fine, I'll drop it. For now. Lucky for you, you're the only person I know to bring this to." She reached into her bag and handed me a bulky watch. "I swiped this from his workbench... which actually looks a bit like yours." Did her eyes narrow at me? Was that a good sign? I'd basically already told her I was a Gnome, too, right? By admitting Gnomes were real, I felt like I had beat her in the face with my own identity.

I turned the watch over. The workmanship was intricate. I saw tool marks, indicating that it was handmade. It was too clunky to just be an actual watch, though. The body was a faint copper hue with a large gray screen in the middle, and the strap had a complex buckle, making it difficult to put on or take off quickly. Unless it was automatically fitting or something. I ran my fingers along its surface and around its edges, noting a fine pattern of ridges all around it. Several dials and switches were laid around the edge and I flipped one, hoping it was a power switch. The screen started glowing, blinking a few times before settling into a series of strange characters.

"Ooh, that's new. An alien—or Gnome—language?"

She was right. It did look like a language; the shapes were strangely familiar. I stared at it and turned the watch 180 degrees. *Ha, I had it upside down. And aha! It is Gnomish.* Too bad my Gnomish was awful, but there was one word I did recognize, and I whispered it out loud. "Gnome."

"Yeah, he's a Gnome, that's what you said."

Ignoring her, I toggled the switch again, and the text reappeared. Most of it was the same, though one word had changed. It no longer said 'Gnome.' I didn't recognize the word, but it seemed to still be in the Gnomish language, so I sounded it out. "Meow?"

Meep stiffened in my peripheral vision. Odd. Did it mean something? If it said "Gnome" when I pointed it at myself, then logically, it stood to reason...

"Are you... a *cat*?" I hoped the disbelief in my voice didn't offend her.

"*What*? No. Why—Why would you say that?" She jumped down from the workbench and paced my small dorm room, mostly on Kyle's side due to the clutter on the floor of my own side.

That's all I needed. I was convinced. It made sense. If I could be a Gnome living a secret life, passing as a human, couldn't there be others doing the same? And if I had found such a person, then surely they would understand the secret. This was the reaction I had hoped she would have had about the Auditor.

"Alright, I'll explain the rest." Taking a deep breath, I remembered the closet doors I had mentally blown off the hinges earlier. I then proceeded to knock out the entire wall while I was at it. "I could tell he was a Gnome because... I'm a Gnome."

Her mouth opened and closed several times, but she said nothing.

"This device displayed Gnomish. I'm not good at reading it, but when I point it at myself, it reads 'Gnome', and when I direct it at you, it says... 'meow'?"

Meep paced silently for a minute. "It probably said 'Mau.' But we use the term 'Lynx,'" she grumbled.

I stared at her until she sighed and continued. "It's M-A-U, pronounced like mouse without the S-E at the end."

The most Gnomish of Gnomes shows up in town with a device able to detect Gnomes *and* Lynx. What did it mean? "I think we both need time to process. Let's meet up later and figure out what we want to do next. Deal?" I asked.

"Fine. Deal. And if you tell anyone about me, and I mean *anyone*, I will flay you with my nails."

I gulped. "Are they sharp?"

"No. They're *dull*." And then in a conspiratorial whisper, she added, "It hurts more."

CHAPTER TWELVE

ESSENCE CONTAINERS

Fashion and Style: Stay updated with human fashion trends and incorporate them into your own style.

BEAU

The watch was my best lead. Maybe understanding the purpose behind it could help me figure out what the Auditor was doing. My Gnomish wasn't good enough to decipher the whole read-out, but I did know someone who could read it. I punched in a familiar number on my cell phone, holding it to my ear with my shoulder as I continued to prod the watch with various tools on my workbench.

"*Bro*regard!" answered a sweet, youthful voice.

"Jo*sis*phina, I have a puzzle I need your help with."

"Ooh, what kind of puzzle?" she asked.

"I have some Gnomish text I need translated."

"Where did you find Gnomish text at your college?" she asked.

"It's a long story. I'll explain later. Let me send you a pic." I sent her a photo of the screen and the text it displayed.

"What the hell is that thing?" she asked, voice tilting up in incredulity.

"I told you, I'll explain later. Can you tell me what it says?"

"Mostly. There is a word here I don't know, but the rest of it says, 'Bio scan complete'... something I can't read at all, then, 'markers found, Gnome signature detected.' Beau, seriously, what is this? I need to show Mom and Dad."

"Wait, promise not to tell anyone. Remember the mystery?" I explained the strange devices, his ray gun, and this watch. I omitted Meep from my story, not to take all the credit and look like a badass to my little sister, but because I didn't know how much I could explain without leaving Jo with more questions.

She was silent for a long moment. I even checked my phone screen to make sure the call hadn't dropped. "That's a lot," she finally said in a near whisper.

"I know. I've been trying to wrap my head around it, too." I collapsed into my beanbag like I had just run around the block, which, for me, was a big deal.

"I've been looking into the roots of that missing word, and it means something like 'essence container.' Though, I'm sure it has a more specific meaning I don't understand."

"Essence container markers found. What does that mean?" I wondered out loud.

"I don't know. But they were found, and it marked you as a Gnome. Give me one good reason not to tell Mom and Dad some crazy guy is running around with proof you're not human? They would freak so hard."

"I'm telling you, this guy is a Gnome, too. He won't expose me. I don't know what his game is, but I am certain. Mom and Dad would just panic, and they wouldn't understand. I *need* to solve this mystery."

"Fine."

"Thank you." I breathed a sigh of relief. I loved my parents dearly, but I did not need them to pull me out of college over this.

"No problem, anytime. And by anytime, I mean tomorrow around three in the afternoon," she said.

I frowned. "What's tomorrow at three?" I fumbled the screwdriver I was using to poke the watch, trying to find a way to open it.

"When I'll be arriving to help you solve this mystery. Aren't you paying attention?" I felt sure my attention wasn't the problem here.

"You are coming here? I didn't ask you to do that."

"Oh please, as if I'd let you have all the fun by yourself."

"What about your schoolwork? Where would you stay? You aren't allowed to stay in my dorm room. You need a plan."

"Let me worry about my school, and I'm sure you'll figure it out. You're good at making plans." She hung up before I could voice any more objections.

Sighing again, I dialed another number. "Hey Meep, got a favor to ask you."

"I don't know. We aren't in the favor stage of our friendship."

"It's to help solve our mystery."

"Fine. Name it," she said, clipped and irritable.

"Can my sister stay in your dorm?"

"Excuse me?"

"I brought my sister in to understand the watch. She is vastly better at Gnomish than I am. Don't worry, I didn't tell her about you. But she's coming into town tomorrow and there is no stopping her. She can't stay in my dorm, though."

"This seems sudden. I don't live in a dorm. I'm not even a full-time student," she said.

"Sorry, I just assumed. Where do you live?"

"Umm. At *home*, with my *entire* family," she said

"Alright then, can she stay with your family?"

Meep sighed deeply. "I'll check with my mom."

"Thank you."

"That wasn't a yes, it was a maybe. Mom has a soft spot for strays."

Hanging up, I turned my attention back to the watch. *An essence container detector, eh?* I turned it over and looked for a way to open it up. It had what seemed to be screws holding it together; the head was unlike any screw I'd ever seen. I ended up filing a metal rod into a screwdriver to match and opened it up carefully.

The insides were nothing I had seen before. Silver wires with purple crystals formed unfamiliar, branching geometric patterns. Of all the things I have taken apart, I have never seen anything that immediately struck me as a chaotic mess before. Never had I felt so incompetent; I didn't understand the principles this thing operated on. Still, I poured over it, looking over every centimeter, noting the structures and how the wires wound around the crystals.

I lost myself in examining the device and passed out at some point. I woke up half on my mattress and one knee kissing the floor as Kyle left for classes. After forcing myself to attend my own classes, I rode my scooter to the local bus station.

While I waited for Jo at the bus stop, I occupied myself by solving a Rubik's cube in my head. Keeping track of colors, understanding how moves would shift them, and focusing on the results of each move was a mentally challenging exercise. I found a single 3x3 to be too easy to visualize, so I'd been trying to do multiple, complex cubes simultaneously. I had eight 6x6 cubes going in my head and didn't register the bus pulling up in front of me until the doors opened with a hiss.

Jo was the first to hop down the stairs, her bright pink beanie covered in emoji pins and neon-green streaked hair kissing the back of her pale neck. Her outfit consisted of clashing pastel colors, denim jeans, an orange-cream backpack, and a hot-pink skateboard tucked under her arm. The skateboard had been adorned with none other than the spelling bee sticker I had sent her.

"*Bro*regard!" she exclaimed, dropping her skateboard to the ground and cheerfully embracing me in a quick hug.

I returned the squeeze fondly. "Jo*sis*phina!"

"Do you have it with you?" she asked, getting right to business.

"It's back in my room. I told Meep to meet us there. She agreed to put up with you while you are here." She had called me between classes to let me know her mom was cool with it.

"Meep? Like the roadrunner?"

I shrugged. "Don't know why she goes by that, but she does. I don't think I would make fun of her for it, though. She can be a little intense. Probably best not to bring up the cartoons."

"Is she your *girlfriend*?" she asked teasingly, like we were fourth graders on a playground.

"No." I hastily reassured her. Jo cocked her head and squinted at me. *Oh, was that too fast?* "I'm more of a dog person," I said, trying to clarify.

"What does that have to do with anything?" she asked.

"Oh, never mind. Let's get going," I said. I hopped on my scooter to head back to campus, while Jo skateboarded beside me.

"You got somebody else?"

"Not exactly," I said through clenched teeth.

"Then, why not Meep? Is she pretty?"

"Every woman acquaintance doesn't need to be a prospective girlfriend, you know."

"No need to be defensive, bro. Just trying to figure out who this random chick you are sticking me with is. Wait, how many 'woman acquaintances' do you have?"

None. I changed the subject. "She's the one who found the watch, so it seemed like it would be good to keep the circle of people involved as small as possible."

"Does she know what it does?" A note of panic crept into her voice.

"Well... yeah."

Jo skated in front of me and stopped, forcing me to come to a halt as well. "She knows it detects Gnomes? How does she even know what a Gnome is?"

"I... told her." I admitted sheepishly, lowering my gaze.

"Beau! That's the number one rule!"

"It's fine. She won't tell anyone."

"And how can you be so sure?"

I floundered for an explanation and came up empty. As the silence dragged on, Jo's eyes went wide. "Holy shit on a stick. She's a Gnome too, isn't she?"

"No."

"So, she's something else. Something like a Gnome, but not." If her voice rose any more octaves, she would be talking only to the neighboring dogs.

"I can neither confirm nor deny," I said, trying to side step her.

"You know that just confirms it, right?" She dropped her voice to a whisper, blushing and perhaps realizing how loud she had been.

"I don't understand how you jumped to that conclusion," I said, rubbing the back of my neck.

"The idea of other hidden communities had occurred to me before. I just thought it was because of all the fantasy books I read. So? What *is* she? I *need* to know. This is so exciting." I had never heard a whispered squeal before, but somehow, she managed.

"It's not my secret to tell." *Other hidden communities? There might be more than just Gnomes or Lynx? That seems logical.*

"I'll ask her, then." She continued skateboarding down the sidewalk, and I zipped along beside her again.

"You know, I could motorize your skateboard for you."

"Where is the fun in that?" she asked, puckering her face and looking at me sideways, as if the mere suggestion tasted sour.

"It's not for fun, it's for efficiency."

"If I wanted efficiency, I wouldn't be using a skateboard," she said with a toss of her head.

We found Meep leaning against the wall outside my room, softly chuckling to herself. *What is she laughing at? Can she hear as well as a cat? Was she hearing private conversations? How had she not overheard anything about secret communities of nonhumans before? I guess those people didn't make a habit of discussing their secrets in public, even if they thought they were out of earshot of anyone.* She straightened as we drew closer.

"Meep, this is my sister, Jo. Jo, this is Meep."

"You are going to be just as weird as he is, aren't you?" Meep asked dryly.

"And proud of it," Jo replied, smiling.

I let them in, and Jo immediately tossed her skateboard to the side and flopped onto my beanbag. Meep looked at my workbench in dismay. "What did you do?" she hissed.

I closed the door and locked it. *Honestly, why Kyle never locked it before doing weird things was beyond me.* "I was studying it."

"You completely dismantled it! I expected you to figure out how it *worked*, not *break* it," Meep said accusingly.

I shrugged, why was she so heated? "I'll put it back together. It's no big deal."

"No big deal? It's in a million pieces," she insisted.

Jo fished a box of candy from her backpack and smiled, she probably didn't see many arguments at home.

"Fifty-seven, actually and—" I corrected.

"*What?*" she roared, baring her teeth.

"I know how all of them fit back together." I said defensively.

She didn't deflate, but she did lower her voice. "What? You're telling me you memorized it?"

"I'm a Gnome, it's what I do. I can hold complex visualizations of gadgets in my mind."

Meep turned to Jo. "Did you come to help him put this back together?"

"No, that's Beau's thing." She popped another piece of bright colored candy into her mouth.

"Then what's your thing?" Meep asked her.

"I'll explain my thing if you explain yours," Jo countered.

Meep spun back on me, face red and eyes bulging, "You told her I'm a Lynx?" Her eyes radiated my impending doom.

I held up my hands defensively. "No! I swear. I made sure not to mention it. She figured out you were *something* on her own."

"A Lynx? Interesting," Jo leaned forward.

Meep glared at both of us, her gaze moving back and forth. Finally, she sighed. "I guess it would have come out, anyway. Fine. I'm a Lynx, and we are like cats, I guess."

I attempted to explain Gnomes to her using an analogy. "Gnomes have a mental workbench. It's hard to explain… Imagine having a notebook. You can write things in it and refer back to it later or draw things. Each Gnome might use it for something different."

Jo chimed in, "Beau uses it for his engineering, and I use it for languages. It's faster for me to store the information there than to learn it normally, but I still have to take the time to study the language. And I'm only sixteen, so I'm not as proficient at it as I will be with more practice."

"How many languages do you know?" Meep asked.

"Fifteen. Well, more or less, but they aren't all equally well-known."

"So, you guys are all just geniuses?" Meep wanted to know.

"No. It's like an expanded mental capability. We still have to work for it, read the relevant material, watch videos and tutorials, and even network with the right people. We just have the ability to store specific information in a special memory bank to recall perfectly whenever we want," I tried to explain.

"Though Beau *is* a genius," Jo interjected.

"What? No, I'm not," I objected.

"You are hella smart, and not because you are a Gnome. Because you are you. I've seen the grades you get and the books you read for fun. Engineering blueprints, physics, all the science stuff. You have loads of important things memorized."

"I just worked hard," I mumbled.

"You are brilliant *and* you worked hard. It's a potent combination." She tossed the empty candy box onto an obvious trash pile beside my desk.

"If you are trying to convince me Beau is cool, it won't work," Meep said.

"Anyway," I cleared my throat. "I can definitely put it back together. The problem is, I still don't know how it works. I'm stumped." Jo and Meep both stared at me. "What?"

"I thought we were going to *use* it, not disassemble it," Meep said, gesturing to my table.

"Yeah, that's why I came, so I can read the damn thing," Jo said, rolling her entire head for emphasis.

I slapped my forehead. Of course. It seemed so obvious now. Why had I fixated on understanding how it was made? "This is why I'm not a genius. Don't worry; I'll get it all back together, but I don't know how many uses we will get out of it. I don't know what powers it, so we won't be able to recharge it."

"Hmmm. Good point. We will need to be strategic," Meep mused. "Maybe we should scan the Auditor with it?"

I desperately wanted to, if only to see if he really was a Gnome, but I shook my head. "Too dangerous. If he sees us with it, well..." I pointed to my ruined drone.

We sat in silence for a moment, mulling over our options.

"I think we are overly fixated on the watch," Jo eventually said.

"What do you mean? It's the only thing we have," Meep said.

"Exactly the problem. It's our *only* lead. Pretend we don't have the watch. What would we do?" Jo prompted.

"We need more information. We are working in the dark," I said, voicing my frustration.

"His tablet?" Meep suggested. My eyes widened. *Now that was an idea.*

"What tablet?" Jo asked.

"He always carried a tablet, constantly typing things into it. If we can get it, I'm sure there will be all sorts of useful information in there," Meep said.

I turned to Meep. "You got the watch. Could you sneak back in and get the tablet?"

"No way. I barely got out the first time. Now his guard will be up."

"Yeah, he has increased his security," I said confidently.

"How can you be sure?" Jo asked.

"Because it's what I would do. Observe." I left the room and hit a hidden switch near the bottom of the door with my toe. When I entered without deactivating the switch, a mechanical arm sprung out from under a pile of junk and launched a net over me. I was yanked off my feet in an instant and dangled from a net.

"Woah." Jo's eyes widened.

"Are you nuts?" Meep crouched in my bed. I noted the irony of having a girl in there, but wisely kept it to myself.

"Chud stole my hat," I explained, slowly swaying in my net, "so I upped security. We can't expect any less from the Auditor."

Meep rose and pushed at the net, keeping me suspended. "You just wanted an excuse to show off your gizmo," she accused.

"Well, maybe a bit. But the point stands."

"We need the element of surprise," Jo said. "He has seen what you two can do and is likely going to be ready. So, we need to find someone he won't be ready for."

Meep batted the net, making me spin wildly. "You can't try to sneak in there, Jo," I objected with an unfortunate squeak as I spun.

Jo chuckled. "I couldn't even if I wanted to. What would I do, quote Shakespeare at him? Speak Latin? No. We need someone with a skill set he doesn't know about. And let's assume he understands normal human capabilities."

"What are you getting at?" Meep asked, taking another swipe at me.

"We need someone else with special abilities. And it so happens we have a device to find people like us," Jo said.

"We can't scan everyone we meet," I pointed out, my stomach gurgling uncomfortably.

"I think she is onto something," Meep agreed. "We can find other people who are weird, then use the watch. Once we know what they are, we should be able to convince them to reveal themselves."

"Sounds like a plan," Jo said.

"Great. Come on Jo, I'll show you where you are staying," Meep said as she ducked under my net and slipped out the door into the hall leaving me swinging sadly in the middle of the room.

"You can release the net with that switch over there," I said to Jo as she moved to leave.

Jo gave me a wicked grin and followed Meep. "Bye-bye, Beau. We'll *hang* out soon." She closed the door behind her.

"Come on, guys! Guys?" The momentum of my return swing made me thud into the door, and I spun again to find my phone where it lay out of reach on the table. "*Guys?*"

CHAPTER THIRTEEN

JUST HANGING AROUND

Home Decor and Design: Embrace human aesthetics when it comes to decorating your living space. Incorporate human-style furniture, decor, and color schemes to create a cozy and inviting atmosphere that resonates with human sensibilities. Avoid overt elements that might draw attention.

BEAU

I dangled in the net, my right leg long since fallen asleep. Apart from the uncomfortable position, hanging here was almost Zen. I was toying with my Rubik's cubes again, trying to mentally design an automated solver.

Finally, the door swung open. "About time," I said, trying to rotate my net to face the door. Standing there was an unfamiliar girl with shoulder-length red hair, thick black glasses, and a shocked expression on her face. She had the height and build to be a runway model, though not the face for it.

"Beau, what have you done?" she asked.

"I'm sorry. Have we met?" Why was this strange girl just barging into my room?

"What? Oh, no, of course not." Her face blushed a bright red to match her hair.

"Look, mind letting me down? There is a release right over there." I pointed with a hand awkwardly jutting out from beneath me.

Her eyes darted back and forth. "Yeah, yeah, let me just—" She pressed her glasses back into her nose and ducked underneath me. She found the release, and I flopped to the ground.

"Ooph," I exhaled and untangled myself from the net. I shook my leg and stretched before extending my hand. "I'm Beau. Apparently, you already knew that."

"I'm Kathleen," she murmured.

"Thanks for letting me down. Now, mind telling me why you barged into my room?"

"I didn't think you were going to be here," she said dodgily. She wasn't wrong. If I hadn't been literally tied up, I would have been out.

"That doesn't make it better," I said warily.

"Oh, I suppose it doesn't. I'm Kyle's... girlfriend."

I narrowed my eyes. "Why did you hesitate?"

"Our relationship is... complicated. I hadn't put a label on it before."

"Uh-huh. And you showed up here alone, without him? Why?"

"I was meeting Kyle... to have sex."

"You are really bad at lying," I observed.

"I'm sorry, Beau. I wasn't expecting to find you tied up. I didn't exactly have a story ready."

"You know what, I'm going to call Kyle and let him sort this out."

"No!" She blurted. "I mean, that's not really necessary, is it?" she followed up, much more meekly.

"Yeah, definitely calling him now." I grabbed my phone from the table, making sure I kept my eyes on her. She was looking around frantically again. I dialed Kyle's number and brought the phone to my ear.

Kathleen's pocket started ringing. I raised my eyebrow. "Why do you have his phone?"

"He dropped it when we were making out. I was bringing it back to him."

"Yeah, nothing you've said is adding up. Let's just wait here for Kyle to get back." I crossed my arms and stared at her.

She stared back, then suddenly tried to bolt past me, out the door. I grabbed her, and we ended up wrestling back and forth. I'm not the strongest guy, but I out massed her despite her height advantage and was doing a good job keeping her at bay. Then she kneed me in my crotch, and I dropped to my knees as bolts of pain shot up from my nether regions.

"Sorry," she said. By the time I could see straight, she was gone. I staggered back to my feet and looked down the hallway. There was no sign of her.

I collapsed into my beanbag and waited for the pain to fade. We were looking for strange things, but I wasn't sure what to make of that particular odd moment. Was she human? Could I find her again? Would I want to?

Eventually, things normalized, and I moved over to my workbench. I needed to put the watch back together. I hadn't been kidding when I'd said I had it memorized, and it was short work to put everything back as it was before. I suddenly had a vision of Chud sneaking in again and swiping it, so I strapped it onto my arm, then pulled my sleeve over it. With its complex latch, I felt confident nobody would get it off me without a fight.

Kyle walked in behind me. "Hey, Beau."

"Kyle, there you are. You won't believe what happened. Do you know a Kathleen?"

"Of course, she is my girlfriend," Kyle said.

"Wait, seriously? I thought she made it up."

"Why would she do that? She was supposed to meet me here. Where did she go?"

"Does she normally walk in here without knocking?" I asked, more annoyed than ever.

"Oh, yeah, it's better than her hanging out in the hall alone, you know?" he said quickly, running his hand through his short red hair.

Do red-heads have a thing for other red-heads? Make sense. I pushed away my errant thoughts with effort. I narrowed my eyes at him and folded my arms. "Why did she have your phone?"

Kyle's brows knit together, and he looked at the floor. "Oh, she found it? I lost track of it after we were making out."

I threw my hands up and cupped my head in defeat. "Wow. I'm such a jerk."

"What did you do?" he asked, sitting on the side of his bed and massaging the back of his neck.

I explained how my sister and Meep was here, though obviously I left out *why* they were here, and then how they left me dangling in a net, which I also, kind of, had to gloss over, though he didn't even show any type of reaction, I guess he just expected weird stuff from me all of the time. He nodded in places, but otherwise twiddled his thumbs around and around as he looked into the space about two feet to my right.

"Beau, can you please learn how to have a normal interaction with a woman? I need to apologize to her. I can't believe you." Kyle shook his head and left.

I was more confused now than I had been before. Kathleen was legit? She was the most suspicious person I had ever met, apart from the Auditor. I needed to find a way to get to the bottom of this. *Even if she is Kyle's girlfriend, something is not right about her.* Still, I recognized our encounter had gone poorly, and she would not be receptive to seeing me again anytime soon. *Best to let things cool off for a while before prodding at it again.*

Maybe I should go for a jog. The exercise would help stretch out my cramping muscles and maybe help clear my mind. I wasn't into exercise, but dangling in a net had made me restless. The cool fall air was invigorating, and before long, I was lost in thought.

I needed to find other potential non-humans. Best to be systematic. I made a mental list of everyone I knew and added everything suspicious I could think of.

Chud: Unusually large and muscular. Bully.

Samantha: Supernaturally hot. Steals stuff.

Kathleen: Sus as hell.

Kyle: Dating Kathleen. Hid something when I interrupted him.

Jeremy: Got really squirrelly when the Auditor asked questions about powers.

I paused. The rest of it was just vaguely weird stuff, and Jeremy being Jeremy. As a bonus, he was probably the easiest person for me to convince to help.

I shot Jo a text. *I think I have a good candidate to scan. Meet me here tomorrow morning.* I thought for a moment. *Oh, and thanks for leaving me hanging. Jerk.*

A simple reply came back. *Lol, you did it to yourself.*

I opened my dorm door and welcomed Jo inside. I poked my tongue out at her briefly, and she giggled. Then I dug up some prepackaged snack food for her to munch on. "How have things been going back home?"

"*Muy bien*," Jo said around a mouthful of chips, "Very good. I'm sure Mom has been keeping you up-to-date with everyone."

"Yeah, she's good at that." I laughed fondly.

"She's worried about you, you know."

"I know."

"She supports you, but she is scared for you. What if people find out you are a Gnome because they can see what you can do?"

"Is Mom worried about me, or are you?" I asked pointedly.

"Can't it be both? I know how I come off; I'm the quirky girl who thinks peppering a few foreign phrases in your speech makes you interesting. You are the weird recluse who makes new inventions in a day other people would spend weeks, maybe even years, on. See, it's a bit more attention-grabbing."

"So, I come off as a genius. That's something modern society rewards, not punishes. I think the world is ready."

"I hope you are right."

"Trust me, I am not doing this on a whim."

Jo finished her snack cake, and I led her through the halls to room 403. "Wait out here for a minute."

"Sure."

I knocked on the door and then I heard a large mass shifting inside before it swung open. Chud filled the doorway, looking down at me. His customary scowl melted away as he saw me, "Beau! I didn't do anything, I swear."

"Relax, I'm not here for you. This time," I said. "I need to speak with Jeremy. Mind giving us some space?"

"Sure, I'll just get out of your hair." He reached over and grabbed his backpack easily with his long arms despite it being all the way back on his desk, and then he left down the hallway.

"What was all that?" Jo asked.

"What was what?"

"That dude looked like he could bench press a car, and yet, he seemed terrified of you."

"Long story. Just know people shouldn't mess with your brother... or his hat." I turned away from her and strode into the room, immediately coughing due to the battle of strong scents punching me in the nose. The overwhelming smell of body odor was forefront. Dirty laundry was strewn everywhere. The closet had been left open, and none of the drawers were fully shut, allowing bits of T-shirts, boxers, and denim to peek out over cheap particleboard. Chip bags, snack wrappers, and cans were strewn about randomly, and the only thing vaguely distinguishing Jeremy's side of the room from Chud's was the prevalence of athletic jerseys on one side. Saying the room was in complete disarray was an understatement, at best.

The only thing in order was a small set of shelves displaying a random assortment of objects. On one shelf was a collection of anime figurines, all cute girls, most of them cat-girls, which identified them as belonging to Jeremy. They were in meticulous order, centered perfectly, and facing forward without a hint of dust. Another shelf contained a collection of rocks, with a dizzying array of colors, shapes, and crystalline structures. He even had a few fluorescent ones, which glowed dimly purple in the light from the window filtered by a heavy blanket tacked over it. Jeremy was proud of those rocks in particular. He'd said he collected all of them himself from exploring a local cave network. The next shelf was a coin collection full of unusually shaped and foreign specimens. Dice, stamps, paperclips, saltshakers... many of these collections were smaller, yet were no less well-organized, and held no evidence of dust.

Jeremy lay on the bed closest to the shelves, only half under the covers, snoring loudly and drooling. I prodded him with my foot. "Hey, wake up."

Jeremy groaned and opened his eyes. "Beau? What's up?"

"Get dressed. My sister is here, and I wanted to introduce you."

"Your sister, eh?" Jeremy sat up, picked a shirt up from the floor and pulled it over his head, "Is she cute?"

"Dude, just no. None of your pervy stuff with her. For one, she is my sister. For another, she is sixteen."

"Alright, alright."

"I mean it, she's off limits." I said, wagging my finger in his face and giving him my best glare.

"I said alright, jeez." I turned around as he got out of bed and finished dressing himself. "Alright, let's meet her. Oh, hold on, wait a sec." He went to his computer and woke up the screen, then closed the hentai he had open. "Alright, ready."

I was going to regret this. I flipped on the lights and opened the door. "Come on in."

Jo walked in and proceeded to gag. "Dude, this is foul."

"What is?" Jeremy asked, looking around.

"The stench. How do you stand it?"

Jeremy frowned. "I didn't notice anything."

"Of course, you didn't." Jo looked around the room. "Is this really the guy?"

I frowned at her tone. *Why is she being like this? I didn't know she was mean.* "Yeah, he's my best friend."

"*Why?*" The repulsion in her voice was clear.

"We have a lot of common interests. Yeah, he has some unsavory habits—"

"Hey!" Jeremy interjected.

"—that doesn't mean we can't be friends."

"Did you just bring her over to roast me?" Jeremy complained.

"No, sorry. Jo, this is Jeremy. Jeremy, this is my sister Josephina."

Jeremy extended his hand. "Charmed."

Jo pointedly left it hanging. "Hi."

Jeremy dropped his hand.

"Anyway," I said, searching for a way to change the subject, "do you have your copy of the fourteenth episode of Windrunners? I wanted to show it to Jo."

"Yeah, give me a sec." He started clicking through folders on his computer.

While he was distracted, I pulled up my sleeve to reveal the watch. I pointed it at Jeremy and flipped the switch. The screen gave its readout, which I showed to my sister.

"Of course." She rolled her eyes.

"What? And will you knock off the attitude? What is wrong with you?" I whispered.

"He's a Goblin." She didn't bother to lower her voice.

Jeremy froze, and then he slowly spun around in his chair to face us. His eyes darted back and forth. "Look, I know you aren't thrilled with my hygiene, but there is no need to throw around insults."

Blurting it out to him wasn't how I had seen this going. I figured she would just whisper it in my ear and I could try to approach the subject more delicately. Oh well, what was done was done. "No insult intended," I said.

"Oh, yes it was," Jo cut in.

I elbowed her in the ribs. "We mean it literally. We know what you are."

"What? Don't be crazy. A Goblin, seriously?"

"It's okay, Jeremy," I assured him. "Your secret is safe. We are Gnomes. We know all about keeping your true nature safe."

Jeremy took a step back. "No shit? How did you find out?"

"You remember the strange guy who was asking all those questions?" I asked.

Jeremy snorted. "Yeah, he was a hoot."

"Well, he had this watch." I showed him the device strapped to my arm. "It can detect people's true species."

Jeremy stepped closer, reaching for my arm. "What? How?"

"I don't know. The guy shows up, starts asking questions, has unearthly technology, and this is just a fraction of what we know he has. Meep says he shot at her with an honest-to-God ray gun. Something is going on. And I need *your* help to figure it out."

Jeremy stared, mouth hanging open, "Is she okay?"

"What?" I frowned. "Oh yeah, she's fine."

Jeremy scratched his head. "You need me? Nobody needs *me*. I'm not going to mess with this."

"Would Captain Rosh shy away from danger?"

"Well, no."

"Would Hiria leave a mystery unsolved?"

"Of course not."

"Would Murakasi leave her friends in a dangerous situation without backup?"

"Never!"

"Jeremy, you are my closest friend," I said, sobering. "I have a mystery, and I will be in far more danger without your help than with it. So, will you help me?"

Jeremy puffed up his chest and set his jaw. "Yes. Let's do this!" We clasped hands.

"What exactly are we doing?" Jeremy asked with determined excitement in his eyes.

"Right now, we are gathering allies. It will all be non-humans, so we can trust each other with our secret identities."

"Oh. Cool."

"I'll let you know when we find more people, and we will have to gather to go over a plan."

"Um, sounds good."

I stood there awkwardly for a moment. "Okay, we're going to head out. I'll see you later."

We left his room, and then Jo gasped in the untainted air. "I can't believe it worked."

"What can I say, I know him. I knew involving his favorite characters would inspire him and put him in a heroic mindset."

"Is he going to be useful?" she asked doubtfully.

"I wouldn't underestimate him. At the surface, he may seem like a gross slob. And deep down, he may be a pervert. But in the middle, there is someone wily and cunning."

Chapter Fourteen

Confrontations

Networking and Alliances: Build alliances with community members who have successfully integrated into human society. Strength in numbers can provide additional support and guidance.

Meep

"He did *what*?" Jo spluttered, choking on a mouthful of hot cocoa. I had just told her about meeting her brother and how he had been trying to get a girl. "I knew he was awkward, but I didn't know he was that far gone."

"Which is why what he said about Jeremy's pervert behavior being 'deep down' is concerning."

"Hmm, yes, those two should be watched."

Jessie entered the room, then. "Your mom took Kip to cheerleader practice and said you should make lasagna for dinner because it's big enough to feed all of us." I didn't necessarily invite Jessie. She had just shown up like she often did. Jo and Jessie had seemed to click, though, so I didn't make a fuss about her being here; we were just careful not to discuss anything about our mystery. "Rays was hiding under the bathroom sink again. Scared the bejeezus out of me when I went to get more toilet paper," she continued. "I'm not sure how she fits down there, much less how she thinks it's comfortable." Jessie sat in the middle of the floor across from Jo and me. Books, nail polish, and my new set of throwing knives were scattered around us.

Rays had come in on Jessie's heels and curled up on the bean-bag bag to watch us chat. She didn't take part, of course—she never did—but she liked to be where people were.

Jo entertained us with stories from home, like how she and her brother, Moe, had grown a nine-foot squash, and then how she had built a crossword that required twelve languages to solve.

"Wait, you have brothers, Beau and Moe?" Jessie asked.

"Don't forget Poe, Roe, Woe, and Zoe," Jo nodded.

Jessie scratched her head. "Zoe doesn't rhyme with the others."

I laughed. "Well, I guess I can't complain about unusual family naming conventions." My senses picked up a soft sound from downstairs, like the rustle of satin against a feather. *Who was that?* My mind flew to the Gnome, coined the Auditor by Beau. My heartbeat quickened. I'd hardly managed to get away last time, and now there were other people to protect. I snatched one of my throwing knives off the floor and jumped to my feet. "Stay here," I told them as I started for the door. But he was already there, managing to loom in the shadows of the hallway despite being three feet tall.

Dammit. How had he snuck up on me?

Jo gasped and moved to Rays, while Jessie, bless her braveness, moved to just behind my shoulder, giving me plenty of room to maneuver if I needed to jump to the side, while still showing support.

"Who are you?" she asked fiercely.

The Auditor glanced at her. "I'm here to talk to this *Kli'zath*." He pointed at me. "And I would appreciate it if *you* did not speak." He glared hard at Jessie.

"Excuse me?" she asked.

"I can deal with these two, but you, I know your kind well enough to understand that if you do not speak, you are less likely to lie to me. Now, be silent." He turned to face me. "Where is it, girl?"

"I don't know," I said, coolly.

"Hold on, what do you mean, 'my kind?'" Jessie asked.

"Where is it?" he repeated, ignoring Jessie.

"Explain yourself. This is important!" Jessie's voice had gone up an octave, becoming uncharacteristically shrill.

"I don't know. Why don't you answer my friend's question?" I replied. He still had not bothered to point a weapon at us. Was that a good sign? Or a bad one?

"*Gornbuckle*, and I was worried about this one lying to me." He indicated Jessie, who was still staring at him, eyes wide.

I searched for words to fill the silence. "You want what I have, and I don't know where it is. I definitely won't tell you if you hurt me or my friends, so... what do we do now?"

He paced around the room, scanning my dresser with his eyes and frowning at the small collection of photographs. "I came to you out of a sense of honor. I will not hurt your friends or you. For now. You are nothing but *Lorkorn* playing with things you cannot understand. But you haven't done anything irreversible. Yet." His eyes darted over me, analytically. "I will find it, one way or another."

He was talking like he was trying to convince himself. Was he a fearsome fighter, or wasn't he? His tone of voice was calm and reasonable, until he addressed Jessie, and then the hatred was clear as day. The problem was this behavior was even more concerning to me than if he had been decisive. I couldn't predict if he was going to be calm and peaceful or start shooting up the place. I had to assume the latter. I fingered my throwing knife and whipped it end over end directly at his chest.

Inches before landing, the knife slowed to a stop and thudded harmlessly to the floor. He sighed almost sadly. "Metal repelling force field, *Lorkorn*." He shook his head slowly. "And now I know your heart, *LorMau*." He took a step backwards, then he was gone.

Jo let out a breath and began to mutter to herself, "*Kli'zath*. Fake one... fake family... not family... false member..."

Jessie stared at the spot he had vanished from, silent and deeply concerned. Rays stared at the window, and I could hear a distant cracking of twigs and crunching of leaves down the street.

Jo's muttering reached a conclusion, and she confidently stated her translation. "False-kin."

CHAPTER FIFTEEN

CHANGELINGS

Personal Growth and Self-Reflection: Continuously work on personal growth and self-reflection to better understand your own identity. Embrace and celebrate your unique heritage while navigating the challenges of integrating into human society. This self-awareness will contribute to your overall well-being and success in the urban environment.

MEEP

"Meep," Jessie whispered, still standing frozen in front of the bedroom door. She knew I could hear her as if she had shouted, not only because the room was small and silent, but because she had a pretty good grasp of my abilities. Although we never discussed them, and *bless her*, she had never asked questions.

I turned to her pleading blue eyes. She had always been so desperate to know where she had come from. "Her kind." It must be tearing her up, and I braced myself, already knowing I was going to have to deny her the one thing she *needed*.

"He knew something... My parents are dead. I have no family, but... he knew 'my kind,'" she whispered as a dreamy and determined expression settled onto her face. "When he showed up asking questions a few weeks ago, he didn't give me any indication of that. I'd brushed it off as an insignificant exchange, just some weird dude not even worth mentioning, but here he was, pissed at you for some reason, and he seems to know something about where I came from."

"Oh no, I don't think he did," I hedged.

"You heard him. I heard him. Who is he? I need to talk to him."

"I'm so sorry. I can't tell you who he is. I don't really know, either. I doubt he will tell you anything. Probably just leave you with more questions."

Jessie whirled on me, "Bull. Shit. What 'more questions' could I possibly have? I've spent my whole life in foster care. Unloved. Unwanted. And now him? He came to *your* door, at *your* house, to speak to *you*. About something *you* have. You know a lot more about this than *you* are telling me." Her voice rose with each syllable until she was shouting, "We've been best friends for so long *you* should know how important this is to me. To have a chance to find out who I am and where I come from? My *family*? *You* have no right to keep those things from me!"

"Jessie," I said soothingly, "I would love to tell you, but it's not entirely my secret to tell."

Jessie stood straight and jabbed a finger in Jo's direction. "It doesn't take a genius to put this together. That guy was new. She's new. So, *she* has something to do with *him*. *She* has a family. I heard you talk about her brother. A big family, she said. Good for her. And *you* have a family. Neither one of you has a right to keep information about *my* family from me!"

"I doubt he'll talk to you," Jo chimed in. "He's not exactly friendly, if you haven't noticed."

Jessie glared at her. *Am I going to have to protect this kid from my best friend?* "Well, maybe he'll talk if I give him whatever it is he wants."

Jo and I looked at each other sideways. "You don't know what you're asking, Jess. You have no idea what I went through to get it," I said, my voice cracking. I wanted to tell her. This was so unfair.

Jessie stared at us in silence for a long moment, her face red. "I thought you were my friend," she said, exasperation and pain in her voice. With tears budding at the edges of her deep blue eyes, she fled.

"Jess, wait!" A moment later, the front door slammed against the wall as she flung it open. I sprinted after her, but she didn't slow as I jogged alongside her down my long driveway. "Jessie, please, let's just talk about this." She slowed to a brisk walk, not looking at me. "I'll tell you what I can, I promise, but it's *not* all *my* secret."

This seemed to finally get through to her, and she came to a stop. "It's not because you don't trust me?"

"Jess, you are my *best* friend. I would trust you with my life." I was *about to* trust her with my life.

She took a deep breath and let it out slowly. "This is important to me. I need to know things about myself and my family. I shouldn't have to beg my best friend. So, I will give you a chance, but so-help-me, if I don't find answers, I *will* try to find him myself no matter what you and your new friends say."

"What I took from him—the thing he tried to kill me over

when I stole it—might be useful. *If* it tells us what we need to know. I can explain more, I promise, but first I need to make a phone call and set it up. Please... trust me."

After a brief and whispered conversation with Beau, I opened the front door about an hour later to find Beau... *and* Jeremy. I groaned. "Fuck, did you have to bring him to my house? I have sisters."

"Jeremy? He'll be okay. We had a talk. My sister is here, too... remember?" Beau asked pointedly with a level look at Jeremy. A reminder to be on his best behavior. I wasn't sure what was worse: letting one or both into my house. At least Jeremy had never sent a spy robot to follow me, and I'd never caught his scent around my house before. He entered slowly, trying to squeeze past me meekly. Could it be even... reverently?

I led the two to the kitchen where Jo and Jessie waited. I introduced Jessie officially. She greeted each in turn and shook their hands, though I did see her surreptitiously wipe her hand on her jeans after grasping Jeremy's hand. He turned away from Jessie to look at Rays, who had also entered the room and hopped up to sit on the counter, curious.

Beau revealed the watch-like device strapped to his wrist, which was, thankfully, back in one piece. He pointed it at Jessie and pressed a button as he had done before then tilted the display toward Jo who stood beside him.

"Fae," she announced to the room.

I breathed a sigh of relief. So, Jessie *was* something special. I could give her the answers she was looking for. At least, some of them.

"Fae? Like fairy? What does that have to do with anything?"

Jessie asked.

"Isn't there a bunch of types of Fae? Does it give you anything specific?" Jeremy asked.

"It means you aren't human." I hushed him with a well-aimed look. "None of us are. I'm a Lynx, Beau and Jo are Gnomes, and Jeremy is a Goblin. You're like us. You're special. You're different." I finally got to tell her the truth about who I was. I relished the truth slipping from my tongue. Of course, I had wanted to tell her, and now finally, *finally*, I was able to tell her.

Jessie took some time to process this. Her features froze, and her gaze lost focus like a computer trying to load too many programs at once. Jeremy continued to look around him at everything, as if the fact we had a toaster was a revelation. Jo decided to get some water for everyone, and Rays actually helped her find the right cabinet for the cups. Under normal circumstances, I would have given more thought to that; she didn't often demonstrate complete awareness of others. But my, and Beau's, attention was focused wholly on Jessie. She sat in the kitchen chair and stared for so long, I started to get worried.

Finally, she nodded. "This explains so much. I've always had this strange ability to look like other people. My foster mom caught me once. She freaked out. She said people would want to kill me if they found out. I've been terrified of it ever since then. I didn't know what it was. Maybe that's why they never adopted me. I thought I was a freak, so I hid it from everyone."

I gave her a hug. It was hard enough growing up a Lynx with a family I could be myself with. I couldn't imagine doing so without any support, or even understanding what I was.

"Sounds rough," Beau said.

"*Schwere kindheit,*" Jo nodded sagely as she set a glass of water in front of Jessie. When we looked at her in confusion, she translated. "Poor girl."

"So, you can turn into other people? Sounds like a Changeling," Jeremy said.

"In the old stories, Fae would trade out a human baby for one of their own." Jo became more animated as she explained. "The stories didn't explain if the babies already looked human or if they mimicked another human baby. And it never says what happens to an adult."

"A Changeling, huh? Yeah. That feels right. I'm a Changeling." Jessie smiled. "Though, does that mean my birth parents were human and their baby was swapped out for me? By Fae... who are my actual biological parents? Who is the family I am looking for then?" Jessie clutched her head.

"We don't really know how this all works, either. But that does sound like a headache," Beau said.

"All of my siblings are Lynx," I said, glancing at Rays. "We have different fathers, but we all share the same mother."

Jo indicated her brother and started pacing, losing herself in thought. "We grew up in a family of Gnomes. I was taught the mother needs to be a Gnome for the child to be. There is so much secrecy. This is frustrating. Gnomes have a strong oral tradition, passing history down from generation to generation, but our origins are a mystery. The few written records we keep are in Gnomish, and they are closely guarded."

"My dad just told me, 'Yer a Goblin, kid. Life's gonna suck,'" Jeremy said. We all stared at him uncomfortably. "My old man wasn't exactly one for 'strong oral traditions.'"

"What about the weird dude?" Jessie asked.

We explained about the supposed 'Super Gnome' and everything we had discovered. Afterward, Jessie declared she had a lot to think about, so everyone said their goodbyes and headed home. Including Jessie, which was uncommon.

Chapter Sixteen

How to Get a Date

Social Etiquette: Study and emulate human social etiquette, including greetings, gestures, and appropriate behavior in various settings. Understanding and adhering to social norms will help you navigate social situations with ease and prevent misunderstandings or conflicts.

Beau

I went to bed early Monday, but sleeping was hard. My restless brain buzzed with excitement. The day had come to finally put my big plan in motion, and by tomorrow night, Samantha would be securely mine. And I would have won.

I lay for hours staring at the inside of my eyelids, but just as soon as time had fuzzed around me, the string I had tied to my leg jerked me awake—the silent alarm I had rigged to not disturb Kyle had deployed. I had no idea how much sleep I had managed to catch, but I had more important things to do than worry about my sleep cycle. I slipped out of bed and grabbed the bags of preparations I had left for myself.

I met Jeremy outside and handed him some of the bags. "Thanks for your help."

"You know I'm always down for some mischief."

"This isn't mischief." I looked at him sideways.

"Then why are we doing it at three in the morning?"

I shrugged. "I don't want anyone to interfere with the setup."

"And *why* would they interfere?"

"Because they would be concerned about someone installing all of these things."

"If you are doing something other people want to *stop*, then it's mischief."

"It is not," I said defensively.

"Embrace it. Come to the dark side. You enjoy breaking the rules, admit it," he said with a bemused grin, and bumped my shoulder with his playfully.

No. This isn't breaking the rules. It's for love... but I couldn't deny it, either. Weren't rules made to be broken? I did get a sort of pleasure from it. There was a thrill in sneaking around and trying to avoid being caught. It wasn't the first time I had used my silent alarm. Last time, we'd broken into the locker room and mixed itching powder into all the soap dispensers, but this was the first time I had used it for something good.

"We need to get this stuff all the way to the quad," I said.

"Ugh, this stuff is heavy."

"Why do you think I asked for your help?"

"Fine."

We made our way to the center of campus. I didn't bring a flashlight because it would have drawn too much attention. Jeremy seized my arm and dragged me sideways up against a building.

"What is it?"

"Shh."

We waited in silence for a moment until I heard the scuff of shoes on concrete. The footsteps grew louder, and then a figure walked by our hiding spot. I hadn't even noticed anyone coming. Had Jeremy seen them when I had not? Was that a thing Goblins could do? We stayed in place until the footsteps faded from hearing.

When we reached the quad, my arms were burning from the exertion, and we both set our bags down gently. After resting for a bit, Jeremy kept watch as I set up my elaborate contraptions.

I had studied the quad after examining Samantha's movement patterns to know just how I wanted things arranged. The tricky part would be keeping all my careful preparations out of sight; fortunately, there was enough greenery to hide my stuff in the bushes.

I paced back and forth, brimming with nervousness. I'd spent so much effort planning, you'd think I would be calm and confident, but no. My mouth felt dry, so I took a swig from my water bottle. Checking my pocket watch, I saw that it was 1:45. *Alright, I've got this.* I checked again. 1:45. *Come on, will she just show up, already?* The suspense was agonizing.

Jeremy sat at a nearby bench, giving me a thumbs-up and a smile when he caught my eye. I gave him a smile I didn't feel and returned the gesture, only half aware. I checked my watch again. 1:46. *Agh.*

I tried to do some breathing exercises to calm down. *Breath in. Hold it. Hold it. Hooold it. And out.* I wiped my palms off on my pants and took another swig of water. I checked the clock again. 1:46. This was torture.

I ground my teeth and looked around. It was still too early for her to show up, and indeed, she was nowhere to be seen. The next few minutes dragged on in the same manner until finally—finally! —I caught sight of Samantha.

I felt a simultaneous wave of relief and nausea. She was finally here. Her lovely hair swayed, and I saw her smile as she chatted with her friend.

Good.

Good.

Wait, no.

Not good. She was deviating from the path. She wandered off, following her friend, but thankfully, they paused at an intersection and continued chatting. My teeth involuntarily clenched, and I thought I was going to black out from a spike of blood pressure. Her friend was not supposed to be here. Samantha was not supposed to be over there.

Finally, they parted ways, and Samantha continued toward her next class, but the damage was already done. She was on the wrong side of the quad now. She wouldn't pass through the sweet spot, and nothing would work.

I tried to think of something to do. If I went over and talked to her, it would throw off the entire thing. I couldn't think of what to do now. Fortunately, Jeremy had also spotted the problem, and he was bee-lining towards her in order to redirect her back into place. *Jeremy, I could kiss you. But I won't.*

Jeremy proved to be devious and showed a level of self-awareness I hadn't realized he had. He didn't talk to Samantha. He approached a girl ahead of her. I couldn't make out exactly what he was saying to her. She seemed uncomfortable, pulling her books to her chest and hurrying on. He moved on to the next nearby girl, who loudly gasped and slapped him before marching on. Samantha paused and crossed to the right side of the quad to avoid Jeremy and the scene he was causing.

Alright, we are back on track!

I took my position and grabbed the button to start things off.

Closer.

Closer.

Now!

I pressed the button. A loud electric bass tone sounded, followed by some power chords from an electric guitar. Smoke billowed across the quad, thick and white.

"SAMANTHA!" My voice boomed out from the speakers, louder even than the music. Her eyes went wide. I hit the next button and ran forward, bursting out of the smoke in front of her and sliding forward on my knees. I held out a bouquet of roses, and then flying drones streamed from behind me, displaying a large banner that read, "Samantha: Will you go out with me?" I said those same words out loud, and then fireworks went off, sending sparks shooting up on either side of me as the music rose to a crescendo.

When the music stopped and the smoke cleared, I remained on my knees, holding out the flowers and waiting with bated breath. Samantha looked around wide-eyed, and I realized a crowd had surrounded us, staring and holding their phones out. I hadn't planned on being a spectacle, of course. *Why wouldn't I be? I had fireworks, for Gnomes-sake.*

After a moment, Samantha licked her lips and said, "How can I say no?" Then she smiled weakly. Some of our audience clapped, and a few people shouted, "Woo!"

"Tomorrow. At 6:00. Signor Bernini's," I said.

"Sure." She smiled, showing an odd amount of teeth.

"Alright! See you there." Unsure how to proceed, I got to my feet, shook her hand, and walked away. *Was there some way to leave that situation without looking like a fool? Why had I not planned my exit?*

Once away from the quad, Jeremy caught up to me, "Dude, that was awesome. Her panties must be so wet right now."

"Hey, don't talk about my girlfriend like that." *My girlfriend? I did it. I really did it.* I started laughing. "My girlfriend. Man, that feels good to say."

"What did I say? You just had to talk to her."

"Just talk to her? No, remember what I said about needing a plan? *That* was a plan."

CHAPTER SEVENTEEN

GHOST, A YETI, AND A DEMON

Social Clubs and Organizations: Join human social clubs, organizations, or interest groups that align with your own hobbies and passions. This allows you to meet humans who share similar interests, fostering connections based on shared activities.

MEEP

"I'm telling you, Kathleen is sus as hell." Beau spoke with uncharacteristic fervor. He loudly told anyone who would listen that he had a date tonight. He even told Kip, and now I heard her off-key musical tones drift playfully through the air. "A Gnome named Beau, wants to be a beau..."

"But is she a *non-human* type of suspicious?" I asked. Beau had some beef with Kathleen, it was clear, but I wasn't convinced that it was relevant. Apparently, Kathleen had claimed to be his roommate's girlfriend and had acted awkwardly. But I mean... had he met himself? The pot calling the kettle names, as Kip would say.

"I don't know, but who else are we going to scan? And do we even need any more people? We haven't been able to come up with any clearer candidates," Beau said, tugging at his beard.

I ticked off on my fingers, "We have a Lynx, two Gnomes, a Goblin, and a Fae. Five is a good number, right?"

Jo snorted. "But we are 'false-Kin,' which implies the existence of the real ones somewhere. Like the Auditor is a true-kin Gnome. So, there are true-kin Lynx, Goblin, Fae, and all that. That kind of sounds scary." She shuddered, a minute tremble of pastel and dark brown hair the same shade as her brother's.

Beau and I both frowned and he said, "Yeah, I say that as long as the scanner works, we should try to scan and recruit as many people as possible."

I nodded in agreement.

"The bigger question is, is scanning someone enough to make them work with us?" Jo asked from my bean bag with Jessie's blanket thrown over her. Jessie wasn't here right now. We weren't sure where she was. She had been quiet the last couple of days since the Changeling conversation. Finding out the people she thought were her birth parents might not have been her biological parents after all must have really messed with her. If I thought it would help, I would have gone to her, but I had my hands full with the rest of this mystery. I couldn't give her any more answers if I stopped now.

"Our true nature is our biggest secret. Once exposed, protecting lesser secrets becomes a lot less important. If we can get Kathleen to admit what she is, we can untangle what she was doing in my room afterward," Beau said.

"Are you telling me you want to expose her identity just to sate your own curiosity?" Jo threw her brother a dirty look.

"No. Maybe. Alright, I have some additional motives here, but that doesn't change her being one of the most likely candidates we have. Unless you want to start scanning people at random and hope."

I wanted to argue, but we didn't have anyone else we wanted to scan right now, and we didn't know how many uses we could get out of it. I sighed. "I've asked around some. Few people seem to know her. I did find one person who saw her at the Wednesday night women's Book Club meeting at the library."

"Perfect, tonight you and Jo can go and scan her." Beau wanted me to scan her instead of doing it himself. He thought their prior interaction "wouldn't be conducive to prying deeply held secrets out of her."

"Ugh, tonight? Sounds miserable," I groused.

"I have a date tonight."

"We know," Jo and I said in chorus.

Jo left, striking out on her own. Apparently, she didn't get much freedom at home, and she was always telling me where she was going, all the details of how she was getting there, and when she was coming back. I mean, I *did* care, but... wasn't it a bit much? Just go. Call me if you need me, and I'll see you later.

About an hour later, Jo flounced into the room and tossed a book at me. Curled into my beanbag, I snatched it from the air and sat up. "What's this?" I asked, irritated that she threw this—I looked at the cover—garbage at me.

"The book for Kathleen's club, of course." Jo sat on the window-sill and opened her own copy. "I went to the public library—it's so small here—and I found two copies of this book. The librarian was confused that I wanted to check out both copies of the same book, but I could check out up to five books at a time, so I don't know what her problem was."

"You're weird."

"You have to read the book, otherwise you won't be able to contribute to the conversation."

"We don't need to contribute."

"What if we scan the girl and she's not human?"

"Then wait for it to end."

"It will be a lot easier to talk to her if we bond during the meeting."

"We can't finish this book in five hours."

"Of course we can," Jo said, and started flipping the pages. I couldn't imagine her sitting still for long enough to finish a whole book, but she was already engrossed.

"Alright, *I* can't finish this book in five hours," I mumbled.

"Just read what you can. I'll summarize the rest for you."

I looked at the book again. It was some trashy supernatural romance. I flipped it over and read the blurb on the back.

My name is Gloria Forevermore. I just moved to a new high school, and I'm already being romantically pursued by a ghost, a yeti, and a demon with a heart of gold. I don't know why—I am just an average girl. The fate of the world rests on my shoulders, but first, I must decide who I date.

My eyes rolled so hard I expected to hear them drop to the floor. This sounded atrocious. I read the first page, then flipped to a random mid-chapter, and after skimming the page, I flipped to the end in disgust. *Nope.* The book thudded on the carpet along with any remaining hope this book club would be tolerable. But Jo was lost in Gloria's pubescent thoughts and didn't notice my silent escape.

The Auditor was following us when we went to the library. He wasn't even subtle about it, just strolling along some distance back. I spent a few minutes trying to evade him, rounding corners then putting on a burst of speed to reach an unexpected corner. Jo had to hold onto me while on her skateboard to keep up, but whenever we stopped and looked back, he was still there.

"What is up with this guy?" Jo asked. "Is he just trying to freak us out? Because it's working."

"I don't know. I don't think he will make a scene with a lot of people around, so let's stick to the crowds." I didn't know what would happen when the crowds thinned and we had to go home—other people couldn't shield us forever. I decided not to voice this concern so as to not worry Jo too much, and instead, I played it by ear.

When we arrived at the library, the Auditor stood outside across the street and watched us go in. He gave a taunting little wave before the doors slammed shut, hiding him from view. We followed some signs to a meeting room filled with women. I recognized Margaret from Clair's, but the others were new to me.

"Oh, new faces! Welcome, welcome, I'm Susan, Susan Bates," a girl with a blonde bob said. I cringed at the obviously fake "customer service" voice; no one was this happy. "Over here we have Margaret, Penny, Kathleen, and Heidi,"

"Pleased to meet you," I mumbled.

"Hi, I'm pleased to be here with all of you. This book was amazing." Jo bubbled over with excitement. I still couldn't believe she had read the entire book with hours to spare to fill me in on all the details. I wished Jessie had been there. She would have gotten a kick out of it.

"Oh, you read it? Excellent," a tall girl with long brown hair said—Heidi?

"Not that it would be a problem if they hadn't, everyone is welcome to join. But it does make it easier to talk about the book if we don't have to dance around spoilers," Susan added brightly.

We took seats, and I managed to sit next to Kathleen with Jo on my other side.

A small girl with mousy hair like mine leaned forward and rubbed her hands together. "Sooo... who was your favorite character?" Penny asked.

"I just loved Prasher. Such a tragic figure, able to love, but never to touch, or be touched," Margaret said. She was heavy-set and wore all black—black slacks and a black turtleneck with black hair to match. Her red lipstick captured my attention until her form fuzzed in my mind so she was just a set of glossy red lips, like the Cheshire Cat without the toothy grin.

"Damian had such a great arc. At first you think he is just evil, drawing in Gloria with his bad boy vibes, but over the course of the book, he grows to be more human and compassionate, and just when he finally becomes worthy of her, that same compassion drives him to sacrifice himself for her. Ironically, by becoming worthy of her, he *cannot* have her," Heidi said, practically swooning in her seat. I struggled with my eyes, trying to keep them from rolling out of my face. Insulting all these ladies was not going to help me.

"But Herschel was what Gloria needed. Prasher might have been an amazing friend, but she can't share her life with him if he doesn't even have a life of his own. And Damian might have been willing to die for her, but Gloria needs someone who can *live* for her. Herschel was the only balance between Prasher's purity and Damian's deviousness," Jo said enthusiastically.

"You are overlooking the biggest problem though," Kathleen

said, tossing her flowing red hair, which contrasted beautifully with her gray off-the-shoulder top. "All of them want Gloria for what she can *do* for them. Prasher wants the companionship she can offer, Damian wants her for her body, and Herschel is just latching onto the only human who treated him like a person. All of them view Gloria in terms of how she can improve *their* life. They don't care about Gloria's happiness for its own sake."

God, this was boring. But Kathleen's rant gave me the chance to activate the watch. I showed Jo the screen, and she nodded at me. *Fuck, Beau was right.* Now I had to sit through the rest of this nonsense.

"That's exactly why I support Damian," Heidi said. "When it came down to it, he sacrificed himself for her. He may not have started out that way, but he ended up valuing her life over his own."

"Does it count as a 'sacrifice' when he didn't actually die?" Susan asked. "He's a demon. I don't think mortality works the same way for him. I bet it was all a ruse. He will be back in the sequel."

"Don't do Prasher so dirty," Margaret complained, turning to Kathleen. "Just because he doesn't have a body doesn't mean his love can't be pure. He is interested in Gloria for who she is as a person. He wants companionship from her. How are you making that sound like a bad thing?"

"It's not that wanting companionship is bad," Kathleen responded. "It's that his relationship is based on what he can *get* from her, not about what he can *offer* her in return."

"A poor man who gives away the only ten dollars he has is worth more than a rich man giving away a hundred dollars he doesn't value," Margret retorted.

I couldn't take it anymore. "Why should she have to choose at all? All of them offer her something different, and this is all about what she will be getting out of the relationship, so why should we penalize them for wanting stuff out of it, too? Just be with all of them, and if it goes south, break up with that person and move on. All relationships are finite. I say get what you can out of them, then get out." Everyone stared at me like I had grown horns and started chanting in Latin. My cheeks heated. "Excuse me." I rose from my seat and fled to the hallway. The room erupted into furious conversation as the door snapped shut.

I shouldn't have said anything. The concept of non-monogamous relationships wasn't a societal norm. I wasted the rest of the hour by using the library database to try to find peer reviewed articles on mythological creatures living among us, but I found nothing of use. Hemmons College did not have a folklore department or anything, and besides, I had the feeling that this kind of research was better suited to someone like Jo.

The door opened about an hour later. "That was a blast!" Jo said. "I wish I was in town longer so I could keep coming."

"Don't let that stop you! Here, take my number." Susan scribbled something on a scrap of paper and gave it to Jo. "Text me anytime and I'll loop you in on the reading list."

"Thanks!" Jo took the paper and stuck it in her pocket. "Kathleen, hold on."

Kathleen paused at the door, then turned and came back over, "You fit right in, Jo. It was so fun to have you. Meep?"

I gestured for her to follow us back into the meeting room.

"We need your help," I said.

"With?" Kathleen asked.

"There's an unusual man in town. We have reason to believe he is dangerous, and we need to find out what he is planning," I said.

"What does that have to do with me?" Kathleen asked, raising one immaculate eyebrow.

"You're an Aethel," Jo said.

"What the hell is an Aethel?" Kathleen asked.

"Arrogant and not nearly as helpful as you'd think," the Auditor said.

We all whirled to find him at the doorway, gun out and trained on us. Kathleen paled.

"I thought you didn't want to make a scene with witnesses," I said, trying to stall while I thought of a plan. I might be able to dodge if he tried to fire, but Jo or Kathleen couldn't. The latter girl dropped to the ground, grabbed her backpack, and crawled under the table. Good, that got her out of the line of fire. One less person to worry about.

"It's quite remarkable, really. You have these libraries," he said, "which contain vast amounts of information sitting there for anyone to access. And yet, it gets ignored. There is barely anyone in this building. In fact, I'd estimate it's a low enough number, I could kill every witness if I needed to. I trust you won't let it come to that."

My breathing quickened as I cast about for solutions. I remembered there being a brief moment between blasts from the gun during my encounter with him in the forest. Maybe if I could bait out an attack, I could slip through that opening and attack him. But how would I ensure he didn't attack anyone else?

Rustling came from under the table, and I leaned back a bit to see Kathleen putting a mat on the ground, followed by several statues. *What is she doing?*

"No more games," the Auditor said. "You have the Zath scanner. It's right there on your wrist."

I glanced down, and yep, there it was. I hadn't taken it off after scanning Kathleen. Stupid of me, in retrospect. I knew that little Gnome had been poking around. I just assumed the interior of the library would be safe. Kathleen was muttering bad poetry under her breath, understandable to me only due to my sharp hearing.

Was this really the time or the place for that? *Well, whatever makes her feel better, I guess...*

I didn't see any options that wouldn't put the other girls at risk. "Okay, you got us, don't shoot. I'm taking the watch off now." I slowly moved my arm in front of me and began carefully unlatching it.

"Hurry up!" he snapped.

"Oh, so you want me to make sudden movements now?"

"Not sudden movements, but stop trying to delay."

Jo was hyperventilating behind me. I couldn't blame her. My heart was racing, and my hands were sweaty, which didn't help me to unlatch the watch. I got it off my wrist and held it up in front of me. "Alright, here it is." Maybe I could grab the gun when he came closer to take the watch.

"Set it on the ground, then slide it over to me."

So much for that idea. I stooped down and set it carefully on the ground. This gave me a good look at what Kathleen was doing. She had statues arranged on a mat in front of her and was reading from a book. Before I slid the watch over, Kathleen stopped speaking, and then a voice called from the hallway. "Hey, you! Freeze!"

The Auditor whirled, bringing his gun to bear at someone in the hallway.

Shit.

I used my crouch to pounce at him as he fired his death ray at the interloper. I wasn't in time to disrupt his aim before he took his shot, but he had no time to turn and aim at me before I slammed into him. We tumbled out of the reading room into the main section of the library as I tried to take hold of the gun.

Perhaps I should have tried to kill him. He was actively threatening me and others, and probably just killed someone else. Yet, I had stolen from him first. And more than that, I had never tried to kill anyone before. I didn't have the instincts for it. So, when my attempt to wrestle the gun from him ended up with the barrel pointing at him, I didn't try to fire it. The realization that I could kill him stunned me, scared me so much that I faltered, releasing my hold, and falling back.

Maybe the moment had terrified the Auditor as much as it had me because he scrambled to his feet and ran towards the exit. I was too shocked to go after him, and it even took me a couple of seconds to remember he had just shot someone.

I looked around for a burning corpse, but instead, I saw a security guard, unharmed and standing motionless with an accusatory finger pointing at the reading room. Behind him, a section of wall was on fire. Before I could check on him, he dissolved into a mist, which quickly dissipated.

"What the actual fuck." My breaths started coming faster and faster, and I felt dizzy. *I just saw someone get unexisted! Is this a murder? But you can't have a murder without a victim and* there is no victim.

My eyes found the flicker of the flames, then my instincts kicked in. I grabbed one of the emergency fire extinguishers before spraying down the wall. My breath slowed as I made sweeping movements like all the training from working at Clair's had drilled into me.

I went back into the reading room to find Jo blocking the doorway, arms crossed, as Kathleen was trying to exit. "We need to talk," she pleaded.

Kathleen's gaze darted between my face and Jo's, then she retreated back into the room and plopped down in a chair, dropping her bag beside her. "Alright, fine, let's start with who the fuck that was?"

"We call him the Auditor, because he's been going around asking people a list of questions, insisting it's for an audit and we must comply." I explained how I had found his base of operations and stole some of his tech. "He's been up in arms about it, literally. He really wants it back."

"Then give it back! Why are you stealing from a guy with a laser gun?" Kathleen asked incredulously.

"It's more complicated than that," Jo chimed in. "He isn't human. He's a Gnome. The watch we stole? He called it a *Zath* scanner, which is Gnomish for kin. Based on other terms he's used, I deduce that 'Kin' is how they refer to different groups of, um, let's call them mythological creatures."

Kathleen lifted a brow. "And you know all this... how?"

"I'm a Gnome. Or at least... I thought I was. We are still sorting out the specifics. But I'm a Gnome, and I can speak Gnomish," Jo said.

"And I'm a Lynx, and you are an Aethel," I added.

"I still have no idea what an Aethel is." Kathleen crossed her arms.

I looked at Jo. "I don't know. I don't know the translation of that word. I was hoping it would be close enough for her to recognize. But regardless, we know you are *something*, and we've trusted you enough to tell you our secrets."

"I'm a human," Kathleen insisted.

"You did something back there, with the statues and the chanting. It saved us," I said.

"I was praying."

"Oh really, and that's why a security guard seemed to be there, but wasn't?"

She lifted her hands innocently. "My prayers were answered, it's a miracle." I gave her a flat stare. After a moment, she relented. "Do you think that guy is going to hurt anyone else?"

"He was willing to shoot the fake guard. He isn't acting like someone who has peaceful intentions. We don't know what he is planning, but it seems really important we find out. We need your help. We are finding people with special abilities to team up against him," I said.

"I can't believe I'm saying this, but I'll help. I'm human, and I really don't know what an Aethel is... but I am a witch."

Jo's eyes went wide. "A real witch? You mean you can cast spells and turn people into frogs?"

"That is a hateful stereotype."

"I know some people who could use being turned into a toad," I said.

"I know, right? But still, the Archmage does *not* allow that," Kathleen said.

"So, there is a structure? Like a ruling body, and a government? Do you have your own language?" Jo asked.

"Look, our secrecy is important. People tend to get burned alive when we are discovered."

"We are all scared of what humans might do to us if they find out what we are," I said, attempting to reassure her. *I wish Jessie was here. I bet she could have done this better.*

"Yeah, well, excuse me if I don't want to implicate anyone else. It's bad enough I outed myself," Kathleen said.

Jo leaned forward. "So, you can cast magic fireballs and stuff?"

"No, magic is more subtle than that. It takes time to set up a spell and pull it off, so if there is someone I need to blow up with a fireball, I'd be better off with a grenade," Kathleen said. "You saw how long it took me to set up that spell. If you had fought him immediately instead of buying time, the fight would have been over before I managed it."

"So... you're what? Not very useful either?" I asked, scowling and folding my arms.

Kathleen shook her head and tucked long strands of red hair behind her ear. "Magic is very useful. It's possible to do all kinds of things. It just takes time and preparation." She brushed her face again, seeming to struggle with a stray strand stuck on the frame of her thick, black-rimmed glasses.

"You said the word 'possible?'" Jo asked.

Pulling her glasses off and blowing a puff of air upwards out of her stuck out lower lip she said, "Well, yes. It really depends on how familiar I am with a certain spell."

"What kind of spells are you good at?" I asked.

Kathleen sighed. "I'm pretty decent with... uh... illusions. It's probably what I have the most practice doing." Jo made her eyebrows disappear under her bright pink beanie and glanced at me. Kathleen tucked the errant strand she had been fighting with behind her ear and stood up, "Look, no offense, but just because I *believe* you doesn't mean I want to immediately tell you all my secrets. I don't even know you. I'm going to go sleep on this, okay?"

Jo and I let her pass. We'd done what we came to do.

Chapter Eighteen

Disillusionment

Emotional Regulation: Practice emotional regulation techniques to avoid standing out or drawing attention due to excessive emotional displays. This can help you blend in better with human societal expectations.

BEAU

While the girls were gossiping at the book club, I sat in Signor Bernini's, gnawing at my umpteenth breadstick as a tuxedoed Italian waiter refilled my water glass. He frowned at the gold and silver balloons I had tied to the empty chair across from me. He also made a point to scowl at them every time he was here like they were some great personal insult. *Did he have a bad history with balloons?*

"Would you like to order yet, sir?"

"No, I'm sure she will be here any minute now."

"Sir, the kitchen will be closing soon. If you don't order now, we won't be able to serve you."

I pulled out my phone. I had sent her a dozen messages on her Nebula profile I had found, all asking where she was, with zero replies. Time to admit it, I'd been stood up. "No, that's alright. If she isn't here, I won't be having anything."

"I will bring your check," the waiter said imperiously.

"Wait, I didn't order anything."

"Sir, the breadsticks are complimentary *with the purchase of a meal*. If you don't order anything, I'm afraid we must charge you for them."

"Ah, right, of course. Sorry."

When the waiter plopped the bill in front of me, I was astonished. "$40 for breadsticks?"

"The sir has consumed quite a few."

Kyle was there when I walked back into our room, and he put his book aside, leaving it splayed open on his table, which was something I'd never seen him do. "Please, tell me the rumors aren't true."

"What rumors? Nobody tells me rumors." I slumped into my bean bag, feeling glum and worthless. What had I done wrong?

"What the hell were you thinking? Fireworks, Beau? Really? You're lucky you didn't get expelled or arrested. Making unexpected loud bangs on school, or any federal property, isn't consequence free."

"You said to be me. I make elaborate schemes. So, I made an elaborate scheme to impress her." Obviously.

"Do you even understand how inappropriate that was?" He swung his long legs off the side of the bed to sit up straight.

"Inappropriate? I thought women loved big romantic gestures."

"Sure, from someone they are romantically involved with. But receiving *that* kind of attention from someone they don't know isn't romantic, it's creepy." He seemed legitimately upset with me. I didn't even know he could get upset, he was always so quiet and level.

"Creepy?" I was genuinely confused.

"For one, you don't *know* her, therefore, you can't be in *love* with her. This means you are in love with the *idea* of her, or lusting after her body, and neither makes women feel valued and loved. That makes women feel objectified.

"For two, you made it a public spectacle. You put her on the spot, which put a lot of expectations on her to say, 'Yes.' There's already a level of risk when turning down a guy because women don't know how he's going to take rejection. Yet here you come with loudspeakers and fireworks. Do you think it represents you being a chill dude who will take, 'no,' for an answer?"

"I didn't realize any of that." I sank my head into my hands. "I didn't mean to make her uncomfortable. I'm a nice guy. Jeremy is creepy."

Kyle sighed. "Just because you aren't as crass as Jeremy doesn't mean you are a nice guy. I hate to break it to you, but most guys think they are a 'nice guy.' What matters is how you *actually* treat women. And Beauregard, my friend, you are not treating women like people. You are treating them as *things*."

"Of course, they are people—"

"Then act like it! Describe Samantha, anything about her."

"She is tall, chestnut hair, a swimmer's body—"

"No! Don't describe her body, describe *her.*"

"She is a great swimmer, and... umm..." I closed my eyes and took a deep breath, letting it out slowly. I was drowning and I knew it.

"Exactly. You don't know anything about her. What is her personality like? What are her interests and hobbies? What are her passions? What does she want to be?" Kyle leaned in closer with each question, until he was poking my chest with a thin finger.

I tried to piece an answer together from the clues I had. She hung out with her friends, she took a biology class, and she stole necklaces? "I don't know," I finally admitted, both to Kyle and to myself.

"Precisely. You don't know her as a person. And instead of trying to get to know her, you decided to do some elaborate scheme to impress her without understanding how she would react to it. She is probably legitimately terrified right now." Kyle seemed to calm down a bit, and his tone went from pure fury to stern lecture. He returned to sit on his bed.

My stomach burned and twisted uncomfortably. I was so sure she was going to love it. "I should apologize."

"Wrong."

"No?"

"No. The last thing she wants right now is to hear from you."

"Then how do I fix this?"

"You don't. You blew it. Now the best thing you can do for her is never speak to her again."

"But—"

"But nothing. Look, I get it, you don't know how to talk to girls." He reached for his bookcase and pulled a few books off the shelf. "Here. Try to read these. They are romance books, written by women, for women. It shows *their* perspectives and explores what *they* want out of a relationship. I think it will help you." He handed me a stack of books.

He retreated to his bed and pulled the privacy curtains closed around him, leaving me with a stupefied expression and a stack of books. I slumped onto my bed, letting the books tumble out of my arms and fall to the mattress beside me. I picked up a light blue one with a silhouette of a man and a woman standing back-to-back. I read the cover, *Love Legit*. I looked at the line printed at the bottom of the cover, which read, "Let him love you as much as you should love yourself." I picked up another one, this one a bright pink that might match my sister's hat and sporting an angry looking explosive that might actually be an emoji. *Love Bomb: Red Flags and Other Signs to Avoid.*

My stomach twisted again, feeling like a black hole, sucking me into it as I crumbled in on myself. *Who am I kidding? Why would she ever even look at me?*

CHAPTER NINETEEN

GROW A BACKBONE

Advocacy: Develop your skills to advocate for yourself within human society. Use your unique perspective and experiences to blend in seamlessly with a diverse human population.

MEEP

The next couple of days were hard for me. I had called out of work since the Auditor's appearance at my house, and I didn't know what else to do. He obviously knew where I lived, where I worked, where I went to school. Nowhere was safe. So, there I was, going through the motions at Clair's with my mind nowhere near coffee. I didn't even register the time and was surprised when Bella came in from the back room with her apron already on, ready to start work. *Was I so lost in thought I hadn't heard her?*

Bella remained still in a stoic silence as I began to clean the equipment. I normally would have had all these chores done before Bella arrived, but not tonight. She seemed to take note of the odd behavior. Bella was always intently quiet. I wished I could read minds, because there had to be something turning behind her normally stone-like mask.

One sound cut through my distraction, piercing me to the heart. The jangle of the Auditor's boots. My blood thickened in my veins, and I ducked behind the counter. Not again. Couldn't he just leave me alone?

Bella looked down at me. "You alright?"

I shook my head as the chime on the front door rang, and I grimaced. Bella set her jaw and casually vaulted over the counter.

"You need to leave," Bella said, her voice steady and firm.

"I have business with your colleague."

"No. You don't," Bella asserted.

"Step aside," the Auditor said, a note of danger entering his voice. I risked peeking through the pastry display and saw the Auditor doing his best to intimidate Bella, a person three feet taller than him. The effect was spoiled by the grimace of strain caused by craning his neck. Bella didn't know how dangerous he was. I couldn't let her put herself at risk like this. I took a deep breath and stood up.

"Leave her out of this," I said.

"Meep, I've got this," Bella said.

"You don't understand, Bella. He's dangerous," I warned.

"Listen to the *Lormau*," the Auditor advised. "We wouldn't want things to get... messy."

"You're right. Which is why you should leave," Bella said.

They continued to stare each other down until the Auditor suddenly reached to his side, but Bella grabbed his wrist. Her hand moved so fast I didn't even see it, and then she was twisting his arm behind his back and manhandling him to the door. I could have sworn she had him lifted completely off the ground as if it was nothing. Then she tossed him onto the street.

The Auditor scrambled to his feet and looked at Bella with an expression of fear before he turned to run away. After a single step, he vanished into the distance.

"Thank you," I said.

"It was nothing."

"No, it wasn't. You don't even know how major that was," I said.

"Forget it. I mean it, forget about this," she said, returning to work.

I dropped the subject and felt safer, able to work more diligently without being distracted. I even managed to smile at the next customer that came in. At the end of my shift, I called Bella to the breakroom.

"We need to talk," I said.

"I told you to forget about it."

"I can't."

"You need to."

"There is more to this than you realize, and I could really use your help," I pressed.

"Not interested." She turned her back on me and started to walk away, but my next sentence made her freeze.

"I know you aren't human."

"And what am I then, a bunny rabbit?" she asked, cocking an eyebrow.

"I... I don't actually know what," I admitted. "But it's okay, you can trust me."

"Meep—"

"—I know, it's a big secret. I'm not human either. I'm a Lynx."

"I don't care." Bella slammed her fist onto the break room table. "Damnit, Meep, leave it alone. Don't make me regret helping you." She whirled and stormed back to the front, leaving a fist-sized dent on the table.

I sighed in frustration. It was obvious she wasn't human, and she would clearly be helpful, whatever she was, if I could just get her to listen to me. I needed something more concrete to convince her to trust me.

Chapter Twenty

Took a Calculated Risk,
but I Am Bad at Math

Continuous Learning: Embrace a mindset of lifelong learning and personal growth. Stay curious and open to new experiences, constantly expanding your knowledge and skills. This not only enhances your ability to integrate with humans but also enriches your own life.

BEAU

Meep told me about Bella's odd behavior and super-human strength, so we decided it was best to scan her. As I pulled open the door to Clair's, my brain poured over the scene Meep had built for me. If someone had come up to me and accused me of being non-human, I'd be scared. I'd feel hunted and pursued, even if I didn't think they had malicious intent. Keeping this secret had been drilled into me from a young age, so I could understand why Bella would be reluctant to cooperate.

Samantha stood in line, her back to me. I hadn't seen her since she stood me up and Kyle told me to stay away. But there she was—chestnut hair cascading down her back like a waterfall, highlighting the curves of her hips. Curiosity drove me to raise my watch and activate it.

"What are you doing?" Jo asked beside me, confusion in her voice. She might not have known anyone in town, but she was aware the girl I aimed at was not wearing enough black to be Bella. I didn't answer as I stared at the readout. It blinked for a moment before displaying the verdict.

I burned the phrase into my mind. I knew Samantha was inhumanly special. She froze after she turned around and saw me there, eyes widening in panic. *Oh no.* I ran out of the store, and Jo left to trail behind me, one eyebrow raised.

"Beau, you good?" Jo poked her head around the alley entrance where I had hidden. "What's going on?"

"What does Hieniol mean?"

"Siren."

A Siren? Of course. I puffed out my cheeks and exhaled slowly.

Jo squatted down next to me. "What's up? Who was that? Why did you scan her?"

"That was Samantha."

"That's the girl you've been pining over? I didn't expect someone so plain."

"Plain? She is the most gorgeous woman I've ever seen. And now... she is terrified of me. She thinks I am some crazed stalker."

"You *are* a crazed stalker," Jo said. "You were *literally* following her with a spy drone, Meep told me."

"But not like *that*! I was just trying to figure out the perfect spot to ask her out."

"Beau, every person in the history of ever has managed to ask someone out *without* building a spy drone," Jo said.

"Yeah... I see that now. God, did you see the look in her eyes?" I took a deep pained breath and closed my eyes.

We sat together in silence for a while longer until I eventually stood up. "She should be gone now. Let's just scan Bella and get out of here."

I went back into Clair's and found Bella at the counter, nonchalantly chewing on some gum. What kind of gum did goth girls chew? Skulls and poison? I was pretty sure she shouldn't be doing that while serving food, but she didn't seem to care, and frankly, neither did I.

"I'll have a whipped cocoa," I said, and as Bella turned around, I activated the watch. Simple.

Nothing happened.

The screen was blank, and I flipped it again.

Still nothing.

I pointed it at Jo to see if maybe it didn't react at all to a human, but it remained stubbornly blank. I fiddled with the dials and buttons, but I already knew. It was dead. I had used up the last of its charge scanning Samantha. If I could kick my own ass, I would.

"What's wrong?" Jo asked.

Bella handed me my drink, and we left after I paid for it. My brain scrambled to come up with the words to explain exactly why I wasn't able to scan Bella.

As we climbed on my scooter with Jo perched behind me, she said, "You fucked up."

"I know."

"On multiple levels."
"I *know*."
"We can't find a new team member now."
"I know!"

CHAPTER TWENTY-ONE

NEXUS

Limited Exposure: Minimize your interactions with humans as much as possible. Avoid densely populated areas or places where humans are likely to gather in large numbers. Keeping a low profile reduces the chances of being detected.

MEEP

We met in my basement again, and a distinctive lack of black clothing and goth attitude advertised itself shrilly. "Where is Bella?" I asked, folding my arms.

Beau looked at his feet. His red low-top sneakers that peeked out from his baggy cargo pants matched his hat in a rare display of fashion.

"Yes?" Jessie prompted poking him in the ribs.

"I wasn't able to scan her. The watch died," he said to the floor.

I narrowed my eyes at him. If the watch died, why was he acting so guilty?

"Tell them why it was out of charge," Jo prompted, her standard pastel-cloud chic look only continuing to highlight the glaring absence of Bella.

Beau signed deeply, "Because I scanned someone else first."

"Who?" I asked, narrowing my eyes.

"Tell me you didn't," Kathleen gasped, and covered her face with her hands.

Jeremy looked confused.

Beau winced, "I scanned... Samantha."

"Beauregard!" Kathleen exclaimed.

"Why am I not surprised," I fumed. "We *need* Bella."

"I know! It's not like I decided to scan Samantha *instead* of Bella. I didn't know I couldn't do both!"

"But you had no business scanning Samantha at all," I shouted, and Beau shrank back. I had to make a conscious effort to slow my breathing and dig my fingernails out of my palms.

"Maybe it will work out? We can invite her instead," he said meekly.

"Oh, no, we won't," Kathleen said, marching up to him. "You are going to leave that poor girl alone."

"I'm sorry!" Beau cried. "I really am. You don't understand how deeply I regret how this has worked out."

"Yeah, I bet he regrets having everyone in the room jumping down his throat. He just wishes he had gotten away with it," Jessie scoffed.

"That's not it," Beau said.

"You fucked up," Kathleen said, pointing at him. "This

obsession with Samantha has affected our entire plan."

We towered over Beau as he shrank back, and then he bolted, running up the stairs before a door slammed above.

"You *may* have been a bit harsh," Jo said tentatively.

"He had it coming," I snapped.

"Guy really needs to learn to respect women," Jeremy said, and I shot him a glare.

Jo sat down across from me. "Look, I know my brother messed up. For a genius he can be a real dumbass sometimes. But you shouldn't attribute malice to what is really just mind-boggling awkwardness."

"What do you mean?" I asked, confused.

"He has a crush and doesn't know how to act on it. And, well, he's Beau. He'll get fixated on some idea and pursue it without thinking about how it looks to others or how anyone else will react to it."

"That girl is not 'an idea,' she's a human-being... or, whatever," I shot at her. "And that's not malicious?"

"No, it's not." Jo shook her head, placing one of her pale hands on my much darker one. "I talked to him about the spy drone."

"Spy drone?" Kathleen cut in.

"Yeah. That spider drone that was following the Auditor? He was using it to follow Samantha first," Jo explained.

"He did what? I didn't even know that part of it. I just thought he had an overzealous date proposal!" Kathleen shrieked.

I looked between her and Jo in confusion. "A date proposal?"

Kathleen waved my question away. "He did some big elaborate proposal with music and banners... It would have been sweet if they were *actually* together, but it came on *waaay* too strong," Kathleen explained. "I tried to explain to him *why* that was problematic and *why* she said, 'yes,' in the moment, and then stood him up later. I thought he understood."

"He did," Jo said softly. "He didn't go out of his way to run into her again. She was just there when we went to Clair's, and... he acted without thinking. You should have seen him. He realized what he did to her emotionally, and he was devastated."

"But a spy drone? Come on," I said.

"If he was malicious about it, he would have been using it to spy on her undressing. For some reason, the way he used it made sense to him," Jo said.

"The date proposal that was an overwrought and horrible idea?" I clarified.

"Look, he made bad choices all around," Jo said. "I'm not saying he didn't. But it's not as bad as it looks. I know my brother. He's sweet. Overzealous and awkward, but he has a good heart."

"He is friends with Jeremy, though," I said, bitterly, crossing my arms over my chest.

"Why is that such a bad thing?" Jeremy asked, exasperated.

"He knows Jeremy is a pervert, and he doesn't think it's okay. But he looks past it," Jo said.

"I'm still here," Jeremy said.

"I'm not trying to excuse him. I just think you guys should understand. I know you are stressed, and the Auditor is scary. But Beau can help."

"We don't need his help. Let's figure out a plan without him," Jessie said. "Have we tried simply *asking* this Auditor what he wants? Now that the watch doesn't even work, we can give it back, right?"

"He was evasive, and he had a 'I'm the one asking the questions' vibe. And if he is as secretive as we think, I don't think we will get much out of him," I said.

"Still, it's worth a try, right?" Jessie asked.

"It might be. I think a better approach would be to steal his tablet. He was tapping away at it when he interviewed us. If we can find out what's on there, it could reveal a lot," Jeremy said.

Kathleen mused, "But we don't want Meep to face him because he knows what she can do, and we don't want the Gnomes to face him because he knows what they can do, and Jeremy... What can you do, Jeremy?"

"I... can see in the dark really well," Jeremy said.

"What else?" Jo asked, unimpressed.

"I dunno, I think that's it," he said.

"Then why are you even here?" I snapped, rubbing my temples. *What exactly is he contributing here?*

"Hey, I was invited. In fact, Beau made it seem like my involvement was crucial."

"That was before we knew you were useless," I said.

Jo cut in, probably to keep the peace. "Kathleen, you said magic was hard and takes time. Can you tell us more about what you can do? About how magic works?" That was a fantastic question, and much more useful than my temper right now, so I perched on the table and awaited our magic lesson. Jeremy remained silent as well. I had probably hurt his feelings; my mother would have an angry word or two to hiss at me if she had heard me call someone else "useless."

"Magic is like matter; it can neither be created nor destroyed. You need a ley line, which is magical energy. Ley lines crisscross around the world, converging at nexus points like the center of a spider web. There is a tremendous amount of magical energy available near a nexus. There is one here in town, actually," Kathleen explained.

"You think that has something to do with why there are so many non-humans here? Why was everyone we have scanned so far, even that random girl, special?" I asked.

Kathleen shrugged and swept her long, red hair over her shoulders. "I don't know. Perhaps. It's the most unusual thing about the town. It's why I am here, at least, although that was a deliberate choice on my part. Maybe it has some kind of uncon-scious effect on the rest of you?"

It was as good of a guess as anything.

"Where does the Auditor come from?" Jessie mused.

"I thought he was an alien" I said offhandedly.

"Maybe some kind of hidden Gnome colony that has developed more advanced technology?" Kathleen suggested.

"Maybe they are inbred, and that's why he seems to be exagger-ated," Jo added.

"And they realized that, so he is scouting out fresh blood to bring back. He is asking about powers and abilities to find the best specimens for breeding. Then he will kidnap them and bring them, and they will be used as sex slaves, bred nonstop day in and day out," Jeremy said, using the tone and rate of speech I associate with insane conspiracy theorists.

I rolled up an old nearby copy of Cat Fancy magazine and leaned over to bonk Jeremy on the head. "No. Keep your gross fantasies out of this."

Returning to a more normal pace, he said, "One moment he was there, and the next, he was far away. He didn't vanish, he just... moved wrong. Who knows what he is capable of."

We sat in thoughtful silence, and I remembered the time at the cafe he had moved too fast with no sound, and how he had van-ished from my room after he'd threatened me. I stood and paced the floor. "Auditor. Tablet. Stealing. Ideas?"

"So, it's just Jessie and me who have skills to utilize?" Kathleen asked. "Do I have that right?"

Jo tried again. "Beau can help. He knows he messed up and was already beating himself up about it. Jumping down his throat is not helping him, or us."

I huffed. "Alright. He can come back." I wasn't thrilled, but I still needed him.

Jo left the basement, and I stopped pacing. Jessie put her hand on my arm. "Meep, why is this bothering you so deeply?" she asked, her voice gentle and soothing. My first instinct was to deny being bothered at all, but this was Jessie asking. Jessie, my best friend. I slumped onto the couch next to Jeremy, whose startled look I caught from the corner of my eye as he fumbled the magazine he had been flipping through.

I took some time to think through my emotions. "I'm terrified, Jess. I thought messing with the Auditor was fun at first, but since then, he has shot at me, shown up every place I used to feel safe, and threatened me some more. I can't go anywhere without looking over my shoulder and expecting him to pop up."

"I'd be scared too if he kept showing up at my door," Jessie said, sitting on the other side of me and putting her arm around my shoulder.

I saw Jeremy on my other side struggling with what to do with this small show of acceptance. I would have laughed in normal circumstances, but I was too preoccupied to do more than note the reaction.

"The only thing that made me feel safer was Bella. The way she faced him down... There wasn't a trace of fear in her. I was thrilled at the idea we would have her on the team."

"And Beau just messed that up for you," Kathleen said, sitting on the arm of the couch by Jessie.

"Yeah," I said. "And for what?"

"It's okay, we are here. You're not alone," Kathleen said.

"Thank you."

Beau came down the stairs, face red and tear-stained. Jo trailed behind him. He stopped at the bottom of the staircase and stood there in silence, perhaps surprised that three girls were sitting on the same couch as Jeremy.

"So... we need to deal with the Auditor with the people we

have now. Any ideas?" Jessie asked. We took some time to explain to Beau what he had missed, about ley lines, nexus, and how magic worked. We also filled him in on Goblin abilities, though I still couldn't see how that would be useful. I did not voice that opinion again. I had been raised better than that.

Beau took a deep breath. "We don't have Bella. But we do have the next best thing."

"And what is that?" I asked, skeptically.

"Jessie," he said. "She can turn *into* Bella."

"I don't... Oh!" The realization struck me. Hopefully, "Bella's" presence would be enough for now.

"Woah, I can look like her, but that doesn't mean I'll get whatever abilities she has," Jessie said in protest.

"Sure, but the Auditor won't know that," he said, his voice calming and becoming more confident. "We also now have a useless watch, which can be a bargaining chip. So, we can set up a meeting to give him the watch with 'Bella' as a dissuasive show of force. That will set us up for the other half of the plan."

"What's the other half of the plan?" Jeremy asked.

"I'm not sure yet," Beau admitted. "Kathleen, I still don't know *what* your magic can do. Any ideas?"

"Well, it's more a matter of what *I* can do with the magic than what the magic is capable of."

"Okay," Beau said patiently. "What can *you* do with the magic that would be helpful?"

Kathleen thought for a moment. "I can make someone invisible."

"That sounds perfect," Beau said, perking up. "Does anyone know how to pick pockets?"

After a moment of silence, Jeremy raised his hand.

I pinched the bridge of my nose. "Do I want to know why you can pick pockets?"

"It's useful for pulling pranks at night," Jeremy said with a shrug of his large shoulders. "I can get keys and such to open locked doors." He looked altogether too big to be sneaky, so I remained doubtful.

"So, we meet him at night and use the darkness, *plus* invisibility, to let Jeremy sneak up on him. He can swap out his real tablet for a dummy I'll make. Meep and Jessie will be the distraction and bait."

"Might work," I said.

We spent the rest of the evening ironing out specifics and laying out some contingency plans.

CHAPTER TWENTY-TWO

SECOND THEFT

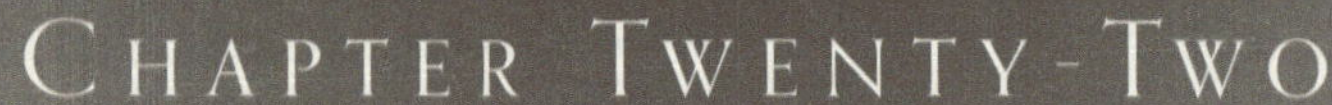

Emergency Exit Plans: Develop contingency plans and escape routes in case of unexpected encounters with humans or situations that may jeopardize your safety. Familiarize yourself with means of rapid escape.

BEAU

The next couple of days, Kathleen gathered supplies for her spell, and I worked with Jeremy and Meep to replicate the tablet from memory. It felt strange to design something with aesthetics in mind rather than functionality. Our replica wouldn't go unnoticed for long; close inspection was going to reveal the fake no matter how good it was. I suspected it was made of the same interwoven material the watch was, and I couldn't replicate that. But I did include a crack in the screen, hoping it would mask the nonfunctional nature for a bit longer.

Meanwhile, Jeremy spent some time practicing his thievery skills to swipe it from us in various configurations: attached to my belt, jammed into a pocket, sitting on a table near me. It was significantly bulkier than what he was used to swiping, but he got the hang of it, and I soon, I barely noticed when he took it. He also practiced walking silently, but he was already good at that. Whether it was from being a Goblin or being mischievous, no one knew for sure. I never heard him sneaking up on me in any of the exercises, despite listening for exactly that. Meep could hear him, but she admitted it was a soft sound normal people wouldn't have been likely to hear.

Jessie spent her time at Clair's, studying like so many other patrons, but she was studying Bella instead of notes. She said she needed to memorize not only her appearance, but her mannerisms, her tone, her cadence, and some other stuff I never would have given a second thought. I didn't know there was so much to wearing black and acting moody, but I wasn't the master of disguise.

We also scouted a location for the meeting, settling on a hill in the woods where we could set up a picnic table. We hoped he would set the tablet down, rather than hold on to it. I found a nearby vantage point and set up a sonic telescope with built-in night vision. My phone buzzed, and I saw a text from Meep. She had secured the meeting for tonight. Everything was going as planned.

I sat in a lawn chair and observed the hilltop with my sonic telescope. Meep sat at the table illuminated by a small lamp and "Bella" stood rigid behind her right shoulder.

Kathleen was setting up the spell a few feet away from where I sat, tucked into a bush that we had scouted earlier for the purpose. She arranged various items around her and laid out a mat on the ground that had a complex symbol drawn on the fabric. She kept referring to a book that seemed really familiar for some reason. The spell wouldn't last long, so we didn't want to cast it before the Auditor showed up. Jeremy crouched near Kathleen with a determined set to his jaw. He had disclosed to me earlier that this was his first chance to show the others he was not useless. He really was a good person with a heart of gold, and really, he was just misguided, but—a pang of hurt burst in my chest at the thought of Samantha—who was I to judge?

Clearing my mind, I checked the sonic telescope again and saw the Auditor appear—not a sudden appearance out of thin air, but rather, he seemed to rapidly approach from a distance before slowing at the base of the hill. Like those supernaturally fast vampires on TV shows, but I thought perhaps it was not *him* that was fast, but those boots he wore. They were the only common denominator other than his hat and goggles. Boots that granted speed made the most sense. Tonight, he wore a mechanical suit that made him look several feet taller, but he still wore those distinctive, curly-toed boots.

"Please sit," Meep said, gesturing to the bench seat opposite her when he got to the table. "I'd like to discuss a few things before I give you your device."

"He's there. Cast the spell," I said, and Kathleen started muttering a mantra, rhythmic and steady. I didn't recognize any of the words.

The Auditor sat down slowly, his gaze fixed on "Bella." "What is she doing here?"

"Protection. Just making sure you don't try anything," Meep said.

"I remind you, *you* are the one who invaded my privacy and stole from me. Also, I recall you threw a knife at me once," the Auditor said.

"And you shot at me with lasers and harassed me. I will give you the watch back. I'm sorry for taking it and keeping it from you. But first, I want some answers."

"Depends on the questions."

"Why are you here?" 'Bella' barked.

The Auditor sat down, placing his tablet on the table in front of him and resting his hand on it. Jeremy wouldn't be able to steal it from there. The plan was already going awry.

"I came to investigate how many Aether crystals had grown since we were last here."

"What's an Aether crystal?" Meep asked.

"If you don't already know, then they are worthless to you. We would have offered you a fair trade for them, too."

"Then why all of the secrecy?" Meep was asking all the wrong questions. I didn't care about crystals. I cared about where he came from and what he was.

"The only thing I have kept secret is my technology. Such as the one you stole."

"Where did you get this technology?" Meep asked. *Okay, better. That is at least the right direction.*

"I already told you, it's mine."

"So, you made it all yourself?"

"Of course, I did." The Auditor seemed offended by the question.

I registered the silence, indicating Kathleen had stopped chanting. The spell must be done, and Jeremy would be on his way over now.

"Of course." Meep tried to recover. "Who wants these crystals?" *That's the right question*!

"My House, obviously."

What the hell does that mean? I wanted answers, not more questions.

"Your House? You mean your family?" Meep asked.

"Of course."

"So, there are more like you?" Meep pressed.

"I didn't spring from a rock." The derision in his voice was clear. "I have humored you enough. These questions are a waste of time. Give me my device now."

"Not until I'm satisfied," Meep said, jumping to her feet and pointing. "Bella" slammed her hands on the table and made the Auditor recoil from her ferocity. As she leaned closer to stare him in the eyes, Meep swung her arms wide and batted the tablet off the table. I watched the tablet halt in midair, then disappear, then reappear, continuing to fall. The trajectory was slightly off, but as no one else was watching it fall, I hoped no one would notice. The fake tablet smashed into a rock.

"What have you done?" The Auditor roared, pouncing on his tablet, and turning it over to reveal the cracked screen, "How *dare* you!"

"I'm sorry," Meep recoiled. "Look, here is your watch. You can have it back." She threw it on the table and made to leave.

The Auditor didn't glance at it as he held out his arms, a weapon held in each hand pointed at a different girl. The one intended for Bella shot a thin spray of silvery mist, whereas the one targeted at Meep dispersed a thick white foam.

Meep rolled to the side, but the Auditor was covering the entire ground around her. She rolled into it, stopping fast. He pointed his ray gun, but 'Bella' kicked it out of his hand. The Auditor turned to her with a look of shocked surprise. Whatever he had sprayed at her was probably intended for Bella and not for someone like Jessie.

A fight was the last thing we wanted. I threw down the telescope and sprinted towards them. That proved to be a horrible idea as I tripped over the first tree branch I came across. I scrambled to my feet and continued cautiously, hearing Kathleen follow close behind.

The Auditor backed away from Jessie, keeping his eyes on her warily. He lunged to the right, going for his gun, but she deftly matched his steps as if in a choreographed dance. After a few attempted feints to get around her, he looked confused. His eyes darted over to the watch, still resting on the table where Meep had tossed it. Shit, he had finally guessed that something was up with "Bella." Jessie couldn't replicate how she behaved in a fight well enough to keep him fooled.

He dove for the table, catching Jessie by surprise. She was slow to lunge after him, and he grabbed the watch, rolling across the table before falling off the far side. He popped up, watch on his wrist, and then he pointed it at her.

Too bad it was out of charge and couldn't scan her.

Except, to my great surprise, it did turn on. He backpedaled away from Jessie and kept it trained on her as she tried to rush him. "Aha! You are the Fae. I knew I couldn't trust you."

The Auditor backed away towards the pile of foam where Meep still struggled to free herself. Without even a glance back, he leapt into a backflip as Jessie's momentum carried her forward and caused her feet to squish into the foam, getting her stuck next to Meep.

The Auditor ran back to retrieve his weapon. With his breath labored, he pointed it at them. "You are more trouble than you are worth," he sneered.

I ran forward, but he was too far away for me to do anything to stop him. I tried to brace myself, preparing to see two of my friends murdered before my eyes. I would probably be next. How could I brace myself for that?

I stood frozen—should I run towards them and get there too late, or run backwards and hide?—and watched a large rock rise from the ground behind the Auditor. It crashed against his armored head. He stumbled, ray gun firing into the sky. The rock lifted again before it swung another blow against his face, cracking the faceplate of his helmet. Off balance and probably dizzy, the Auditor fell, rolling down the hill a few feet before coming to a stop.

"We have to get out of here," Jeremy's disembodied voice yelled.

Taking advantage of the situation, I scooped up the Auditor's weapon as I jogged past his prone figure. At a glance, it looked like his helmet had absorbed the worst of the blows, but I wasn't about to stop and give him a thorough examination.

I assessed the situation; the Auditor had sprayed some kind of fast-acting adhesive foam around Meep. Kathleen was tugging on Jessie's arm, and Jeremy was trying to help Meep, but both of them remained stuck firm into the solidified substance.

I aimed the ray gun at a patch away from my struggling friends and pulled what I assumed to be the trigger. A foot-wide hole burned through it easily. I fiddled with dials inlaid into the grip and narrowed its beam, creating a more precise cutting tool. Then I flipped the table, creating a bridge I could cross to get close. After that, I set to carefully burning away enough foam to free the two trapped women, and together, we raced from the scene right as the Auditor began to stir.

"You are all dead! Dead, you hear me! No more courtesy from me, no more holding back. I will wipe all of you from the face of this planet. I know you, Meep. I know where you live. I know your family. I know your friends. You can't hide from me." He was struggling to his feet, but we soon put him out of sight before he could actually chase us.

"That was awful!" Meep screamed. "He is going to be coming after us even harder now!"

"We need to figure out what we are doing next," Jessie puffed.

"We need a place to hide," I said, trying to keep up.

"I know a place. Follow me," Jeremy's voice said.

"Um, Jeremy, we can't *see* you," Kathleen reminded him.

"Oh, right. Um." I felt hands on my shoulders—I guessed he didn't want to touch any of the girls—and he turned me to face a direction into the woods. "This way."

Jeremy guided us using my body until we found a cave entrance.

"A literal hole in the ground?" Meep asked.

"At least it's not a figurative one," Jessie quipped.

"Hey, it's sheltered, and he won't be able to find us here," Jeremy said defensively.

"He is right, this is perfect," I said and entered first. It was pitch black inside, but I had a small portable flashlight that I used to help guide the others. The cave was cramped and narrow, but it quickly opened into a spacious cavern with a high ceiling.

"How did you find this place?" Kathleen asked.

"Found it when I was rock collecting earlier in the year. I liked it here, so I set up some supplies."

I moved the flashlight around until I found a single sleeping bag and a few boxes of snack cakes.

"We can't live like this," Meep complained.

"It may be the only way we *can* live," Jeremy countered. "You heard him. He is going to be gunning for us, and he knows where we live. We have to hide. We can investigate his tablet, and maybe that will give us a new course of action, but for now, all we can do is survive."

PART
TWO

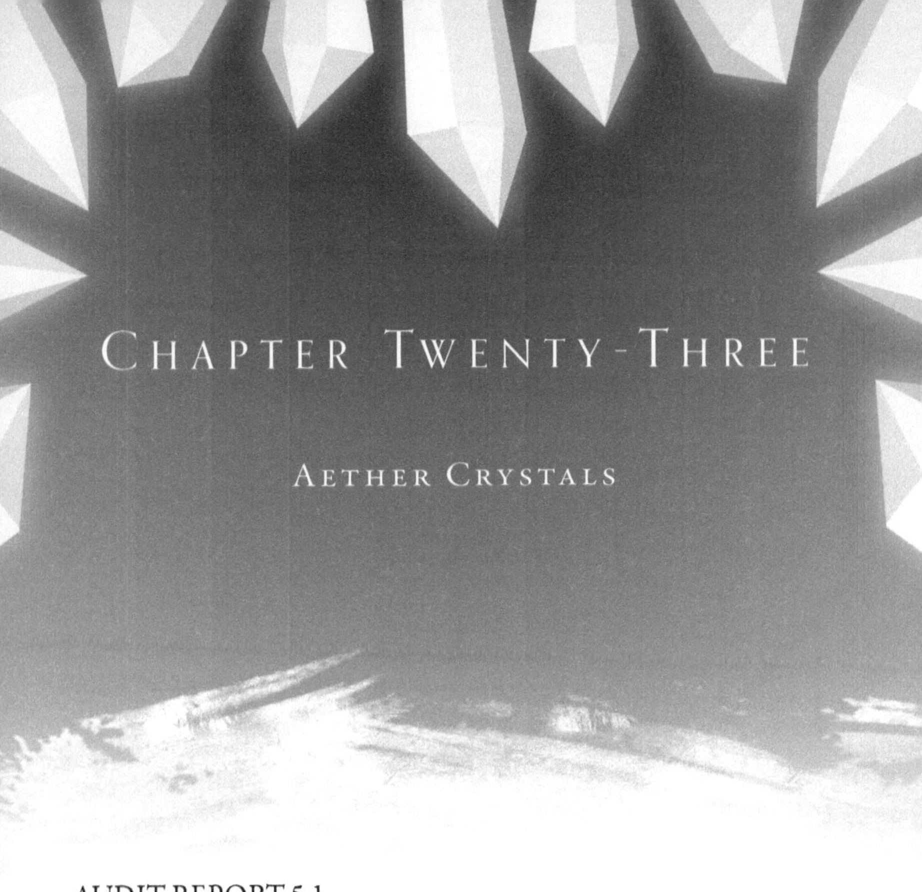

Chapter Twenty-Three

Aether Crystals

AUDIT REPORT 5.1

CYCLE: 1000 YEARS

NAME: Auditor Phelony Adalbert Jaroba Opunkele IV

OBSERVATIONS: Upon arrival to this realm, preliminary observations revealed a population estimated to be upwards of 20x that of the last report.

First surveys indicate no aether crystals in the immediate vicinity. A sharp decrease of 100% from expected yields. Further investigation will determine the source of the discrepancy. This auditor has sensed several ley lines, the largest of which is the "town" that now serves as this auditor's base.

Other observations reveal the technology level is higher than expected, though much less than gnomish technology, of course. However, the implication is problematic. Therefore, i am extending this audit to study these current advancements.

MEEP

Normally, I was used to the ghostly glow of streetlamps that managed to sneak into my room through my curtains, so when I opened my eyes to complete blackness and the dank scent of Earth in my nostrils, I was disoriented, to say the least.

Where...? Oh, right, the cave.

I sat up and took stock of my body. I found no bruises or soreness, but my clothes did stick to my skin in uncomfortable ways. The soft breathing of six other people around me informed me that we were all together and they still slept. I had called mom last night and begged her to leave town. She hadn't understood at first, but eventually, she'd complied with my out-of-character panic. I had to go get Rays though. She didn't travel well in the car. It was just as well because I had to get Jo and bring her here as well.

We didn't think he knew where anyone else lived, but the others had still tried to send warnings to those close to them. Beau couldn't reach Kyle, though Kathleen had managed it.

Despite the warmth of the heavy sleeping bags Jo had brought—where had she managed to find six in pastel colors? —bitter ice slipped through my veins. Stretching my limbs, and needing to pee, I felt around in the dark until I could follow the smell of dew-covered trees outside.

The morning was still dark with the sun playing coy games of shyness in the sky. I breathed in the fresh pine air and listened to the birds calling; this was my favorite time of day. After relieving myself and doing some stretches to get my blood flowing, I found my way back to the others. Along the way, I passed several other tunnels in the stone, which twisted sharply into the dark so I could not see down them. Cats are known for their uncanny sense of direction, so I guess I could thank my heritage for not getting lost. When I rejoined the group, everyone was sitting up inside their bags, except Jeremy, who was still lying down under his sleeping bag.

"So, what is our next move?" Kathleen asked. Her red hair was already showing signs of neglect, sporting knots and tangles from being slept in and not brushed. There was even a twig stuck in it, a memento from our midnight dash through the woods. Just another reason I kept mine short.

"It's obvious," Jeremy said, not bothering to rise. With his voice partially muffled by his sleeping bag, he added, "We read the tablet. That's what this was all about."

"Where is the tablet?" Beau asked.

Jeremy fumbled near him, and Kathleen scooted out of his reach. He grasped the tablet and held it lazily upwards. Beau handed it to Jo, our resident translator.

Jo looked it over and found the power switch. Symbols appeared on the screen, and she started tapping around. "I was afraid of this."

"What is it?" Beau asked.

"Linguistic drift. The version of Gnomish I learned and this version are different. I saw signs of it with the watch, but the text was so simple, it wasn't a problem," Jo explained.

"Alright, so, can you read it?" Beau asked hesitantly.

"It's just going to take me more effort to translate it. Give me some time," Jo said, already staring intently at the screen.

Beau turned on his flashlight, and I examined myself in the light. Chunks of the Auditor's foam was stuck to my clothes in large patches, it had hardened almost instantly. It was no longer sticky, thankfully, or I would have been stuck inside my sleeping bag. The foam was flexible, not as stiff as insulation foam, but it seemed like the same concept. I looked at Jessie who did not look any better than I did.

"Great, how are we going to get this off?" Jessie asked.

"Really depends on what it's made of," Beau said. "I was hoping it would decay on its own by now. This is chemistry, which isn't really my thing, but we need to find something to dissolve it. Starting with water as I guess it would be the easiest and safest option. If that doesn't work, we will escalate to harsher options."

"So, I need to take a bath," I said dryly.

"Yeah." His eyes widened. "Do you hate baths, or something?"

I stared at him. *Did he just ask me that?* And Jessie was laughing so hard, she had doubled over.

"I need one, too," she sobbed out between fits. *I guess you have to take the chance to laugh whenever you can. She does.*

We shared a look, thinking the same thing, then I asked, "Where can I bathe in the middle of a cave?"

While Jessie said, "I see nothing but rocks and dust, too bad we're not Chinchillas."

"There is one here," Jeremy said, finally sitting up. He crawled out of his sleeping bag, exposing his nakedness to us all, and we all exclaimed at once as we all turned our backs to him.

"Dude!"

"What the hell!"

"Ugh!"

"What? This is how I normally sleep," he said.

"In the privacy of your own room! Not with six other people around you! Maybe leave the pants on," Beau said.

"I'm not ashamed of my body," Jeremy said.

"Yeah, but we are," Jessie said.

"I have pants on now, you can all turn around. Babies," he added. I risked a glance back, but he was indeed clothed. He had on the same stained t-shirt from yesterday and his black hair was rocking an impressive case of bedhead. "Come on, follow me." Beau handed Jeremy his flashlight as he passed, and Jeremy led us away into the dark.

Rays decided to follow behind us, likely not wanting to be alone, but equally as likely, playing the big sister role.

"This path can be a bit confusing, but I marked it earlier with chalk on the cave wall. See here?" Jeremy pointed at a chalk arrow, "Make sure you follow the markers and you'll be fine. Wander off, and you could get seriously lost." He turned to face me. "And getting lost in a cave network like this can easily be the last thing you ever do. Understand?"

"Yeah, I get it," I said.

Jessie nodded beside me, and Rays acted like she would never leave my side again.

"Good." He took us further into the caverns, passing a few more marked intersections, before it opened up into a large chamber—much bigger than where we were camped out. "Before you ask, I didn't lead you all here last night because it's hard to navigate. Moving a group of panicked people further inside the cave could have been catastrophic."

We passed a few more twists and turns before reaching a cavern that took my breath away. Purple crystals jutted from the wall, glowing with a soft lilac light to illuminate the rest of the room. They were mesmerizing. Their light wasn't all that bright, but against the absolute darkness of the cave, they seemed like brilliant beacons. I clicked off my flashlight to appreciate it better. Sunken into the floor was a pool of water, reflecting the shimmering light of the crystals. Wisps of vapor rose from the surface, and I could feel the heat as the entire room was extremely warm.

"What are they?" I asked in wonder.

"I don't know," Jeremy replied.

"I thought you said you collected rocks?"

"Just because I collect them doesn't mean I know what they are. They don't match the descriptions I have in my guidebooks. There are a huge variety of luminescent gems, but they don't behave like these. I was never able to figure out the cause of the glow for these. I stumbled across them one day while searching for rocks. I kinda felt drawn to this chamber, and I knew I had found something special when I saw it. I've never shared this with anybody before."

"They are beautiful," Jessie said in awe.

"The hot springs are a perfect temperature to soak, and the heat might help dissolve the foam faster. I'll be a few caverns away if you need anything."

This reminded me of why I was here, and who I was with. "You aren't going to spy on me, are you?" I asked.

"Of course not. Look, I know I have a reputation for being a pervert, but that doesn't mean I'm going to violate anyone. Especially not you," he said, wincing.

"And are you sure you think of spying as a violation?" I pressed.

"Look. I want sex. That is no secret. But just because I'm open about it, I get called a pervert. Every other guy wants sex too, but they don't admit to it as readily," Jeremy said.

"It's not that you want sex, Jeremy. It's that you are *crass* about it," I said.

"You say crass, I say direct and honest. I'd rather be honest about it than lie to conform to a social norm," he said.

I wasn't sure how to respond to that. "Just... sing a song or something so I can hear where you are," I compromised.

"I can do that." He headed down the tunnel and started singing something I didn't understand. Was that... Japanese? Oh, God, he was singing an anime opening, wasn't he? I waited until his voice was far enough away, and then I turned and stripped down as far as I could. Which wasn't terribly far—my shirt and pants were stuck to my skin.

Dipping my toes into the water to test the temperature, I sighed heavily and sank into the water to let it embrace me. Rays crouched nearby, silently watching us. The light from the crystals was the perfect mood lighting, and for the first time in weeks, I relaxed. The tension in my muscles melted away like butter left on the counter on a hot day, my breathing slowed, and my mind drifted with thoughts blowing away like a dandelion wish.

"Meep, check it out." I opened my eyes to see Jessie in the neighboring pool. Her flesh shifted and bloated until she looked like Jeremy. "I'm not a pervert, I just like sex," she said, mimicking his voice perfectly, but adding a mocking tone. I snorted in laughter as she took on the exact likeness of Beau. "I'm not a stalker, I just build spy drones for girls I like."

I choked with laughter as I scrubbed at my face.

"What is wrong with those two?" I asked once I stopped coughing. "They act completely inappropriately, then make it seem like we are the bad guys for calling them out on it."

"I think it's pretty obvious. They are virgins and get all tangled up about sex," Jessie said, still wearing Beau's face and using his voice. "I mean, like full on, never even kissed a girl. I swear, it messes with their brains." Even knowing the person who was talking was Jessie, watching the likeness was surreal. The illusion was so realistic, I bet I could touch her and everything.

I found the foam was dissolving in the hot water, and a bit of scrubbing was enough to get the remaining bits off. We floated in silence for a long time—the water never cooled—and it was the best worst experience of my life. Hunted, yet relaxed. When we were finally done, Jeremy led us back to the others, complaining that he'd almost run out of songs.

When we got there, Jo perked up. "Excellent, you are just in time. I translated the first part."

"Part? What's on the tablet?" I asked.

"It's a series of reports. The Auditor—his name is Phelony—is making reports about us. I'm not sure who he's reporting back to, but you have to hear this." She proceeded to recite her translation, not even glancing at the tablet. "Audit report 5.1…"

When she was finished, Beau pinched the bridge of his nose and flopped back onto his sleeping bag. "I have more questions than before."

"Let's take it from the top. 'Cycle: 1000 years.' And he says the population is 'twenty times higher.' Is he actually saying it's been 1000 years since the last time one of these reports were made?" Kathleen asked.

"It didn't say *he* made the last report, just that the last report was 1000 years ago. Twenty times the population compared to 1000 CE? I think that's about right, actually. If they stayed hidden for those 1000 years, no wonder we haven't heard about Gnomes like him," Beau said.

"Would explain the linguistic drift," Jo confirmed. "He mentioned Aether crystals, just like he did yesterday. What is an Aether crystal?"

"I have a theory," Kathleen said. "Wizards call them mana crystals. They are a way to store the raw energy of ley lines for later use. They are pretty rare."

"What do they look like?" I asked, already suspecting the answer.

"They vary in size a lot, but their signature quality is a soft inner glow. They only glow when charged, so identifying empty ones can be tricky," Kathleen explained.

"Are they purple?" Jessie asked.

"I'm not sure if they come in different colors, but yeah, the one I have seen was purple."

I looked at Jeremy and Jessie and nodded. "I think we found some."

Kathleen's eyes bulged, "Individual crystals are rare, are you sure?"

Jeremy retreated back into the tunnels and returned with one of the crystals and held it up. Kathleen took it carefully. "This is one all right, I can feel the power. Why would there be so many here?"

"The report made it seem like he expected them to be here," Beau said.

"1000 years is a reasonable timespan for crystals to grow," Jeremy said, "So maybe he came here, expecting to find new crystals, and he couldn't find any?"

"He didn't do a great job of looking," I said. "There must have been dozens in there."

"Unless they are normally easier to find?" Beau posited. "If Kathleen can sense their power, maybe he has a scanner for them. But being underground shielded them from detection, possibly."

"Where did they go then?" I asked.

"It has been 1000 years. Lots of things could have happened in that time," Beau said. He gestured for the crystal, and Kathleen handed it to him. "I've seen this before. The Auditor's—I mean Phelony's—watch had shards of this in it. It must be a key part of Gnomish tech."

"That would explain why he wants it so much," I said. "But why was he surprised by our technology advancing? Especially since their technology is even more advanced?"

"I don't know, but I'm hoping more reports will shed light on this," Jo said.

"They can shed light on it from back home," Beau said. "This has gotten way too dangerous, and I can't let you stay here. We are getting you on the next bus out of town. Take the tablet with you and keep it safe."

Beau continued to argue with his little sister until he won, and Jo left the cave with a pout. We sat around in silence for a minute.

"So... truth or dare?" Jeremy asked, brightly.

"No," we chorused.

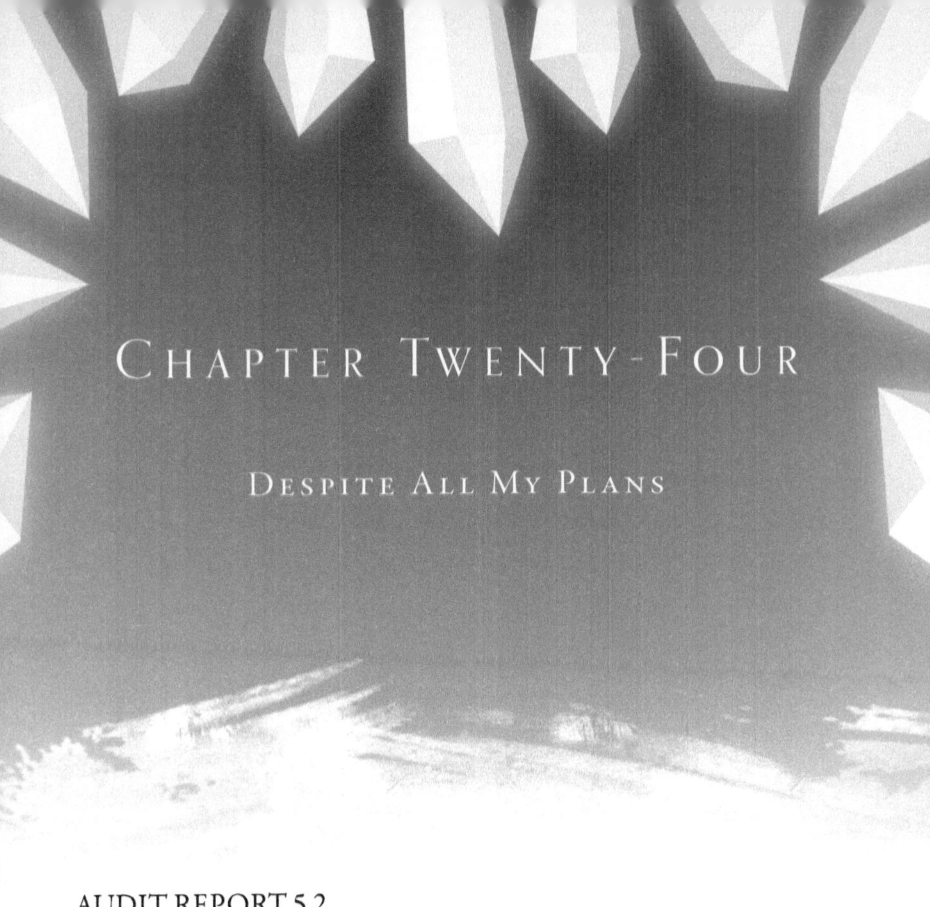

CHAPTER TWENTY-FOUR

DESPITE ALL MY PLANS

AUDIT REPORT 5.2

CYCLE: 1000 YEARS

NAME: Auditor Phelony Adalbert Jaroba Opunkele IV

OBSERVATIONS: A troubling trend has been noted. The average lifespan has been expanded to just over 2x that of the last report. An increase from 35 years to about 79 years of age. Can you even imagine? Kin have barely learned to use their abilities much less govern themselves at that age.

The extended lifespan does not necessarily explain the

technological or societal advancements. The advancement of this society seems to come from the newly identified adults (referring to their own perspectives) while it is overwhelmingly ruled/owned by the elite near expiration. This is contrary to the development of kin species. The average elder here seems largely ignored, packed into special housing, and has little to no say in even their own lives.

Some good news is that human birth rates have decreased, so there is still some hope for a self-contained population going forward.

The search for aether crystals is ongoing, and results are being checked and rechecked for accuracy. However, so far, they are not promising. Even perched on the largest nexus in this region, no crystals seem to be forming. Interviews with the local population do not indicate any knowledge of the existence of aether crystals nor magic in general.

However, certain inconsistencies within the interviews that have been already conducted do indicate a larger question. If kin are unknown as well as magic, who then are these people?

Beau

The cave felt like a cage. I wanted to pace, but there were only narrow tunnels. I wanted to work, but there was only darkness. I wanted some privacy, but there were only people.

"We've backed ourselves into a corner," I said to nobody in particular.

"You don't think I made the right call with this cave?" Jeremy asked.

"No, the cave was perfect. It's exactly what we needed at the time. We are here and we are safe—probably safe, at least—but it's not conducive to action."

"We have been in here for less than a day," Jessie pointed out.

"I have ideas. I want to study the Auditor's weapon, and I want to work on defenses, but I need better light, tools, and materials."

"These caves probably have more than one entrance, so we could use another exit more freely," Jeremy said. "Then we can send someone into town for supplies. Even if Phelony spotted it, finding this particular cavern would be improbable."

Jessie gave him a grin.

"I thought you said we shouldn't wander in the caves," I said.

"I said *you* shouldn't wander. *I* can navigate in the caves easily," Jeremy said. "I can see in the dark, which helps a lot."

"I thought you meant like, see with little light, like an owl," Meep said.

"No, I meant dark-dark. Don't ask me how it works. But even beyond just seeing the caves, they all seem distinctive to me. I can easily keep track of where I've been and what connects where."

"Jeremy, did you ever consider that might be part of your Goblin skills?" I asked. "Goblins have an association with mines."

"Yeah, I just never thought it was going to be useful for anything," Jeremy said.

"Okay, let's assume we can get supplies in and out that way. I need power. We have hot springs... A geothermal power plant, maybe?"

"That sounds difficult," Jessie said.

"Depends on how hot they are," I said.

"They are cool enough to bathe in," Meep pointed out.

"Ah. Right. That's... unfortunate. Hmm," I said. "I don't suppose there is an underground stream? No, that probably wouldn't have enough flow. A gas generator is out due to air quality concerns. A battery with a deep cycle lead-acid technology could be the solution, since we don't need to create energy just have access to it when we need it—"

Two small pebbles thrown from the directions of Meep and Jessie bounced off my skin, and I stopped to take a breath. "Hold on, I'm planning," I said, irked at the interruption. "Jeremy, you should start looking for a back exit." Then I lost myself in the world of my mind.

Those types of batteries were designed to discharge their power over the course of many hours. If we could get one to last a day, that sounded sustainable. Low power consumption would help. LEDs were great for that. We could spare a light to illuminate the cavern better, and I could use the rest to power any supplies I needed. No cooking with it though, that would use too much power. We also needed food, but it needed to be nonperishable and precooked. Trail mixes and pre-packaged granola bars would be good. Wait, of course there was a way to cook food. MREs were designed for scenarios exactly like this.

That left the issue of communication. There was no reception in the cave, and we needed to be able to contact Jo. An antenna and some wire could let me get reception inside without being too noticeable.

Additionally, Meep needed armor. I didn't know how to protect against the ray gun, but that foam was what had really caused her trouble. Something it wouldn't stick to would be ideal. An ablative coating that could break off would help. It could leave the outer layer stuck behind her. I didn't want it to be single use, so

I'd layer it. If the segments were small and overlapping, it would be like scales. *Hmm.*

"Alright, I know what I need. Let me write down a shopping list." We scrounged up a pen and some scraps of paper from people's pockets, and I wrote it out: bulbs, wire, tape, food, metal... This would be challenging to transport it all by hand. My scooter would help move it to the cave, and once here, we would have more hands available to help carry stuff down the tunnels.

"I could disguise myself so the Auditor won't recognize me. Then I can bring back the supplies," Jessie said.

"Perfect." I handed her the shopping list.

Jessie read it over. "This is a bit pricey."

I handed her my debit card. "I can afford it."

"Just like that? Are you secretly rich?" Meep asked.

"I sold a couple of patents and earned enough money to be comfortable. It's not a bottomless well, though, so don't go crazy."

When Jeremy got back, he said, "Good news. I have found another exit, and it's far enough to offer protection without being infeasible to get to. There are probably tons more off all the side passages I haven't explored yet. I can guide people there and back whenever you are ready."

"Let's go," Jessie said.

Jeremy saw how long the list she held was. "Really, Beau?"

I shrugged. "I was thorough. When she gets back, leave the stuff inside the entrance and bring a load back. Then, we can all come help move the rest."

I was left to sit with Rays, Meep and Kathleen. The latter two were chatting, but Rays sat hugging her legs to her chest and staring at me. Unsettled under her stare, I asked, "Are you alright?"

Looking up, Meep squinted at me. "She doesn't speak."

"Why not?" I asked.

"We don't know. Mom said she was born that way."

"Not all babies speak," Kathleen pointed out.

"Yeah, but it's more than that. She really embodies the Lynx traits. We haven't taken her to a psychologist to get a concrete diagnosis since, well, it would be hard to explain that she really is cat-like."

"That doesn't sound fair to her," I said.

"She seems happy enough. Well, most of the time. This situation is freaking her out. But yeah, it's not fair. I don't think this secrecy is fair to any of us. I bet it's easier on us than some of the others."

"How so?" I asked.

"You don't even realize it, do you?" Kathleen asked. "Most of us live in constant fear. Every time we use our powers, it's another chance to be discovered. Your power is subtle, and you use it brazenly. Even when you make your crazy shit, nobody can be sure it's anything supernatural because it's indistinguishable from genius."

"And we have a similar freedom as Lynx," Meep added. "Most of my abilities can be explained by my gymnastics training. I still have to restrain myself, though, and I'm always worried about presenting an unfair competition to others." Meep looked me up and down. "You don't seem to be worried about that."

"I guess I don't really think about engineering as a competition," I said.

"Isn't it, though? You will be competing with others for jobs after college. Even now, you have a leg up from normal college students because you have already sold patents," Kathleen said.

"I guess. But engineering is about creating things that will change the world, not being better than anyone else," I said. "We all have to work together and build on each other's work to help society as a whole reach the stars. It's not about any one of us, but all of us together."

"That's exactly my point," Meep replied. "You have the freedom to fully embrace your abilities, and we don't. Imagine not being able to use your mental storage *at all* without risking discovery."

I thought it through. "That would feel extremely oppressive," I admitted. "I wish we didn't have to fear humans."

"Don't we all," Meep said, sighing.

We sat in silent contemplation of a world that didn't need secrecy. The silence dragged into uncomfortability. Everyone got up and drifted away until it was only me and Kathleen.

I gathered up my nerve, and asked softly, "Can you help me? With dating, I mean. I thought I knew what I was doing, but I keep screwing it up. I get that I was doing it wrong, but I'm still not sure how to do it right."

"Yes, I think this is the perfect time to really talk about it. Do you think about her when you do these things?" Kathleen asked.

"Of course I did. I thought about her the whole time," I said.

"No, you *fantasized* about her the whole time. I'm not talking about *imagining* her, I'm talking about considering her point of view. What *she* wants. How *she* would feel about things. You put in all this effort planning a huge production, but did you think about what *she* would like?" Kathleen asked.

"No. I guess I didn't. I was just focused on trying to impress her," I admitted, hanging my head.

"Did you think about her perspective when it came to a spy drone following her?" she continued.

"No."

"How do you think *she* would have felt?" Kathleen pressed.

"If she doesn't find out—"

"*Bzzzt*, this isn't about what she does or does not find out. Hiding your transgressions doesn't make them better."

"Alright. I suppose... I'd have to say... she probably wouldn't be too happy about it," I said.

"Better. But stop evading the answer. You know it, so just admit it," Kathleen prodded. Meep paced back to us and sat next to Kathleen.

"She would hate being spied on," I said, and Meep huffed.

"Damn right, she would have," Meep said.

Kathleen made a shushing gesture with her hands. "Bingo. So, if you like her, why would you want to do something she hates?" Kathleen held up a long, thin, finger. "This one concept will get you far. Always consider her wants and needs and strive to meet them. How do you think she would like to be asked out? How do you think she would want to be treated? That can be a guiding principle from a first date all the way through decades of marriage."

"Sounds a bit one-sided. Where do my wants come in?" I asked, and Meep sniffed.

"This goes both ways. You focus on her wants, and she focuses on your wants. I should clarify," Kathleen said hastily, "this doesn't mean you need to be satisfying their every whim. Your own boundaries are important, too. My point is, their wants, needs, and well-being should be a key factor in what you do."

This made sense. *But how would I know what she would want?* Before I could ask, Meep interjected. "That's not how the world really works."

"Oh?" Kathleen asked.

"Nobody gives a shit about you. You gotta look out for yourself. This overly romantic crap is for kids."

"Ah. Your outburst at the book club makes sense now. I think that's a really sad way to go through life. Sure, a good romantic relationship may be hard to find, but that doesn't mean it's not worth striving for," Kathleen said. "And if you assume it's impossible, you might miss it when it happens."

"Is that how it is with you and Kyle? Do you put each other's needs first?" I asked.

Kathleen laughed. "Our situation is... unconventional, but

yeah, I exist to fulfill his desires."

"That's a creepy way to put it," Meep said darkly. "But maybe you have a point. Maybe I am so resigned to not finding a good fit for me that I just break up with guys before giving them a fair chance. Maybe there is someone out there that wants to give a shit about me, and I am the one stopping them." She slunk off to sit in silence.

Eventually Jessie got back, and we unloaded all the stuff. The trip through the caves took a solid half hour, but such is the price of security.

The first thing I did was call my sister. "Jo, I managed to get us reception. Did you make it home yet?"

"Almost there. But listen, you won't *believe* the next report," Jo said, and proceeded to relay the contents in a hushed voice. I put her on speaker so we could all hear it at once.

"The eldest Kin are millenia old? Am I understanding this right?" I asked.

"Looks like it," Jo confirmed.

"They are fundamentally different from us to the point where they don't even understand basic things about how we live?" Kathleen asked, sharing a look with Meep and Jessie.

"Beau... are we real Gnomes?" Jo's quiet voice echoed the thought that had been haunting the back of my mind. "He called me false-Kin, like I was the fake version of himself."

"I'm not sure anymore. These reports seem to be our best hope for answers. Keep at it," I encouraged.

"About that... Nah, it's probably nothing, I'll get started on the next one," Jo said.

I hung up and got to work setting up our temporary living space. The light made a huge difference, immediately making the space feel more open and comfortable. A bit ironic, because everyone was tired by this point, so I had to turn the light off so we could sleep.

CHAPTER TWENTY-FIVE

JUST A CAT IN A CAVE

AUDIT REPORT 5.3

CYCLE: 1000 YEARS

NAME: Auditor Phelony Adalbert Jaroba Opunkele IV

OBSERVATIONS: A strong sense of community and nationalism has become evident throughout my investigation. Most troubling is the existence of a large military presence not governed by one stable body, but by several small, oft-opposing, bodies.

WEAPONS ARE IN USE BY COMMON SOLDIERS THAT ARE STRONG ENOUGH TO POSE A THREAT TO SOME KIN.

Vehicles (referred to as tanks, planes, submarines) operate on land, in the sky, and underwater respectively, are mass-produced, and include weapons that can pose a threat to some kin.

Extra-large weapons can easily destroy entire cities and can pose a threat to some kin.

There are always at least two local countries* involved in a war at a time. There have also been instances where most, if not all, countries in this realm have been involved in the same war. And yet, other instances where one country decided to fight itself and its own people.

As a reminder, none of the advances were made with aether crystals (no knowledge of their existence nor the use of ley lines has been evidenced) leading to the conclusion that these advances were created outside of aether influence.

The combination of the population numbers, the level of technology, the warfaring mindset, and the threat level of weapons present in this realm indicate a frightening possibility for all kin if left alone.

This auditor will continue to investigate these people's culture in an attempt to discover how this rapid advancement was made possible despite their short lifespan.

Note country/countries are groups that beings associate themselves with, like a house, but on a larger scale.

MEEP

I went to the neighboring chamber with a flashlight to do my morning stretches; being in these caves was frustrating, but facing Phelony seemed daunting. How could I protect my family from a threat I did not understand? I finished my stretches and grabbed a granola bar for breakfast. Then, the others started waking up.

Beau didn't bother waiting for Jeremy to wake up before switching on the new cavern light. But Jeremy merely groaned and rolled over in response. Beau wasted no time getting to work by cutting rolls of aluminum foil into little pieces.

"What are you doing?" I asked him.

He didn't respond, only continued staring at his work, brows furrowed. *I'll leave him to it. Whatever it is.* I slumped next to Jessie. If sucking on a lemon was a mood, I thought this would be it.

"How are you feeling?" Jessie asked.

"Trapped." I set my chin on my knees. "This is awful. I should be out there, doing something."

"You should? Why you? And what do you think you should be doing?" Jessie asked with pursed lips, tapping a nervous rhythm on her hip.

I swallowed hard and felt my mouth go dry as desert sand. "Yes, me. I don't know. Protecting my family, you, the people I love."

Jessie shook her head softly. "But why *you*?"

A shiver crept through my body. No, not a sandy desert, but the *polar* desert. The largest desert in the world was Antarctica by definition, and I was entrenched there. I trembled in my apprehension and dread. "Why not? Who else is more capable?"

Jessie scoffed. "Um, okay. Ow." She pulled her blonde hair over her shoulder and twisted the tail of her braid.

I cringed at the insult I just handed my best friend. "I'm sorry. I meant that you're an actress, not a fighter."

"You're a *barista*, not a fighter," Jessie retorted caustically, turning her body to face me more directly. Her deep blue eyes seemed to bore into me, like she was searching for my soul.

"But I am so... agile. I can dodge and avoid getting hit, and I have seen enough movies to know the basics of hurting people. I'm not trying to offend you. I am the least likely to get hurt, and who else is going to step in and save us?"

"We don't even know what we need saving from." Jessie's fingers fluttered against her denim clad hip, a sure tell of her level of agitation.

"Maybe the tablet will tell us what is going on. And maybe then we can turn it over to someone more capable. But until then, it's just a barista, an actress, a bunch of nerds, and my housecat of a sister."

Kathleen sat across from Jessie and me, making a triangle. Her long red hair had only gotten messier, and I winced at the thought of having to brush out all of those knots. Kathleen looked into my face, and I felt the heat creeping into my cheeks. *Did I offend her with my rant?* "You don't have to do this alone. The rest of us might not be as capable of front-line assaults or anything, but we can be useful too. I was thinking about that foam stuff, for instance, and I think I found a spell that might work." She held up a thick book. "Using a new spell on another person can be risky, and it takes time to perform, so it's not for all situations..."

Of course she was useful. She had magic. Magic was useful, right? But I was touched by the show of acceptance and friendship. She had thought of a way to help me. With emotions overwhelming me, I flung my arms around her, nearly knocking her onto her back. Laughing, Jessie joined in the hug, and Kathleen melted into the show of affection.

More conversation distracted me for a while as Beau continued to work in silence on the other side of the chamber. Jeremy still slept in his bag, and I looked at him, considering.

"You should go with Jeremy to explore some more of the tunnels," Jessie said, following my gaze.

My eyes widened and my brows knit together. "Why would I want to spend more time with him?"

"Would you rather sit around instead?" she retorted.

"I'm going to stab someone if I have to stay in here much longer." I walked over to Jeremy's bag and nudged him with my toes. "Yo, wake up."

He looked at me.

"I want to go with you to explore the caves." The look of pure joy on his face was unsettling. He leapt up to his feet and, before I could avert my gaze, I got an eyeful of him. I was pleased to see he had pants on.

"Of course, let me get ready," he said, digging through his pile of stuff for a shirt and pulling on his shoes. He even took a moment to run his fingers through his hair, which was much more effective than I would have expected. "Let's go."

I snagged a flashlight from Beau and followed Jeremy into the blackness, while he enthusiastically explained the nuances of spelunking. He rambled about the rocks and what various striations meant. I nodded along, not paying complete attention.

"And this striation is limestone," he said, gesturing to a section of rock.

"Hey, can I ask you something?" I asked.

"Sure. Was my explanation of limestone versus sandstone unclear? I don't think I explained it well."

"No, not about that. Why don't you put more effort into...?" I trailed off. I didn't think this through. How could I politely ask why someone is revolting or repugnant? He seemed to know where

I was going anyway, and his face fell. A pang of guilt punched me in the throat. Other than being unattractive, this guy had done absolutely nothing to me for me to be so rude to him. Well, except that one time, and he never did that again. Was I subconsciously mad at him for the entire female gender?

"Of course I put effort in, what do you mean?" he asked.

"Well, like, you—" I stuttered, fumbling around for words to say before finally deciding to just finish what I had started, resulting in a crashing wave of words that erupted from my mouth, "—don't shower, and your clothes are always a mess."

"I shower."

"The smell." I wrinkled my nose.

"Ah. Yeah… it's not a lack of hygiene. I could shower five times a day and layer on deodorant, and the smell would still knock out a rhino. I think it's because I'm a Goblin. It's just how we smell," he said.

"Oh. I'm sorry." And I was. My mom had always told me that commenting on someone's body, especially when it was something they couldn't help, was hurtful.

"I can be sloppy, but it's because even if I *was* meticulously clean, it wouldn't help. Why put in the extra effort?" He shrugged. I bet he got this a lot when he was younger.

"What about perfumes or colognes?" I asked, ducking around a long stalactite.

"That just makes it worse. I've tried explaining to people they'll get used to it. Chud, my roommate, doesn't notice anymore, but that's not exactly a winning pickup line."

I thought about it for a bit and connected some dots. "Is this why you don't care about meeting social norms?"

"Yeah. Doing the whole song and dance people expect from you seems pointless when they will just think you're repulsive anyway. So, why put on airs? It is freeing in a way," he said with a sigh. Then he added quietly, "Still, I'd trade the freedom for acceptance. It doesn't matter how polite your pickup lines are if they find you gross." After a few steps, he muttered, "Some of it is depression."

I eyed him sideways. A part of me was annoyed at discovering this level of depth. Then, I was annoyed over feeling annoyed. Why shouldn't he be his own person, with complicated thoughts and emotions? "You always have a smile on your face."

"Only when you're around."

Poor guy had a crush on me. Not sure why I hadn't noticed earlier. He didn't exactly hide it. Seemed obvious in retrospect.

"I'm really jealous of the rest of you," he said. "You get cool athletic abilities or sweet magic, and I get to be stinky."

"You can navigate caves."

"Oh, wow, how amazing. It's a miracle it was useful," he said with bitter sarcasm.

When we finally returned to our cavern, I found Beau sticking tiny pieces of foil to a—mannequin? —also made of tinfoil. Jeremy drifted back to his sleeping bag to rest, and I approached Beau curiously. "What the hell is that?" I asked.

"Your armor," Beau said.

"But it looks like *trash*."

"I made it in a cave with a box of scraps. What do you expect, a perfect Ironman suit?"

Jeremy's voice called from where he lay. "He made that in a cave, too."

"Do you want it to look fancy or stay alive? If I make it look cooler, it will either have a fraction of the protection or weigh a lot more."

I couldn't believe it. Beau had started messing with foil before my conversation with Jessie and Kathleen. This little nerd was a step ahead of me, and a surge of fondness rushed forward to swell inside my heart.

Beau's phone rang. He answered, "Ah, excellent, I'll put you on speakerphone."

"Hi everyone," Jo's voice said. "I made it home and translated the next report." She read it aloud.

"Realms?" I asked. "There are multiple realms of Kin? Where?"

"I have a theory," Kathleen said. "There aren't many places on earth where you could hide a kingdom, much less multiple. So... maybe they aren't from Earth?"

"I knew he was an alien," I muttered.

"Yeah, them being from Earth seems less and less likely... but if not Earth, where?" Beau mused aloud, tugging at his beard.

"Phelony referred to multiple kinds of Kin. I think it's a reasonable assumption to assume Gnomes aren't the only kind, and from there, we represent other ones. So, Fae and Goblins and... whatever Kathleen is," Jessie said. "Well, think back to stories about Fae. They talk about them as if they existed in a separate world you could slip into."

"Like a parallel dimension?" I asked incredulously.

"They are scientifically feasible," Beau said. "I mean, not proven or anything, but definitely not ruled out."

"So, he isn't just a diplomat from some small Gnome village somewhere? He is a scout from an entirely different world?" Jeremy asked.

"Seems so," Jo said. "And they don't like what they see."

"I'm worried about other types of Kin," Kathleen said. "He makes it seem like some of them would be immune to tanks."

"A sobering thought," I said.

"There is something else I should mention," Jo said. "It's gotten harder for me to translate these."

"What? Why?" Beau asked.

"My understanding of them... collapsed," Jo admitted.

"What do you mean collapsed?" Beau asked, sounding concerned.

"I wasn't sure at first, but I had to forget French to re-learn new Gnomish," Jo explained. "It wasn't immediate, but it's been noticeably diminishing since I left. I had been pushing the limits of my extra mental storage to keep track of the new Gnomish. When I was there with you, I could hold it all, no problem. But it's been getting harder the longer I've been away."

Beau paled slightly and stared ahead, unfocused. "I've been doing more complex things since I got here, but I thought it was just the extra experience and practice I'd gotten," Beau said.

"Something about being in your town seems to make our abilities work better," Jo said.

"It must be the nexus," Kathleen said. "Your abilities must be powered by the same energy mine are."

"Why haven't the rest of us noticed it?" I asked.

"Well, I never tried to use my powers much before, so I don't have a great point of comparison," Jessie said. "Jeremy's powers barely do anything, and Meep has lived here her entire life."

"I've left town before," I said defensively, and shot Jessie a glare. *Ixnay on the Eremeyjay.*

"But for how long? It took Jo a while to notice, and who knows how it would compare between different kinds of Kin," Kathleen said. "If Aether is fueling your powers, your body could be storing it, like a giant crystal. Then you drain slowly, or at different rates, by using your abilities. You could have enough stored compared to how long you were away, and then you wouldn't have noticed."

"So, what do we take away from this?" Beau asked.

"We are dealing with magical enemies from another dimension

that are potentially immune to tanks?" I summarized. "We are *so* out of our depth. We need to tell someone else. Like, the government or the military."

"Tell them what, exactly?" Beau asked. "The only evidence we have for this is a tablet with a language they won't understand. It would just be our word to prove it says what we say it does."

"So, we just hide in this cave forever?" I asked.

"I'm preparing us to face the Auditor again," Beau said. "We've gotten by with the element of surprise, but I think we are out of that. It takes time to do all of these preparations."

"I can't just sit around much longer. We need to do something," I said.

"Well, you can try on the armor. I was going to apply more layers of foil to it, but it's complete enough to test," Beau said.

"Fine." It would be something to do, at least.

The armor was designed to fit over my clothes, but it was snug. Still, once it was all in place, it felt pretty natural.

We moved to the adjoining cavern where I did my stretches, and I tried doing some basic gymnastics. It didn't hinder my range of motion, and I adapted to the weight easily.

"It's actually great," I said, grudgingly.

"Are you trying to fight or win a fashion show?" Beau asked.

I sighed. "I'm not vain, but this literally looks like a pile of trash."

"Fine, fine, I'll make sure the final layer gets smoothed out and polished," he said.

"One thing I'm confused about. You are making me armor from tin foil. How is that going to protect me?"

"Oh, it's not. Not like that," Beau said. "If someone stabs you, it will protect you as well as you'd think tin foil should. But that's not the point. I still expect you to evade the attacks. This is to protect you from the foam. See, the layers of foil can flake off and free you from getting stuck."

"Oh." I paused. "That is useful. I *would* prefer something that prevented me from getting blown up, though."

"So would I. But this is what I can do right now."

We returned to the others, and I sat down on my sleeping bag. Beau pulled something out of the pile of supplies and tossed it to me. A deck of cards.

"You really did think of everything, didn't you?" I smirked.

"It's what I do," he said, and he turned his attention back to my armor.

I gathered the others and started dealing out some hands.

Chapter Twenty-Six

Beau Learns Magic

AUDIT REPORT 5.4

CYCLE: 1000 YEARS

NAME: Auditor Phelony Adalbert Jaroba Opunkele IV

OBSERVATIONS: Large repositories of knowledge have been discovered, which are not considered rare, but are considered to be "dying" by locals; which is confusing since these repositories do not appear to be alive in any sense of the word. In addition to these repositories, it is echoed in their technology. The result is an abundance of information that is available to anyone, at any time. For example, while writing this report, this auditor has

SEVEN ACCESS POINTS TO THE SHARED KNOWLEDGE. THE WIDE-SPREAD ACCESS TO ALL THE INFORMATION OF THE WORLD BY EVERY BEING ALIVE IS TROUBLING; EVEN THOSE WHO ARE LONG SINCE DECEASED HAVE THEIR KNOWLEDGE AND INFORMATION PRESERVED FOR FUTURE REFERENCE.

FORTUNATELY, FURTHER INVESTIGATION REVEALED ONLY A SMALL AMOUNT OF THIS POPULATION TAKES ADVANTAGE OF THIS ACCESS; AND EVEN THEN, ONLY A SMALL OF THE KNOWLEDGE IS CONSUMED BY ANY ONE PERSON. I HAVE HEARD MANY LOCALS REFER TO THIS PROCESS AS 'SCIENCE.' THE PRACTITIONERS OF SCIENCE ACTIVELY SEEK TO DISPROVE PREVIOUSLY SHARED KNOWLEDGE; THE IDEA IS THAT ONLY THE STRONGEST IDEAS SURVIVE, CONTINUE TO BE SHARED, AND BUILT UPON. THERE IS A LARGE POOL OF KNOWLEDGE ABOUT THE FUNCTION OF THEIR BRAIN IN WHICH THEY SELF-DETERMINED THAT NO ONE BRAIN CAN RETAIN ALL THE AVAILABLE KNOWLEDGE.

THEREFORE, THEY ONLY HAVE A PARTIAL UNDERSTANDING OF ANY GIVEN TOPIC AT A TIME, AND THEY ARE BIOLOGICALLY HELPLESS IF A COMPLETE UNDERSTANDING REQUIRES MULTIPLE TOPICS. THIS IS A SERIOUS FLAW IN THEIR KNOWLEDGE TRANS-MISSION. IN FACT, SOMEHOW, MULTIPLE PEOPLE CAN ABSORB THE SAME INFORMATION AND COME TO DIFFERING CONCLUSIONS, SOMETIMES RESULTING IN VIOLENCE AND EVEN WAR. PLEASE REFER TO PREVIOUS REPORT FOR INFORMATION ON WARFARE CAPACITY.

IN CONCLUSION, THIS INVESTIGATION EVIDENCED THIS ABHOR-RENT KNOWLEDGE SHARING IS THEIR FEEBLE ATTEMPT TO OVERCOME THEIR ADORABLY SHORT LIFESPANS, WHICH HAS LED TO THEIR RAPID TECHNOLOGICAL AND SOCIAL ADVANCEMENTS.

Good news for us is that an identified weakness can be exploited if necessary. There is so much contradictory information available that present-day beings seem to have a difficult time finding the most accurate and up-to-date information. For example, the majority of people have information that has been previously disproven, however they also seem to be the loudest in the population, resulting in the spread of inaccuracies, which again, results in violence and warfare.

Beau

I stared at the gun in front of me. I had memorized every detail of its shape, toyed with all of its adjustments, and done everything except fire it. I had to open it up, but I was putting it off. What if it just had a pile of nonsense inside like the watch did? I was not sure why the idea of not understanding it bugged me so much. It was literally running on magic. Why should I understand it? But Phelony did. It was knowable.

I pried the casing open. Lenses and gearing stared at me, and I sighed in relief. Finally, something I could understand. Nestled inside the handle was a purple Aether crystal wrapped in wire that led to the main chamber. Okay, so it was still magic, but more of a hybrid. That was perfect. It gave me an angle to understand it.

I started with the mechanical side. I looked at each piece, fitting them together in my mind, and then letting them interlock and interact. I could see how the dial I had used earlier adjusted the spread of the beam by narrowing the output aperture. I could see how it would build up a charge in a central chamber, then discharge it when the trigger was released. I didn't know what the chamber held exactly, but by the behavior of the weapon and its mechanical function, I could deduce some properties of it.

I turned my attention to the Aether crystal. The silvery wire it had been wrapped in split into various loose ends rather than forming the closed loops used in normal electrical systems. I froze as the realization struck me.

Not just silvery, I realized, but *actual* silver. I needed a better understanding of how Aether functioned.

"Kathleen, can you please come here?" I asked.

She was sitting on the same sleeping bag as Jessie, who was brushing out her hair and putting it into tidy braids. She waited until Jessie finished her current braid and then came over. "Yeah?"

"Can you explain how magic works?" I asked.

Kathleen chuckled, "Oh, sure, it's not like that's a topic I have had to study my *entire* life."

"Can you explain the basics?" I asked.

"Why should I trust you with that knowledge? I don't know you that well," Kathleen said.

"We are stuck in a cave together being hunted by a homicidal Gnome. If now isn't the time to trust me, then when is?" I asked.

She chewed on her lip thoughtfully.

"Look, I know we haven't exactly gotten off on the right foot. I would ask Kyle, but he isn't here," I said. This was the first time Kyle had come up since we set up camp here. I didn't want to involve any more people than strictly necessary, and maybe, similarly, Kathleen wanted to keep him safe too. Besides, I doubted the Auditor could figure out who my roommate was even if he was able to identify my dorm building.

Kathleen looked puzzled. "Why would you ask Kyle?"

"He's a Wizard, too." Her look of shock was over-acted. "Oh, spare me the dramatics. I saw your spell work, and it was the same type of setup I caught Kyle with. Plus, you two are *dating*. I know it's encouraged for Gnomes to date other Gnomes, so I assume that it's common for others?"

"Wizards dating Witches is common, yes," Kathleen admitted slowly.

"So, do you think Kyle would show me magic?"

"He would love to," Kathleen said.

"Then show it to me on his behalf?" I pleaded with her.

Her defensive posture relaxed, her hesitant expression melted, and she took a deep breath. "All magic stems from Aether. It's the raw power of creation. When it's in a ley line, it flows through our world but doesn't interact with it. It's stable and inert. Witches and Wizards can sense it. It's like feeling the sun with your eyes closed. You can tell there is a brightness, and you can feel the warmth, but you can't see any details."

"And that is what's in the Aether crystals?" I asked, trying to keep up.

"Yes. It's much weaker—more like feeling the heat from a small animal in your hands—if I pay attention, I can tell something is there."

"What do you do with Aether once you find it?" I asked.

"I can reach out to it, and it will flow into me. I can't hold it for long before losing control of it. I have to do *something* with it, and when I release it, it's no longer inert. It wants to change things and will do so wildly if not directed with exacting precision. If not, it's pretty much always lethal for everyone nearby."

"Yikes," I said.

"Yeah. So, we have to take it in with a purpose and release it quickly. Properly directed, it can produce the exact change we want. It's tricky though. I can't actually see the Aether, yet I have to shape it precisely. It's like trying to make a statue out of clay when the clay is invisible and likes to twist around like plasma."

"That sounds incredibly difficult," I frowned.

"If I tried to do it just by feel or intuition, it would be nearly impossible. The greatest masters can accomplish that, but everyone else needs to use the rituals," Kathleen explained.

"The rituals give you a set of instructions to follow to get the outcome you want, despite not seeing what you are doing?" I guessed. "Like a recipe?"

"Exactly. I think of it as being a blind knitter. You can't see the yarn, you don't know the colors, but if you follow the patterns properly, you can still make an elaborate sweater. But deviate even slightly, and you won't even know what the result would look like."

I showed Kathleen the interior of the ray gun. "From what you are saying, I think these wires are used to channel the Aether and direct it into the desired shape. Does that sound right?"

She frowned deeply. "Maybe as a first approximation. The clay analogy is probably a bit misleading. Aether isn't a static thing; it moves and shifts. A major component of any ritual is the timing, and you need to apply your influences at the right moment when the Aether is doing the right thing. Chants are often used to give a rhythm to all the steps, for instance. Some Wizards prefer to use music."

I studied the wiring closer. These weren't wires like I was used to, mass produced and uniform. The thickness of the silver varied from place to place, and the loose ends had subtle imperfections, some fraying while others were capped with bits of rubber. If timing was so important, maybe the thickness of the wire controlled how fast the Aether flowed, and the ends impacted how the Aether was released? It also worked a lot faster than her spell did, so maybe the mechanical precision could shape the Aether more quickly than Kathleen could manage by hand. That probably meant her set of timings and effects wouldn't translate directly to a device. If only I could figure out what configuration served what function, I thought I could replicate this weapon. More or less.

I planned out a new design and made a shopping list.

"Jessie, mind going to town again?" I asked.

"Of course not," she said brightly, tossing her long blonde braid over her shoulder. "What do you need?"

I handed her the list. "Just a few more items. These should be a lot easier to carry by yourself."

Jessie began to shift, a smile broad across her face until she was a cheerful middle-aged man with a beer belly. "How do I look?"

"Like you should be grumpier," I said.

Jessie's face fell into a scowl.

"Perfect."

When Jessie returned, I took the new supplies into the adjacent cave for safety. I tried to reproduce the wire harness with one of the Aether crystals from the hot springs. After figuring out how I could stretch the thin silver wire to achieve different thicknesses, and how to use a silver solder to join the wire, I began to grow more confident in my ability to replicate this.

By the time I had finished, I had a copy of the original Aether harness. I just hoped it was precise enough. I swapped out the original setup from the gun and inserted my own. I wanted to test fire it, but given what Kathleen had said about uncontrolled Aether, I didn't want to be holding it when I did. So, I clamped it into a stand and used a string to pull the trigger.

With a *wee-whoomp,* my target burst into flame. Not exactly the clean hole the original had left through things, but I was getting a heat blast. I examined my setup for differences and was able to clean up a few of them, which improved the result, but didn't get it up to the same power of the original. I could get it to burn through the target on the narrow beam setting, but the wider settings couldn't do it.

It would have to be good enough. I didn't know how to improve it any further. I turned my attention to making a new housing for it. I simplified Phelony's design, removing most of the adjustable settings. I basically hardwired it to be at the narrowest, most intense setting since it didn't have the power to do anything useful with a different setting, and it made it a lot easier to fabricate.

I did make one improvement, though. The Gnome's gun didn't have a way to take out the Aether crystal. I presumed he knew how to recharge them, but I didn't. What I did have was a stockpile of charged ones. So, I designed it to reload similar to how a pistol can reload its magazine, inserting a new crystal in the base of the handle.

A test fire of the new gun showed it working at an acceptable level. I got to work making more so we could arm everyone.

Exhausted, I brought my work to the others. "I made us weapons."

"We all get ray guns? Sweet!" Jeremy exclaimed. He took one of the guns and started making *pew pew* noises. Surprisingly, he maintained good trigger discipline and firearm etiquette by not pointing it at anyone and keeping his finger off the trigger, like he had at least used a normal gun before.

"I'll set up some targets in the other cavern for you to practice on tomorrow," I said. "I'm too tired to do it now."

Kathleen stared at the pile skeptically. "Are you sure those are safe? I warned you about the outcome of uncontrolled Aether."

"Absolutely, positively, mostly sure they are reasonably not lethal to use," I hedged.

"Reassuring," Kathleen said, rolling her eyes.

"I've tested them all, and if my understanding is right, they should be perfectly predictable."

Rays cautiously crept forward toward the pile of guns and sniffed at them. "Ah, no, I don't think you should mess with those," Meep said, gently guiding her away.

"Jo called, by the way. You were busy, but I wrote down the report for you," Jessie said.

I eagerly took it and read through it. "So, he figured out the scientific process," I chuckled as I waved my phone in the air searching for enough signal to call Jo back.

"And is baffled by it," Meep pointed out, rolling her eyes.

"What they do know, they learned on their own. I can't even imagine how much work that would take," Kathleen said.

"Millennia, apparently," Jeremy quipped.

"No wonder he's so pissed that we keep taking his stuff. I thought it was just that he made it himself, but this goes beyond that," I said thoughtfully as Jo answered and I put her on speaker to join the conversation.

"The Gnomish way of advancing sounds horribly inefficient. Everyone is reinventing millennia of progress," Jo said. "Do they ever get time to relax? To be themselves? I don't want to be a real Gnome if I have to be in school all the time."

I frowned at her use of the term "real Gnome." We were real. I didn't care what anyone else said. Right? "It's no shock that he is flabbergasted by humanity. Imagine getting a degree, then working for decades in your field, only to find a baby is somehow nearly as knowledgeable as you."

"That would be so weird," Jo agreed. "Still, his stuff is so advanced. How will we cope with it?"

"He may know a thing or two that I don't, but I'm going to show him just how far you can reach from the shoulders of giants."

CHAPTER TWENTY-SEVEN

UNWELCOME

AUDIT REPORT 5.5

CYCLE: 1000 YEARS

NAME: Auditor Phelony Adalbert Jaroba Opunkele IV

OBSERVATIONS: THE INFORMATION HUBS, KNOWN AS SCHOOLS, PRESENTED A NON-CHALLENGE AS THE "STUDENTS" SEEM TO BE CONDITIONED TO ANSWER QUESTIONS QUICKLY. AN ADVANCED SCHOOL, CALLED A UNIVERSITY, IS LOCATED DIRECTLY ON THIS NEXUS. IT APPEARS THAT IF THE AETHER WERE INTERACTING WITH AND/OR ENHANCING KNOWLEDGE OR TECHNOLOGY, EVIDENCE WOULD BE FOUND HERE.

The purpose of schools are to share education, similar to the large knowledge repository in the last report. Schools are places the public is forced to attend until adulthood, and then it becomes optional. Perhaps many locals do not know what to do otherwise, spending their youth learning only how to be in school.

Do these people not understand the advantage knowledge gives you over your competitors? To give it freely is unthinkable.

It appears that no aether exist in their knowledge or technological advances. Original speculations appear correct in this regard.

Meep

For the past week, stuck in the cave, trapped in my head, all I had was exercise and stretches to numb the minutia and nattering doubts plaguing my mind. This entire experience was a nightmare. I wanted to be *doing* something productive, like Beau and Kathleen with their preparations, or Jessie with her ability to shift and venture from the cave. Or even Jo, who wasn't here anymore, but got to eat hot, homemade meals and still be useful all the same. All I had was Jeremy, who said he felt just as useless as I did.

No. Not useless. He was *not* useless. And although my bitter thoughts stood up for Jeremy, there seemed no scrap of grace for my own contributions. Probably because there were none.

But today.

Today we got guns.

And I was *good* with them.

The ray guns were a blast. Thankfully only metaphorically, and nothing exploded in our faces. The death rays were much easier to aim than real guns. We didn't have to account for how a bullet took a curved trajectory, or how recoil would throw off my alignment, or wind resistance, or whatever. We all practiced using the guns, except for Beau, who was manically writing a new order for gizmos, gadgets, and probably more tinfoil.

After a few rounds of target practice, Jessie left to head into town. I did not find it fair that she could leave this stupid cave whenever she wanted, and I was stuck in here. Maybe I should sneak out, risks be damned.

"Check this out!" Jeremy said, his back to the targets and his gun held by his face, pointing up. He whirled around, landing in a wide stance with his hand stabilizing his wrist, aiming at one of our makeshift targets, and promptly shot *over* it. "Ummm, pretend I hit—"

I placed my hand on his wrist. "Aim lower, directly where you want to hit." I put my head on his shoulder. The smell that would have normally assaulted my nose seemed muted, like the scent of mildew after leaving your clothes in the washer on a hot day. "And fire. Okay, you hit a bit off, so just adjust your aim sideways and try again."

I heard Jeremy's breath catch, and realized I was pushed against him. I took a step back. "Yeah, you've got the idea."

When had I gotten so comfortable with him? Kathleen shot me a raised eyebrow, and I could only shrug. We fired a few more rounds before deciding it was enough for today.

"Hey, Meep. Can you follow me? I want to show you something," Jeremy said.

"I swear to God, if you pull down your pants..." Kathleen said over her book.

"Can we drop the 'everything Jeremy does is perverted' shtick, please?" he asked.

"I'm sorry," I said, shooting Kathleen a glare, and she refocused her ice blue eyes onto the text propped in her lap.

Jeremy led me into the tunnels and through a twisted path of caves and caverns. "I know you have been cooped up in here, and it's been harder on you than the rest of us. I'm used to sitting around in a dark room. Jessie has left, Beau has been building things, and Kathleen seems happy sitting alone and reading the books Jessie brings back for her. But you, you're active. You do gymnastics and shit. You've just been prowling back and forth like a caged animal."

"You aren't wrong, but I don't know what to do about it."

"I had some ideas." We entered a larger cavern, and Jeremy messed with a battery on the floor. Suddenly, light spilled through the spacious cavern, illuminating various poles and beams set up to form the familiar shape of gymnastics equipment.

I wandered through the maze of beams, shocked it was here. It wasn't standard stuff—it was clearly handmade. But I tested it and found it to be perfectly stable. "How...?" I asked in amazement.

He shrugged. "I asked Jessie to pick me up some things during one of her outings. It didn't take much to convince her to go along with it because she knew you would love it. I'm not nearly as good as Beau at making stuff, of course, but I do know how to build things."

My lips parted slightly, and my throat tightened. My words felt thick in my mouth and came out in a near whisper. "It's wonderful. Thank you. Seriously, thank you." I reached for his arm and let my fingers slide down his skin, leaving behind goosebumps in my wake. I entwined my thin fingers with his thicker ones, feeling the many calluses. *How many did he get just for me?*

"It was nothing," he said, ducking his head. Was that a bit of red on his face?

I gave his warm hands a quick squeeze, and then sprinted at

the overhead beam, jumping to grab it. I used my momentum to carry me up and around before I struck a handstand at the top of my arc. Then I swung back down, landing into a somersault before leaping onto a balance beam made of wood.

I found it easier to push off a rock floor instead of soft padding. It would suck to slip and fall here... but I never slip.

As I sprinted from the balance beam and leapt to the pommel, I realized that I could fully let loose here. I did a complex routine from the pommel, and then flipped off it, twisting and spinning through the air to land at Jeremy's feet. "This is the best thing anyone has ever done for me." I sounded winded, but it was from excitement instead of exertion.

He beamed. It was the first time I had ever seen him smile so genuinely, and I noted the crinkle beside his eyes. "Feel free to spend as much time here as you want. It's not like we have anyplace else we need to be."

I grinned and ran back to the uneven parallel bars—if they were to continue out into infinity, they may at some point cross, but they were parallel enough for me.

Overall, the handmade equipment presented a more interesting challenge than the boring, standard, and safety-regulated equipment anyway. The bars were not perfectly smooth, the beams slightly narrower, but I was in pure play heaven.

We returned to the main cavern, and I felt properly worn out. That exercise was just what I had needed, and a soak in the hot springs sounded divine. Jessie was back and standing in the middle of the room. As soon as she saw me, she rushed over and pulled me into the neighboring chamber.

"We have a problem," she hissed in my ear.

My good mood vanished like the popping of a soap bubble. "What's wrong?"

She pulled a paper out of her pocket and handed it to me. MISSING, it read. Jeremy Vimes, Kyle Moolin, Beauregard Cornelius, Samantha Dent. It had a picture for each, which looked like it had been pulled from the school catalog. It had a number to call printed at the bottom.

"Jeremy and Beau missing makes sense. Why is Kyle missing? That's Beau's roommate and Kathleen's boyfriend, right? And Samantha is the girl Beau's been stalking, isn't she?" I asked.

Jessie nodded. "I called the number. These posters were put up by Chud."

"Chud?"

"Jeremy's roommate. He said he noticed Jeremy hadn't been around for a couple of days. At first, he didn't think much of it because of college shenanigans, but eventually, he became concerned and tried to find him. Kind of sweet, actually. He found out that Samantha, Beau, and Kyle were also missing. He seems more frantic about Samantha, truth be told, but I think he is actually worried about everyone. That's weird, though, because Beau says he's a bully. But he seemed honestly protective, in a way."

"It has to be Phelony, right? He couldn't find us, so he tracked down Beau's roommate and crush?"

"It must be."

"Should we tell Beau?" Were we ready to come out of hiding? We all had guns now.

"He's completely unreliable where Samantha is concerned."

She had a point. I didn't know of a single time Samantha and Beau had been involved where it had gone well.

"Alright, fine, but I am going to go out and scout the Auditor. I can't just let that poor girl get dragged into this mess and do nothing. Have you told Kathleen about Kyle? She'd want to know."

"Yeah. But she didn't seem overly concerned."

"Her boyfriend was kidnapped by a crazy Gnome, and she *wasn't overly concerned?*"

"She pretended to be. I pushed her on it, and she just said Kyle can take care of himself, so why worry? I don't know. I think she is hiding something from us." Jessie sounded just as upset about this deceit as she was about someone being kidnapped.

"That's strange, but I don't know what to do about it."

"Neither do I. Look, if he does have hostages, I don't know that we can end this without a fight. I think I'm going to try and get Bella to join us."

"But we lost the watch during our meeting with Phelony," I pointed out.

"I know, but I don't need to convince her to reveal her secret. I just need to convince her to come help rescue Samantha and Kyle." I didn't see the distinction, but it didn't hurt for her to try.

After everyone had gone to sleep that night, I got my armor and smuggled it out of the cave. I hadn't seen it since Beau had me test it out, and I was surprised to find that he had actually fixed the aesthetics. It no longer looked like it was covered in crumbled foil, but instead, had smooth metallic scales.

It looked pretty sweet now. I fitted the armor on and strapped a ray gun—which I had also smuggled out—onto my upper thigh with a length of rope.

Let's do this.

I stepped into the forest with my heart pounding. It was wonderful to see the sky again. I raced through the trees, reveling in the feel of the stretch of my legs as my pace ate up the ground below me. I only slowed down when I reached the tree line near the warehouse district.

I squinted down the hillside at the lights on in the Auditor's base but was unable to make out details inside. I crept forward slowly, my heart loud in my ears, my eyes darting around frantically trying to spot any traps. This caution proved wise when I came across a thin wire stretched across the opening between two buildings. If I had been going any faster, or could see less well at night, I would have stumbled into it. I gingerly stepped over it, not wanting to trigger the trap or disarm it and alert him of my presence.

Peering around a corner, and checking to make sure the path was clear, I sprinted up a wall then flipped onto the roof. My muscles burned, sore from my physical exertion earlier. It didn't help that I'd been stagnant for a week before that, but I pushed on anyway. The skylight was ahead, and with it, a clear view into the warehouse.

Phelony was at his workbench where behind him, spheres littered the floor. He had another one disassembled before him, and all of them looked like the floating eye I had dealt with the first time I'd been here. Samantha, was in a tall cage behind him, talking to him. I couldn't hear what she was saying from here, but she looked a bit stressed. Thankfully, she didn't appear to be hysterical, which was good. She'd be easier to work with this way.

I inspected the edge of the skylight, and as suspected, there was a device attached to it. He had seen me leave through the skylight the last time, so of course he would guard it. I had other plans for tonight, though.

There was a big ventilation box nearby, and with a few well-placed blasts from the heat ray, I was able to pry open the cover and remove the fan blocking the way. A brief flash in my mind of Jessie playing with a stick, pretending it was sonic and able to unlock doors and fix machines, invaded my mind. You don't need screwdrivers when you can *melt* metal. Grinning and excited to tell Jessie about my "sonic ray gun," I slowly lowered myself into the vent. It was one of those big suspended vents they use in industrial spaces, and it let me get close enough to hear what was being said.

"I'll give you anything you want, just let me go," Samantha said with a sob.

"I want Meep, Jessie, Beau, and Jeremy," the Auditor said.

"I have no clue who those people are! Please. I promise I won't tell anybody. Just let me go."

I moved further along the vent until I reached a grate over some shelves, which I then melted open. Thank God these things were silent. I lowered myself down and climbed to the floor.

"Do you want money? I don't have much, but you can have all of it," Samantha sobbed. "I could get even more if you let me go."

I tried to creep towards Samantha's cage, but a loud clang startled me as I passed one of the Auditor's strange machines. I leapt backwards, pushing myself flat against the shelves and froze. When nothing else happened, I inched forward to investigate what the noise had been. A hollow half-sphere, about the size of a grapefruit, sat in a tray below it, like some kind of gumball machine. Was that a part of one of those robot eyeballs?

"What makes you think I care about money?" Phelony asked dryly.

I reached the cage, caught Samantha's attention, and placed a finger over my lips. Her face lit up, and she edged closer to me.

"I don't know who you are, but you've got to get me out of here. This guy is crazy," Samantha hissed at me.

"Don't worry. I'll get you out. Where is Kyle?" I whispered back.

"Who is Kyle?" she asked.

I looked around and frowned. "The boy."

Samantha cast her eyes around, too. "What boy?"

"I knew something was up when she stopped prattling," Phelony said behind me.

My hair stood on end, and I whipped around, crouching low as if ready to pounce.

The Auditor aimed a death ray at my chest, and several of the eye drones hovered menacingly behind him. "It's why I let her keep talking."

"Let her go. She has nothing to do with this," I demanded.

"I didn't want to hurt anybody, and I am here as an observer, not a warrior. This is only happening because of *you*," Phelony said.

"I was only curious. You attacked me first," I snarled.

"I came to negotiate in good faith after you stole from me, then you attacked *me* and stole from me *again*," Phelony sneered back, gesticulating wildly.

I took the chance to run sideways, darting behind a shelf. Samantha yelped, pressing herself against the edge of the cage as the floor melted in several places. Those shots had come from the eye drones. Shit, were they armed now? I fired a few shots behind me as the drones rounded the corner.

I winged one of them and darted around another corner as the shelf behind me burst into flames. Those things took some time to aim and fire, it seemed.

I sprinted through the maze of shelves, catching glimpses of the eye drones fanning out in various directions. I was so busy trying to keep track of them that I lost track of Phelony. When he reappeared in front of me, he sprayed foam on the floor around me, trying to cut off my escape.

Hoping for the best, I sprinted across the foam. The look on Phelony's face—the initial smugness of success followed rapidly by shock—was almost worth the mortal danger. A tiny tug later, small silvery scales were left in the places where my body had touched the foam.

My armor had worked! And Phelony was *not* happy about it.

Seeing the spot where I had come down from the vents, I leaped into the air, grabbed the bottom of the shaft, and used my momentum to swing myself in.

The tight confines of the shaft would make shooting those drones like the infamous fish in a barrel.

On silent feet, I retraced my steps, moving backwards to keep my eyes on the entrance. Phelony must have realized that sending his drone into such a small funnel would most likely result in his loss. I couldn't say that the Gnome was stupid—crazy as a kitten in yarn, yes, but not stupid. A memory surfaced in the back of my mind of Kip misusing that phrase to say, "...crazy as a yarn cat." I gave the memory a smile and a fond pat on the head as I shoved my family into a box in the corner. I needed to focus.

A faint sound, like the echo of a groan, had me turn my back to the entrance I had been guarding. A small pin hole appeared in the metal floor of the vent shaft. And then another, coming closer to where I crouched. A third and then a fourth. They were not appearing in a straight line, more like a zig-zag pattern about five inches apart. Judging by the angle of the exit hole from the beam itself, Phelony did not seem to be moving.

As I watched, I created a beat in my head to anticipate the next shot. If I waited until the last moment, I could roll out of the way.

Thank God he was not shooting randomly, and the heat ray was not a rapid-fire weapon.

I waited, holding my breath. *Three. Two. One.* As the last beam shot less than an inch from my knee, I rolled forward. In the process, I dropped my gun, and it clattered against the metal floor of the shaft. *Shit.*

However, the shots stopped. *Maybe he thinks he finally hit me?*

Snatching my gun, I continued forward, hoping he didn't see any shadows passing over the holes he had punched through the vent.

I could see my exit before me, and once I got outside, the trees would provide more cover so I could make it back to the others. Because honestly, I didn't know of anywhere better to go.

At the last minute, I heard an echoing shout from Phelony. I risked a look back to see his face contorted in rage as he saw me escaping.

Shit. Shit. Shit.

I rounded the corner and rolled through the exit, already running for the trees as I dropped to the grass. Before losing sight of the warehouse completely, I risked a glance again to see Phelony rush out, fully armored, with all his flying drones buzzing around him. I sped up, pushing my already overworked muscles to go even faster as Phelony began the chase.

CHAPTER TWENTY-EIGHT

LASERS AND TREES ARE NOT FRIENDS

AUDIT REPORT 5.6

CYCLE: 1000 YEARS

NAME: Auditor Phelony Adalbert Jaroba Opunkele IV

OBSERVATIONS: As stated in the previous reports, my original intention was to investigate the transfer of knowledge. However, the goal of this investigation shifted due to the startling realization of what I can only call "false-kin." They do not seem to know about the kin, who are, at most, only referenced as myths and legends. No one seems to believe the kin are real.

I have looked into these myths and found contradicting information. I expect nothing else from these people. For example, they seem to think gnomes are small and cheerful with lots of hair, and pointy hats that they use as decorations for their homes. It is insulting.

They do have one record about an "ancient" civilization who worshiped the mau. However, that term is only found in a small number of records. They think this is amusing because they have changed the word "mau" to mean "cat," and therefore think this ancient civilization worshiped domesticated house cats—an entirely different species.

I have created a device to detect all forms of kin in order to collect evidence to confirm my increasing suspicion.

Due to the lack of aether crystals, my efficiency is slightly reduced. However, it is not to a degree in which I cannot overcome with time and gnomish ingenuity.

I did not realize any kin had come to this realm to breed. Why was this even possible? What are the implications of mating with humans? How does that affect the natural order in this realm? These are questions others in the family will be better suited to answer, due to this auditor's dedication to engineering in lieu of biology.

BEAU

"Wow," I said.

"I know," Jo said. "I started getting an idea of where this was going and had to finish translating it as fast as I could."

"This answers so many things," I said, excited. "We are half-Gnome, half-human. No wonder he felt so much more Gnomey. Though, this must have been centuries, if not millennia, ago. Wouldn't any traces of Kin have been bred out by now?"

"It's not just us. The others are descended from Kin, too. There must have been a lot of contact between realms in the past, and our folklore and mythology sprung up around it. He's quite irate about pop culture Gnomes," Jo giggled.

"But seriously, how are we not just one-millionth Gnome by this point? I don't think this is how genetics work," I said, rubbing my temples under my hat.

"I don't know. There is only one more report. I am going to see if I can translate it now," Jo said.

"Good luck." I hung up the phone, lost in thought and trying to solve this giant Rubik's cube of a mystery. An entire realm of Gnomes existed out there, and they seemed to be some kind of highly competitive, anti-collaborative meritocracy. Great. They came here looking for Aether crystals, which they used to make magitech, and somewhere along the way, interbred with humans to create false-Kin Gnomes, like myself. And there were other mythological creatures who created other types of half-breeds. Not only that, but I had managed to gather a bunch of them up and go camping in a cave with them. Something was still missing from the picture. It didn't all add up right. Was I just so good at identifying half-breeds that everyone I scanned turned out to be exactly that?

I sat for a while digesting this. The bit about the Mau was interesting. Meep would want to know about it, so I drifted into the adjoining cavern to find the others.

Meep wasn't there. Neither was Jessie. Jeremy sat in the corner with a dreamy look on his face, and Rays was crouched next to him, her head cocked as she stared at him. Kathleen scowled at a paper with some weird circle diagram on it before scrunching it up and sketching a new one.

"Where's Meep?"

"Don't know. She was whispering something with Jessie," Jeremy said. I noticed Kathleen wasn't just staring at her paper anymore but seemed to be avoiding looking at me.

"Kathleen?"

"She... left," Kathleen said reluctantly.

"What? Without a plan? She's going to get herself attacked," I said in a panic. *Fuck. What is she doing? I'm going through all these measures to make sure we stay safe, and she just runs off.*

"What do you mean? Is she in danger?" Jeremy asked, the dreamy look gone and pure concern covering his face.

I stormed back to my workshop and grabbed a bandolier of Aether ammo for my weapon. I'd been working on improving our equipment in case of a conflict, but I hadn't finished these for anyone else.

I came back and tossed Jeremy a ray gun. He clumsily caught it. "Come on, let's go find her," I said, and headed for the cave entrance. Jeremy followed on my heels and so did Rays. "No, Rays, you need to stay here."

The intense glare surprised me. She normally looked so innocent, wide eyed, and naïve, but right now she looked as fierce and determined as any hunter. But I didn't need another person to protect. She was just going to be a liability. "No, Rays. Stay. Um, bad kitty?" *How do you get a cat to mind you?* I think there is a saying about how impossible that is. So, all I could do was hope she listened to reason.

The dilemma soon became moot as a crashing sound approached us, and I looked around in time to see Meep burst out of the forest.

"I'm sorry! Duck!" she shouted, diving behind a rock. Flying spherical drones shot out of the trees behind her, and Jeremy and I dove for cover. But Rays leaped into a nearby tree instead. *Will she be safe up there? God, I hope so.*

"Dammit, Meep, why'd you have to run off alone?" I shouted, leaning out to take a quick shot at a drone.

"Doesn't matter. Phelony is coming here. Now. The flying robot things aren't a great shot, just don't stand in the open," she said.

I peeked out from behind the rock, watching how the drones flew. I focused and made a mental model of the battlefield. I visualized every tree and rock I could see, striving for the utmost accuracy, and placed each drone in its current position. The movements were predictable; they were mechanical after all, and I focused on anticipating their positions. If I aimed just right...

I pushed my arm out from the rock's rear and twisted the gun to the correct angle, firing at each drone in rapid succession with what I calculated to be the right trajectory.

One.

Two.

Three.

Four.

"What are you doing?" cried Meep. "You can't just fire randomly! Aim, goddammit!"

My chest puffed up. "I *am* aiming. I just took them all out, didn't I?"

"No. You didn't," Jeremy said, taking careful aim and pulling the trigger. I heard the drone hitting the ground shortly afterwards. A sound that was markedly absent after my attempt. I glanced back out and saw the drones, still in the air, moving in the pattern I had predicted. So much for theory. Apparently, I couldn't actually aim blindly as precisely as I could imagine it. I thought through their movement patterns again, forecasting even further.

"Dammit. Everyone scatter! NOW! They will flank all of us at once from here." I hopped over the rock and darted behind a tree, and saw the others reposition out of the corner of my eye. The drones broke their movement pattern, following different people.

By the time Phelony arrived, I had taken out two of the drones while darting between tree trunks. He hovered forward in a stately manner, light reflecting off his orange armored suit. Parts of it articulated and moved around, shielding his joints as he moved. *Badass.* Together, we opened fire at him, but each shot fizzled harmlessly against him.

"It was bad enough that you stole my weapon, but you dare to copy it!" he screamed. "You filthy false-Kin. You haven't earned that."

Copy, shmopy. Just because he didn't appreciate the value of learning from others didn't mean my accomplishments were worthless. I was proud I could make these from a complex jumble of nonsense.

But that armor was amazing. And also, problematic, I thought furiously. His armor was shielding him from the heat rays, but the energy had to go *somewhere*. Either his armor had enough thermal mass and insulation to protect him, which meant a high melting point, or it was using Aether to negate it. Aether was limited, and there could only be so much stored in his crystals, which meant thermal mass could be overwhelmed.

"Keep shooting at him. His armor can't stop this forever!" I shouted to the others.

He flew towards me, and I ducked back behind a large rock, giving Meep an opening to fire at his back. When he went for her, I popped out of cover for another volley.

This might work.

Phelony apparently agreed, as he switched tactics and flew to the side, no longer surrounded, and fired foam around the tree Meep was using for cover.

"Meep, move!" Jeremy shouted, and she darted out, crossing the foam and leaving a trail of aluminum behind.

Jeremy tried to shoot at Phelony, but his gun didn't fire. "I'm out!" he shouted, so I unclipped a crystal from my bandolier for him. He caught it and reloaded.

Phelony noticed the exchange. "You *do* have Aether crystals! Where have they been hiding?"

He changed direction and rushed at me. It was all I could do to grab his gun and twist it away from my body, but we were soon locked in a grapple. Either Phelony was stronger than me, which I doubted due to how much smaller he was, or his armor enhanced his strength. Either way, I couldn't fend him off, and I felt his hand grasp my bandolier. "I'll just be taking these."

Then Phelony was knocked backwards, my bandolier still clutched in his hands. As he hit the ground and tumbled, I saw a figure standing over me. Her stance was wide and stable, battle ready, with fists raised. Her long black and red hair waved in the breeze, and her skin gleamed red in the firelight. Bella had arrived.

Wait, why was Bella here? Jessie stood at the edge of the clearing and gave me a thumbs up. I waved back, and she moved towards the cave where I could see Kathleen poking her head out.

Where had the firelight come from?

I scrambled to my feet and found flames reaching for the sky, eating foliage on the forest floor, and licking up trees all around us—the consequence of heat rays.

"Don't touch them!" Bella snarled, then she charged at Phelony.

He raised his arm and shot a shiny mist at her, and as Bella ran into it, she stopped and clutched at her face, letting out a cry of pain. Was this what the mist should have done to "Bella" the night we got the tablet, or was this a different mist since the first one apparently hadn't worked?

"You think I wouldn't be prepared?" Phelony spat as he rose to his feet.

Damn. Maybe Bella wasn't the trump card we had assumed.

Bella took her hands from her face, which was red and swollen with tears streaming from her eyes like she had been maced. "You think that's going to stop me? Now I'm just pissed."

She kicked him in his chest, sending him flying into the dark. He stopped in midair and rose higher. A small swarm of silvery insects flew from his suit straight at Bella.

They buzzed around her, dive bombing her face and arms, and she twitched away, as if being stung. I raised my gun to continue firing at him, but it wasn't my gun. It was Phelony's. I must have had it in my hand when Bella had tossed him away.

I doubted I could overwhelm his armor without my stock of Aether crystals unless his gun somehow did not run out of charge. I needed a new plan. I cast about frantically as if I could find one lying on the ground. His armor was too strong, the rising flames were going to be a problem soon, and we didn't have fireproof armor like the Auditor.

With Bella distracted, Phelony had turned his attention to Meep, shooting globs of foam at her. At least the foam had a side effect of putting out some flames as she dodged, occasionally forced to leave some of the tinfoil scales behind. Worry gnawed in the back of my mind. Her armor didn't have an infinite amount of those.

Phelony launched another glob of foam, and this time Meep

didn't dodge fast enough. It hit her, pinning her to a tree. Thankfully, it wasn't one that was on fire.

"*Askerbin*. You have been a *flurgle* in my oil for too long." He leveled my death ray at her and fired.

"No!" Jeremy screamed, diving in front of Meep. His belly burst into flames, and he collapsed to the ground face first.

My blood froze in my veins. *No.*

I wasn't close enough to see the gory details, but my mind's eye filled it in for me, extrapolating the effects of that much heat dumped onto organic flesh, like bacon sizzling on high heat. It would be horrifyingly gruesome, the moisture super-heating with steam and exploding outwards. My brain rendered every detail of it for me, whether I wanted it to or not.

I had never wished for my brain to stop so much before in my life. "You bastard!" I flipped the beam-size dial on his gun to full strength and fired.

But nothing happened.

"Raaargh!" A guttural, primal roar filled the air, and Rays pounced from her treetop directly at Phelony. He fired a glob of foam into her chest, but her momentum carried her forward, slamming into him, and driving them both to the ground.

CHAPTER TWENTY-NINE

STUCK, LITERALLY

MEEP

Time is such a silly thing. A linear pathway flying forever forward, except for times like this. I tried to lift my aching arms but was stuck fast. My armor, too wasted of tiny scales, did nothing to free me—the aluminum trash I had made fun of. More of it would have been useful right about now. *Fuck, Beau was right.* My thoughts were bitter as I tried to fight the foam, to tear myself from this trap, but it was futile. And I was tired. I was so tired. All the agility in the world could not make up for the endurance pushed far past its peak.

A soft groan beside me snapped my attention down, and my

head swam with a jumble of partial memories in the present. I had taken a serious knock to the head, but what had happened right before? My eyes struggled to focus. Was that a body next to me?

Oh fuck, Jeremy.

My mind sluggishly recalled what had happened. Out of time. Out of endurance. Out of defenses. A vision of myself mid-leap as I knocked two of those drones out of the air to explode against a nearby tree. The Auditor, with a wicked little smile, waited for me to land, and then blasted me with foam to trap me against this tree. Even if I had scales remaining, I doubted the armor could have gotten me out of this. He had hit me with a direct spray to my torso, locking my arms to my side. It had secured my back against the trunk, and now the foam securely held me against this redwood.

Jeremy lay at my feet, inches away, yet it could have been miles, and the result would have been the same. *I am useless once again.* I couldn't help him, couldn't save him. Fear and worry gripped my heart. The present continued to catch up with me slowly. After being secured to this tree, the Auditor had leveled his ray gun at me, a smug look playing over his face as time had seemed to slow in proportion to how far the trigger was pressed.

Was that Beau's gun?

Phelony himself had seemed to slow down, and the peripheral action sped up. As the gun had fired, a figure had dived in front of me.

Jeremy. He had saved me. The realization struck me with a wave of emotions. Fondness for him and a pang of something more than fondness that I wasn't willing to name yet swelled inside of me. Worry for him, fear for his safety, and gratitude for him followed closely behind.

I heard him breathing, but the sound was so faint and uneven to my ears that I worried. He lay crumpled, face down. I saw no blood, but I could smell it.

How much? I couldn't tell. Without knowing where he'd gotten hit, or how much blood there was, I had no idea how long that ragged breathing was going to last. I didn't want to lose him. *Lose him*—such a strange thought. I had never even realized I *had* him until he was about to be taken from me.

I cast my eyes around, looking for help. Not for me. For him.

Wait, where is the Gnome? There. On the ground, ten yards from my tree, he was stuck to an extremely irate Rays. *How in the hell?* At least Rays seemed okay. I didn't think I could have handled her being hurt as well.

I spotted Beau on top of the hill near the center of the clearing, taking out the rest of Phelony's drones. The size of the beam extending from him indicated that he had somehow gotten Phelony's gun.

Jessie? There in the trees, Jessie was standing over Kathleen protectively as the Witch worked a spell with trembling hands. Kathleen's pale skin glistened as the flames grew around them.

Beau dashed to help Bella, who was surrounded by what appeared to be tiny silver flies buzzing around her head. Everything was happening so fast. How long had Bella been dealing with those insect-bots?

A hissing roar made my eyes fly back to Rays, still stuck to Phelony. I struggled harder than before against my foam bonds. The brief respite had done a bit to restore some of my endurance. The space around my right hip loosened. I must have had a few more scales there, but was it enough? Everyone needed my help, and I couldn't give it. Frustration brewed in my gut.

I fought the urge to call out to my sister as she grappled with Phelony on the ground. I was stuck here, and there was nothing I could do to help her. I did not have a clear view of what was happening, but I knew she was in a dangerous position. If I called out to her, if I distracted her at the wrong time, I could get her killed.

I looked back to where I had last seen Beau. He was pretty far away. Would he be able to hear me if I called to him? I needed to get someone's attention to go help Rays. Luckily, it looked like all the drones were down, including the little silver fly-sized things that had been harassing Bella.

My throat was dry, congruent with the feeling that I had been on this tree for the past ten years, and I found myself unable to yell.

"Help Rays!" I tried to cry, though it predictably and most disappointedly, came out in a horse croak. The hope that Beau would hear me died instantly as my sister's name left my lips. And yet, to my intense surprise, I got someone's attention.

Bella jerked her head in my direction, making eye contact. Her reaction was the same as if I had yelled at her across the kitchen at Clair's. *Oh, she's never met Rays. She's never even heard me speak of her.* I tried to gesture with the small amount of head movement available to me, with little success. However, I saw Beau step up beside her and point in Rays' direction, who was still tangled with Phelony and growling wildly.

Bella got that annoyed stance she took when a customer was acting up, grabbed his arm as if to tug him behind her. They both *blurred*, moving too fast for my eyes to track. Then they came to a stop beside Rays and Phelony. *What in the hell...?*

I felt my phone buzz in my pocket. Well, I couldn't get it now. I hoped Kathleen was working on that unsticking spell because I needed to get off this tree. What would happen if this tree caught on fire, too? Would the foam burn away? Would it burn away before I did? Ironically, it would not have been a human who would have ended my life in a blaze.

Bella reached down and pulled a panting Phelony up by his shirt, sans metal suit. He must have already been trying to escape his armor and Rays would have been fighting to hold him. Bella lifted the Gnome to eye level and snarled in his ear, "You again, little man. Why do you smell so delicious?"

But my attention was once again ripped away as a new sound from Jeremy drew me back to him. A buzz sounded from his jeans pocket.

With my right leg, I stretched toward him, trying to nudge him with the toe of my boot. I could still hear him breathing, at least. But he lay just out of nudging distance. I let my body sag completely against the foam. I might as well use it to my advantage and stretch the remaining few inches to Jeremy.

My booted toe just barely made contact when I suddenly, and painfully, found myself on the ground. My breath was forcefully pushed from my lungs, lips unable to snatch any of it back, and a stinging sensation crept up my backside. My left ankle throbbed. Had I fallen?

I never fall! I am a Lynx, a mighty Mau! I can't fall!

Hot blood pooled beneath my cheeks at the indignation of being molested by gravity. *And what the hell is wrong with my ankle? Is this what happens to everyone when they fall?* I heard a snicker and jerked my head up to see Jessie pulling Kathleen to her feet. The two of them sprinted in our direction. I was sure the snicker had come from Jessie when I had fallen, but the amusement was brief, and now her expression was back to determined and worried for her friends.

Now free of the foam and able to move, I crawled closer to Jeremy to roll him over. This close, I did not have to feel for a pulse. I could hear it, a faint throbbing of his heart. His big heart, full of untapped love and self-sacrifice.

My breath escaped my lungs once again in a hiss when I saw the singed wound under his ribs. The wound seemed shallow. It obviously needed a good cleaning and some stitches, and hopefully that was it. I was just relieved it wasn't worse.

I let my eyes flick to Rays. Beau had pulled Rays free, and

now that he was closer, I saw several holes in his once-red beanie, blackened as if it had been on fire at some point.

Jessie and Kathleen arrived, panting at my side, Kathleen clutching a stitch in her ribs. "If you don't know how to help Jeremy, then go secure the Gnome," I said decisively.

Kathleen looked down and frowned. "I'm sorry."

Jessie gave me a look that seemed to say, *He's going to be fine. Why are you so worried? Also, I saw you fall on your ass, and it was the best thing I have ever seen. Ha. Ha.*

I sighed. "Can you check on my sister, please?" I asked her with an equal look meaning, *I don't want to talk about it. Ever.* Having a lifelong best friend was perfectly, conveniently annoying sometimes.

They ran off, and I turned my attention back to Jeremy. His breathing and pulse seemed to be stable, but he was getting paler because of the consistent blood loss. I pulled off my spent armor, freeing my t-shirt and my cargo jeans. In my pockets, I carried my small pocket knife and my phone, which vibrated again.

Ignoring the phone, I unfolded the knife to slice strips from my shirt. I tried my best not to jostle him while I attempted to bandage his wound. After that was done, I leaned over his head and lightly brushed strands of hair off his forehead. He felt clammy under my fingers. *Probably not a good sign.* "Jeremy? Jeremy, please wake up. I'm sorry I was so mean to you. Jeremy, please. You can't die on me now. I've gone nose blind. You hear me? I can't smell you anymore." I knew I was babbling.

Jeremy's eyes fluttered open, and relief flooded through me. "Are you alright?" he asked me.

I laughed. "Of course, I'm okay, dodo. You're the one who got shot."

He had taken a blast meant for me, and his first thought was if *I* was safe? That was just... I leaned over and locked my lips on his.

He responded immediately, overzealously trying to return the kiss. I pulled back quickly, smirking.

Jeremy attempted to sit up but let out a groan and sank back to the ground. "That got me good."

"It's not nearly as bad as I expected, honestly."

"Still, I think I'll just lie here in your arms for a while." His phone started buzzing.

I reached into his pants, and Jeremy's eyes widened in startlement. Pulling out his cell, I recognized Jo's number. I noted that he didn't even have it saved as a contact.

As soon as I answered, Jo began an onslaught of verbal abuse in various languages. I could only assume she was saying bad words. The girl cussed like a sailor, only in languages you can't understand. "I've been calling everyone for the past twenty minutes and NO ONE HAS BOTHERED TO ANSWER THEIR PHONE!"

"WE'RE A LITTLE FUCKING BUSY. WHAT DO YOU WANT?!" I yelled back as Bella spiked Phelony into the air like a volleyball. But Jo was yelling at me again, so I refocused on her voice.

"... to destroy the entire realm. Do you understand what I am saying?"

"Wait. What?"

"I finished the last report. We can't let him go back. He is going to destroy Earth." She quickly informed me of the contents of the last entry on his tablet. Yeah, this was bad.

Time seemed to slow again. I felt just as helpless as I had while stuck against the tree. I saw Phelony hit the ground. Saw his broken and bleeding lips turn upwards into a half grin. Saw him scramble to his feet, hands clutching Beau's bandolier. Saw his dumb-looking boots as he took a *single* step.

Then I saw him no more.

He vanished into the trees, moving so far in a single step that not even Bella, with her obvious super speed, could keep up. The phone slipped from my hand. When had I climbed to my feet?

With a thunk followed by a grunt, the phone dropped onto Jeremy's chest. "Shit, I'm sorry," I gusted out. "Can you stand?" I shoved his phone into one of my pockets then helped Jeremy into a sitting position. Beau arrived to take his other side, and we worked together to haul him to his feet.

"This isn't nearly as bad as I had imagined… as I thought it would be," Beau said, looking down at the hastily bandaged wound with an expression equal part shocked and relieved.

The group gathered near the cave entrance, exalting after what they saw as a stunning defeat of Phelony. I set Jeremy down against the wall inside the cave and cleared my throat. I relayed the dire warning Jo had given to me. Stunned silence followed. Jeremy groaned, and Jessie, Bella, Kathleen, and Beau all forgot what they were doing and dropped their arms to their sides, eyes gone dull and fixed into the middle distance.

Finally, it was Beau who spoke first. "We n… We need to follow him. Where would he go?" Beau asked no one in particular.

I knew where he would go. I just wasn't sure I was ready to follow him there.

CHAPTER THIRTY

PORTALS

BEAU

I ran through the forest. The stakes were so much higher than I ever could have imagined. Before, I had just been curious about what I was. How had it led me to trying to save the world? *And how is Jeremy not a singed corpse?*

Meep, Bella, Kathleen, and Jessie ran alongside me. Well, in front of me, actually. Meep looked exhausted, and she limped a little, but she was still running ahead of me.

Did I have a plan? Not at all.

How was the Auditor going to return to his realm? I wasn't entirely sure what a realm even was. An alternate dimension?

Another planet? Was he going to crawl into a mirror? All we could do was find him and try to take it from there. And that was my least favorite type of plan.

Unfortunately, all the determination in the world couldn't push me past my limits, and I collapsed to my knees. I tried desperately to breathe life into my burning lungs and numb muscles. The fate of the world was at stake, and my lack of exercise would spell our doom.

Bella stopped running and came back to me, crouching. "Get on," she said in a lifeless tone.

"What?"

"I'm giving you a piggyback ride. So shut up and get on."

I did as she demanded, and then we were off, still easily keeping pace with the others. Bella was amazing and showed impressive strength and endurance.

Meep eyed me sideways.

"Shut up. Not everyone is a star athlete," I grumbled at her.

We continued running, and I took stock of our assets. I had Phelony's gun, and the ones I had made were now all out of charges. Phelony had taken the reloads with him, so his gun was now our only working weapon. Meep's armor was spent, and she had discarded the greaves and forearm pieces for the sake of movement. We really didn't have much, come to think of it. Yet here we were, charging in any way with nothing more than stubborn determination. *And how is Jeremy not. A. Singed. Corpse?*

"So, what are you?" I asked into Bella's ear.

"Jessie said there would be no questions if I helped."

"Alright, forget I asked." My curiosity was burning, but if that was the price for her help, I'd have to respect it.

We left the forest and spotted the buildings beneath, as Meep had said. The skylight of the warehouse at the edge was illuminated from within, and we jogged down the incline to the wide warehouse doors. Bella placed me down like a child, and told us to get into position.

Meep and Kathleen stood on the right side of the door, with Jessie, Bella, and I grouped together in the middle. Bella flung the large doors open, and I had a quick glimpse of an irritated Gnomiest Gnome before a clatter above me caused me to involuntarily duck. In my periphery, I saw Meep shove Kathleen into the building as bars snapped down in front of us.

Bella grabbed them with her hands, but she flinched and made a vexed sound as she contacted the metal. She reacted like they had burned her, but I couldn't see any physical reaction on her pale skin. Phelony turned from his workbench where he had been prying Aether crystals from my bandolier. "Can't you people just let me do my damned job?"

He had no armor. I could stop him now, bars or no bars.

"Not when your job means our extinction." I aimed his gun at him through the bars and squeezed the trigger.

Phelony looked wholly unimpressed. "Did you really think it would be that easy?" He casually picked up some of the Aether crystals and strode to one of his machines on a central dais. He started pulling open doors and inserting the crystals. "I should thank you. When I didn't find any Aether crystals myself, I was worried I'd have to disassemble my inventions to scavenge enough crystals to get home."

I tried to fire again. Absolutely nothing happened when I pulled the trigger. I looked over its settings, confused.

Phelony sneered. "I will admit you are clever, false-Kin. Do you think I would allow one of my *own* guns to fire at *me*?"

Phelony inserted more crystals into the machine, and I searched for a way past these bars. They extended from floor to ceiling with no way of jumping over them or crawling beneath them. "Stay here," Bella hissed at us, and then she turned around and walked away. Was she going to find another way in? That seemed more productive than staring at these bars.

I started to turn away when a voice in the corner caught my attention.

Samantha.

Trapped in a cage like an animal, she looked unharmed. Not even one strand of her perfect curls seemed out of place. *Beau, focus*, I admonished myself. Think about what *she* would want. She would want to be out of that cage. She would want the world to not be destroyed... probably.

How could I get to her? I examined the bars that met the floor closely. Bella did not want to touch these. Were they a trap for her? I thought back to the other traps that had been deployed against her. The little fly-sized drones earlier had been silver. I didn't know what was in that spray, but I could bet it was also silver. Was she a Werewolf? I bet these bars were silver. The past week's activities flooded my mind. Silver. Of course. *Silver* interacted with Aether. Was that a clue to solving the Bella riddle? Was she somehow made of Aether, and the silver disrupted that?

In the corner of my eye, I saw Meep reach Phelony as he placed his last crystal in a drawer. She decked him square in the face. I paused my internal ramblings to admire the sound of her fist crunching into his nose before I shot another furtive glance at Samantha, who cheered, "Woo, hit 'im again!"

I filed thoughts of Bella away for another time. I needed to get to the other side of these bars to get Samantha.

No. To save the world.

Maybe I could melt a hole through the bars with this gun. Phelony's gun, unlike the alteration in my versions, had the option to blast a wide beam of heat into the bars that might make a me-sized hole. However, I didn't want to risk any unabsorbed heat rays to shoot between the bars and hit an ally in the room. I thought better of it and turned the beam size down.

It took a longer time for the smaller beams to melt a hole into the bars that was large enough to squeeze through, but I eventually got it. Jessie, Kathleen, and I hurried through the gap, and I glanced to my side again to see Meep actually fist fighting with Phelony. Though her height and agility definitely gave her a distinct advantage over him, she didn't look like a skilled boxer. Thankfully, neither did he. Her wild and reckless swings kept him busy and unable to move to his other gadgets, and I watched as he took another blow to his temple. Undisciplined or not, that had to have hurt.

Kathleen moved away, heading into the maze of shelving. "I need to find a safe place to cast spells. Keep him distracted."

Jessie was already trying to get Samantha out, so I joined her. Meep already had the distraction thing covered. I didn't know how to fight. I would only get in Meep's way. I still didn't have a plan, but one thing at a time. He was distracted now, so I decided to get the hostages free. But there was only one cage here. Where was Kyle?

An alarm bell rang through the warehouse, and glass shattered overhead. I looked up, cursing myself the next second as I looked back down. Curiosity, broken glass, and gravity were not an awesome mix. In my peripheral vision, Meep jumped out of the way as a body landed next to her.

Bella brushed herself off and straightened, an imposing figure among the pile of glass shards.

Bella snarled and lunged at Phelony. And Meep gave her own growl and jumped in to help. If he wasn't trying to destroy the world, I might feel bad for him. How pissed off does someone need to be to bust through a skylight just to get the chance to fight someone who was half their size?

I saw a keypad lock on the door to Samantha's cage. I didn't suppose Phelony would stop to give me the code, so I gestured to Samantha to stand as far into the other corner as she could squeeze herself into. Then I melted the lock with a heat ray blast.

A crash had us all ducking as Phelony flew into a nearby shelf, knocking over cans and boxes filled with unknown contents. Bella was strong, but she needed to learn that throwing people around like dolls only gave them the space and time to do something we didn't want them to do.

Phelony rose into the air, dangling from a hoverboard, then reached into his pocket to withdraw a remote. He activated it with a push of his thumb.

The dais in the center of the room hummed, and several pinpricks of light, like stars, appeared and expanded towards the middle.

Samantha yanked on my arm. "We need to go."

I shook her off, transfixed. The light, like a paint blotch now, shimmered like a fire opal, iridescent blues and greens swirling together in a gentle embrace. Samantha's tugging at my arm slacked, as she was also staring at the display in the center of the room. We all were. We were mesmerized completely.

Phelony managed to remount his hoverboard and rode it towards the... portal? Was that a portal? I'd expected it to be more of a solid color, either orange or blue. It was the size of an average-sized person, about five and a half feet tall and about four feet wide.

This new piece of information clicked into place in my brain, and I started trying to connect it to any science I knew on the matter. Hypotheses about many worlds, the multiverse, and extra dimensions ran through my head. None of them were helpful.

How could I shut down an interdimensional portal? I had seen him put in those crystals. Could I take them back out? Could I just shoot the device? But what if the portal stayed open without the crystals, and we needed the device to close it again? Maybe this was like a rip in spacetime, and the portal device stabilized it. Was it possible that destroying it would let it spread, unraveling all of reality? Okay, probably not that, but... I couldn't be sure. Too many unknowns to risk random destruction as the answer.

While I stood there contemplating the metaphysical implications of a literal portal, Bella, Jessie, and Meep rushed forward to guard it like goalies in a sports-ball game. They forced Phelony to retreat and circle overhead.

That just left me to close the damn thing. I was the obvious choice to do it. Too bad I didn't have a clue how. I talked Samantha into taking cover behind some crates as I continued to contemplate the device on the dais. This had to be more Aether tech. I needed to talk to Kathleen. She was the only one with any idea how Aether worked. I needed her expertise. Where had she run off to?

As I thought about her, she reappeared out of the maze of shelves across the room, farthest from the door. Meep, Jessie, and Bella were still warding off Phelony, as he tried to circle around and feint to the left. All the while, Kathleen was walking slowly towards the iridescent opening, seeming oddly detached from the fighting around her.

And from that moment on, everything happened so fast it took me days to piece it all together.

A group of large boxes flew off the top of one of the nearby shelving units, crashing down right where Kathleen stood. She tried to jump out of the way, but one of the boxes hit the floor behind her and exploded. The concussive blast hit Kathleen's back and propelled her forward, directly into the portal. Jessie screamed and tried to grab Kathleen as she fell in, but her hands grasped thin air as she, too, fell in after her. They both disappeared with a scream that no one could hear.

Phelony froze, looking both horrified and confused as he watched the girls disappear. Meep turned to stare wide eyed, then lunged at the portal. Bella caught her and held her back as Meep repeatedly screamed Jessie's name, tears pouring down her face.

Kyle appeared then, running out from behind the shelves near where Kathleen had emerged, screaming in disbelief and pain.

Phelony seized the moment the girls were distracted and raced forward. Bella tossed Meep aside and grabbed his ankle as he went in, but she only grasped a boot, which came off in her hand. The portal snapped shut behind him much faster than it had opened, like shutting off a TV.

Click.

Gone.

All three.

Gone.

We all stood in shock. In a moment, just one moment, three people had gone through the portal, and everything that was left felt distant and unreal. The anguished screaming around me seemed far away, the words muffled and indistinct.

We'd failed.

We'd failed in a more spectacular fashion than could ever have imagined.

Meep was shaking me and screaming in my face. With an effort, I focused on what she was saying. "Open it back up! You have to open it so we can save her!" Tears stained her face, and her mousy brown hair was wild.

"Right. Yes, of course." I shook myself. Of course, we had to open it up. It was the only option we had left. We could still save Jessie and Kathleen, still stop Phelony. We just needed the portal open.

I looked at the control panel on the portal device, finding a button marked "open," in Gnomish, of course. I pressed it.

Nothing happened.

I was getting real sick of buttons not doing things.

I pulled open one of the drawers and looked inside. The Aether crystals were not glowing. they were used up.

"Kyle!" I called and had to bodily drag him over because he was too busy weeping on the floor to listen to me. "Kyle, look at me. I want to rescue Kathleen as much as you do, but I need your help. Can you recharge the Aether crystals?"

Kyle gulped in a few breaths of air and visibly concentrated. "No. The entire nexus is dry. There's no Aether left."

"You can't open it?" Meep demanded.

"No, there isn't enough power," I said weakly, understanding what Kyle was trying to say.

"What good are you, then? You are supposed to be the smart one who fixes everything! Why can't you fix this?"

I didn't answer. I didn't have one to give. She was right. I wasn't smart enough to fix this. I lacked the cleverness to put a stop to it. I hadn't even been much help during the fight. I was a confirmed failure. Now, Kathleen, Jessie, and probably the entire world would suffer for it.

CHAPTER THIRTY-ONE

AFTERMATH

MEEP

essie was gone.
   Jessie.
Was.
Gone.

No, she can't be. My mind rejected the idea. Any moment, the portal would open, and Jessie would saunter out, as confident and in control as she always was.

Any moment now.

The moment never came.

This was Beau's fault. He should have been able to open the

portal. What good was he if he couldn't?

This was Bella's fault. If she hadn't held me back, I could have saved her.

This was Kathleen's fault. If she hadn't fallen in, neither would Jessie.

This was my fault. If I had stopped Phelony earlier, the portal wouldn't even have opened.

I screamed and started grabbing boxes from the shelves and smashing them on the ground. I didn't know nor care what was in them. I turned towards the portal device. That's what I really wanted to smash. It had taken my best friend.

As I approached it, Beau caught my arms. "Stop. Meep, listen to me." I didn't want to listen. I wanted to smash. "I can't turn it on now, but studying it is the best chance we have of helping her."

I shook myself free from his grasp, but then I just turned and started pacing. Each step sent a spear of pain through my ankle, but I welcomed the discomfort. I deserved it. There had to be something we could do. A spell? Kathleen could... No, she couldn't. Damn it all, why did I have to be a Lynx? Being a Lynx was useless. Why would I want to be super agile when I couldn't open a magic portal?

Kyle sat on the floor with his head in his hands, and Bella sat nearby, looking exhausted. She looked even paler than she normally did, and even her makeup couldn't cover the bags under her eyes. She clambered to her feet and came over to me.

"So... sorry about your friends. Um, yeah, I'll just leave you to it." She gestured behind her vaguely, then walked towards the door. I glowered at her as she left, but I didn't know what else I had expected from her. She slipped through the opening in the bars, which caused Beau to stare for some reason.

"I'm sorry to interrupt," a voice said, "but I'd really like to go home now."

I turned to see Samantha. "Oh, you want *to go home*? You know who else wants *to go home*? Jessie. But she can't, can she? She can't go home—" I broke into tears again.

Beau came up to her. "I'm sorry. I can't do anything more right now. I'll walk you home." He guided her to the door, and they slipped out.

That just left me and Kyle. I sat down next to him.

"I'm so sorry," he said. "I didn't mean for this to happen."

"But it did. At least Kathleen managed to save you."

"Right. Yeah, she did that. I wish she hadn't. I should have stayed locked away and none of this would have happened."

"Shit," I said, leaping to my feet.

"What?"

"Jeremy. We just left him there. He needs help, and I'm not ready to lose anyone else." *Jeremy, yes.* I grasped onto that thought like a lifeline. It was something I could do. I ran to the door, and Kyle followed behind me.

Kyle was out of breath quickly. "Go on ahead I'll catch up. Don't let me slow you down."

I didn't need any more encouragement, and I took off at a run. My ankle was screaming at me now, but I could worry about it later. I pulled out my phone as I ran and dialed 911.

"911, what is your emergency?"

"My friend is hurt. He has a bad burn on his stomach, and there is a forest fire. We are in the woods near the Thornton hiking trail."

"That has already been called in, the paramedics and firefighters should be arriving shortly."

I hung up. *Who had called?* I silently thanked whomever it was and focused on getting there.

I arrived at the scene of our battle and found firefighters putting out the remnants of the blaze. A number of paramedics were next to Jeremy. And there was Jo, looking way too cheerful in her pink and blue pastels.

"Jo? What are you doing here?"

"I was already on the bus back when I called in the last report. It's so much easier to translate the reports here. I had just pulled into the bus station in town when you finally answered. When I got here, I found Rays trapped and Jeremy injured. What the hell happened?"

With all the injuries and dea... loss, I had forgotten about Rays being stuck. She had gotten herself in that position to save me. What a rotten sister I was to not even give her a thought.

I hobbled over to check on Jeremy, but he was unconscious. I didn't know if he had passed out or if they had already given him something for the pain. I was so useless. Why hadn't I called 911 sooner?

One of the paramedics noticed me limping. "Ma'am, are you okay?"

"No." My ankle felt like it was on fire. I let the medic sit me down and inspect me.

"Good news is, I think it's just a sprain, but judging by the amount of swelling, it's pretty bad. Have you been running on it?" I admitted I had, and he *tsked*. "That's a good way to permanently weaken your ankle. I'll stabilize it for now, but you should come with us to the hospital."

I nodded, "What about Jeremy? Is he going to be okay?"

"I won't lie, it doesn't look great. Looks like a third-degree burn to the belly. But he should live now that he is getting care. What caused the injury? I have never seen anything quite like it."

"You wouldn't believe me."

Kyle arrived, panting, and stopped to lean against a tree and catch his breath. He looked over at Jeremy being lifted onto a stretcher and asked. "Is he going to be okay?"

"They think so."

The paramedics finished strapping Jeremy to a board and carried him over to the hiking trail, where a quad was waiting. I sat on the back of a second quad, and we set off for the hospital.

BEAU

I walked alongside Samantha, my mouth dry. "I hope Phelony wasn't too hard on you."

"It sucked." She watched her feet as we walked, but also looked over her shoulder every fifteen seconds.

"I'm sorry you got roped into this."

The sound of crunching leaves was loud in the silence that spread between us. Samantha kept glancing over her shoulder as if she expected Phelony to pop up at any moment. It made me nervous, but I didn't say anything. I couldn't even think of any words to comfort her. And I thought I could have been her boyfriend? I was a joke. I could see that now.

"Okay, I have to ask. What the hell happened back there?" she demanded.

"I take it Phelony didn't explain anything?"

"Only that I was bait for *you*."

"Well, the short version is that he is a Gnome from another world who came here through a portal. Apparently, he intended to find crystals that store magic, but instead he realized that humanity was far more advanced and populous than he expected. So, he wanted to go home and convince Gnomes, as well as a bunch of other mythological creatures, to come and wipe us out."

She took a moment to let that sink in. "So, him getting through the portal was bad."

"Disastrous," I confirmed.

"Well, that's something else to keep me up at night."

"You believe me? Just like that?"

She shrugged. "After everything I just saw? Sure, why not. I don't have a better explanation."

We rounded a curve in the road, and the town came into view. At one time, I would have thought it looked peaceful, nestled in amongst the trees. Now it just looked vulnerable, unprotected, and unaware. I had utterly failed to stop Phelony from returning. Was he giving his final recommendations to his people right now?

"So," Samantha said slowly. "I feel like I'm supposed to reward you for saving me. I suppose we could go on that date."

My heart leapt. She wanted to go on a date with me! Finally! But Kathleen's words still stuck in my mind. "*Their wants, needs, and wellbeing should be a key factor in what you decide to do.*" What did she want?

I looked at her again. She didn't seem like someone excited at the prospect of going out with me. She didn't even seem to be happy about being on this walk with me. I didn't want her to *reluctantly* go out with me because she felt some kind of obligation.

"No, that's okay. We don't need to do anything like that."

Samantha let out a sigh of relief. "Oh, thank God."

Ouch. I grimaced.

"Sorry, I didn't mean to say it like that. It's just... you really aren't my type. I prefer my men to be big and strong."

"Like Chud."

"Too bad he turned out to be a pervert. Ponies, seriously? Who carries that with them in public?"

"Um, about that. It's quite possible—probable even—that... he was framed," I admitted.

"What?"

"*Someone* may have planted that on him and arranged to have it exposed."

"Oh no."

"Yeah. So, maybe he's worth a second chance." I'd messed up her life enough, I didn't need to sabotage her romantic prospects, too.

"Thank you for telling me. I wouldn't have thought…"

We finally arrived at her sorority house, and we said awkward goodbyes. As I walked away, my phone rang. "Hello?"

"It's Jo. You should come to St. Christine's Hospital. They just took Jeremy back for surgery."

"Jo, what are you doing here? Never mind, you can explain later. I'm on my way. Is he going to be alright?"

"They seem to think so."

By the time I had walked across town at a sloth's pace, Jeremy was out of surgery. I arrived in his room and collapsed into a chair, exhausted. "How is he doing?"

"He'll be fine. Some scarring, but he'll live. They said there was no damage to his internal organs, and it didn't penetrate his belly fat," Jo reported. *How was Jeremy not a singed corpse?*

Meep sat by the head of Jeremy's bed, running her hands through his hair. She had a pair of crutches, and her ankle was in a big blue boot. Kyle sat in a chair next to mine, looking glum.

"Why are you here, Jo? I thought we sent you back home," Beau said.

"It was too hard to translate it there. The nexus made a huge difference. Sounds like I wasn't fast enough."

"Doesn't really matter now, does it? We didn't stop him from going back," I said.

"No, Beau. There is more. I didn't have time to give you the full report."

AUDIT REPORT 5.7

CYCLE: 1000 years

NAME: Auditor Phelony Adalbert Jaroba Opunkele IV

OBSERVATIONS: I regret to bring this dark news to the family, yet I must.

Based on the last report, you now know of this auditor's investigation into the false-Kin plaguing this realm. The kin detector mentioned in the previous report was completed and scans taken. The results are far beyond this auditor's original suspicion.

No natural humans were found in this realm called earth.

Read the above line a second, third, and fourth time. Let the horror fill your head, as it does mine.

Every single being in this realm is a false-Kin of one kind or another. They are grotesque. A bastardization of everything which makes us grand. A living caricature to mock us.

Reference all my previous reports and you will see their warfaring nature and capabilities, their explosion in population and technology, their complete ignorance of the kin, and their sickening way of transmitting knowledge to others with no sense of family, honor, or preservation. It is disgusting and disturbing.

THIS REALM, EARTH, IS POISED TO BE AN EXISTENTIAL THREAT TO ALL KIN, SIMILAR TO THE TAI'TAN. THIS REALM WAS ONCE VALUABLE TO US DUE TO ITS ABUNDANCE OF AETHER CRYSTALS, WHICH NO LONGER SEEM TO BE PRESENT. THEREFORE, THIS REALM HOLDS NO FURTHER INTEREST TO THE KIN.

YET, WE MUST DEAL WITH THIS THREAT IMMEDIATELY. THEIR RATE OF ADVANCEMENT CANNOT BE OVERSTATED, AND IT WILL ONLY CONTINUE TO INCREASE OVER TIME. WE DO NOT HAVE THE LUXURY TO DEBATE THIS FOR DECADES. THESE PEOPLE LIVE TOO FAST.

BASED ON THIS FINAL PIECE OF EVIDENCE, THE RECOMMENDATIONS ARE AS FOLLOWS:

WE CAN AVOID CONFLICT AND HOPE THEY DO NOT DISCOVER US ON THEIR OWN. HOWEVER, THIS OPTION COMES WITH MANY RISKS. MUST I REMIND YOU OF THE PREVIOUS REALMS AND ENTIRE SPECIES LOST DUE TO OUR OWN ALOOFNESS? THIS SHOULD NOT BE ALLOWED TO HAPPEN AGAIN.

WE CAN FOREVER ELIMINATE THE THREAT THEY POSE BY WIPING THEM TO EXTINCTION. THIS OPTION DOES COME WITH SOME RISK DUE TO THEIR CURRENT WARFARE CAPABILITIES. HOWEVER, RISKS COULD BE MITIGATED BY SWIFT ACTION.

WE CAN BRING THEM TO A MANAGEABLE POPULATION. THEY CALL THIS PROCESS "CULLING", WHILE UNDERMINING THEIR TECHNOLOGICAL PROGRESS AND WORKING WITHIN THEIR EXISTING STRUCTURES TO SPREAD FALSE INFORMATION TO MISLEAD THEM. WE CAN THEN MONITOR THEM FOR FURTHER ADVANCEMENTS. THIS POSES INCREASED RISK OF REBELLION

OVER TIME, AS WELL AS THE NEED FOR CONSTANT OBSERVATION BY KIN, PREFERABLY GNOMES. CLEARLY, A 1000 YEAR AUDIT PERIOD MAY SEEM REASONABLE TO US, YET FOR THEM, TEN YEARS MAY BE TOO LONG. KIN SHOULD BE STATIONED HERE FULL TIME, WHICH MAY NOT BE SUSTAINABLE DUE TO THE LACK OF AETHER CRYSTALS.

THE FAMILY COULD CONVENE WITH THE AETHEL TO REQUEST AID TO RESET THIS REALM IN ITS ENTIRETY, WITH THE ADDED BONUS THAT THE AETHER CRYSTALS MAY BE RETURNED. HOWEVER, THIS AUDITOR IS NOT CERTAIN THAT THE RESET OF AN ENTIRE REALM IS WITHIN THEIR CAPABILITIES. NOR HOW REASONABLE IT WOULD BE THE MAKE THIS REQUEST. HOPEFULLY, THESE REPORTS WILL CONVINCE THEM OF THE SERIOUSNESS AND URGENCY FOR THIS SEEMINGLY DRASTIC ACTION. THOUGH I FEAR THEIR ARROGANCE WILL BLIND THEM TO THE THREAT.

My mind reeled. No more humans? Literally everyone was a false-Kin? That changed everything. All of the secrecy, all of the hiding and pretending had been for nothing. We could openly be ourselves. Everyone could be. This knowledge would revolutionize the world.

The Kin already feared us. That was why they wanted to destroy us. If we could stand together, could we fight back?

We might have a chance after all.

CHAPTER THIRTY-TWO

WHAT COMES NEXT

BEAU

Days later, I stood in the center of the warehouse, looking at our failure. I kept replaying the events leading up to this, thinking about what I could have done differently. I should have taken it more seriously. Even when Meep had first shown up with the watch, I'd known that Phelony was dangerous and violent. What had I done to protect us? Run around and try to get a date? I hadn't even spared a moment of consideration for protecting us from heat rays, or for finding methods to capture him.

I knew I was being too hard on myself. I could only have acted with the information I'd had at the time, and I had been woefully uninformed.

And yet, I still felt like I hadn't done enough.

I couldn't fix those mistakes, but I could avoid repeating them.

Phelony had left behind all manner of strange machines. I was sure that hadn't been his intent, but we hadn't exactly given him time to bring anything with him. These were captured spoils, a small victory snatched from our defeat, and I could take full advantage of them. It wouldn't be feasible to move them from here, but there was already a comprehensive workshop set up. I had a few adjustments in mind, but it should do nicely.

The first thing I did was try to turn on the portal device. It did nothing, just like last time I'd tried. Popping it open, I found a number of brightly glowing Aether crystals. Huh, I had thought they would be empty, like maybe opening the portal took enough energy to drain them all. I traced the wires and tried to figure out how it worked, but with little success. I still couldn't understand these designs.

I moved on to the other machines. One seemed to spin the wire harnesses that underpinned the Aethertech. The controls were obtuse, with no feedback on what they did, so I left it for later while I continued taking stock.

The next several contraptions were more straightforward. One was basically a table saw, only instead of a spinning metal blade, it cleanly separated things with no visible mechanism. I presumed it was doing something with Aether. Another seemed like a hydraulic press, but without the hydraulics. The next was some kind of welding kit.

The final machine caught my interest the most. It was the 3D printer that made the strange material Phelony's stuff had been made of. The controls were as obtuse as the harness spinner, so all I managed to make was a few oddly shaped blobs, but it was fascinating to watch it work. Multiple heads darted around, each emitting their own stream of material and moving in three dimensions with varying angles. They wove the strands together in a way that I still thought was impossible even with the extra control.

I also had Phelony's shed armor just begging to be reverse engineered, as well as one of his boots.

This might be the biggest opportunity any engineer has ever had. Even the discoverers of electricity hadn't had examples of complex machines to learn from. With this, I actually could change the world.

There was boundless potential at my fingertips. I wasn't going to let it go to waste. I just had to figure out what I could make that would defend against attacks by the Kin. I didn't know their capabilities, and I didn't know their plans. I didn't know how long I had to complete my tasks.

All I could do was prepare.

MEEP

I took a deep breath and let it out slowly. This was ridiculous. I didn't get nervous, especially not about some boy.

But most boys hadn't been hospitalized for me.

This had been easier when all the others had been here too, and it had been a communal show of support. Today, it was just me. Well, it wasn't going to get any easier standing around. I pushed the door open and entered his hospital room.

Jeremy looked frail, his skin pallid. Various tubes ran into him—or came from him, I didn't know the difference—and a too-thin blanket covered most of his body. I couldn't help but glance down at his belly, which was hidden away underneath the blanket.

"Meep-Meep!" he said, a smile crossing his face despite every-thing. He used a remote to turn off the TV that had been playing.

"Hey there, champ." Champ? What was I, his dad? *Let's go out and toss the ol' pigskin, champ.* I didn't have a cute nickname for him. I'd never given any of my boyfriends a pet name, and apparently, my instincts for it were garbage.

I sat down in the chair next to him and squeezed his hand gently. "How are you feeling?"

"Pretty good, actually. They have me on so many pain killers—"

"I just wanted to say I'm sorry. It's my fault you ended up in here, and I should have fought better, taken him down quicker, not gotten myself stuck..."

"Hey now, none of that. You were amazing. I'm here because I chose to be."

It was a nice platitude, but he wouldn't have had to make that choice if I hadn't messed up.

"I was terrified I would lose you." Lose him like I had lost Jessie. That still didn't feel real, but every time I thought about it, I felt the world closing in around me. I should never have messed with that stupid Gnome. None of this would have happened if I had left well enough alone. And Kathleen... I'd only known her for a short time, but she hadn't deserved that either. Three people had been lost or injured, if not worse, and it was all my fault. I wanted excitement, damn it, not people getting hurt. I felt tears well up inside of me.

"Woah, I'm okay. The doctor says I'll be out of here in another week, maybe two. I'll be fine—it will just leave a scar. And scars are sexy, right?" His comforting tone shifted to a more worried one. "You do think scars are sexy, right?"

Despite everything, I had to let out a small laugh. "That one will be," I promised.

"The doctor wants me to go home to be with family while I

recover. Which is a horrible idea. My family isn't exactly the caring type, but I couldn't convince him that being alone in a dorm room with Chud would be better. But, when I get back... when I get back, I was hoping you would, I mean, you and I could..."

"Are you fumbling over asking me out? What happened to the overly confident guy who would proposition anything that moves?" I asked with a wave of my hand.

He blushed and threw me a silly, lopsided, grin. "I never thought there was a chance they'd say yes, so I didn't have anything to lose. And... I never cared so much about what their answer would be." His grin wavered as he looked at me.

"Well, the answer is yes." I wasn't entirely sure how I felt about him, still. Fondness, yes. Appreciative, sure. Preferring him alive to dead? Of course. But romantically? I didn't know. But figuring that out was the point of dating, wasn't it? I'd certainly gone out with guys I had far less interest in.

The grin on Jeremy's face was as wide as the Atlantic. "I'll make sure it's great."

EPILOGUE

JEREMY

Mom was going to come pick me up. *Bleck.* At least she wasn't bringing Dad with her. The doctors thought it would be safer to heal at home rather than alone in my dorm room, but they didn't know my family.

Of course, Meep wanted to come visit me—I was only a couple hours away from her—but that was not a great idea for multiple reasons. She had even volunteered to drive me, but I'd rather have dealt with Mom's attitude than have Meep find out how we lived.

It wasn't that I thought she would look down on me if she found out where I lived; it wasn't embarrassment over the two-bedroom trailer I shared with my parents that made me nervous. She accepted me for who I was, somehow, and I didn't want her perception to change when she met my family.

Looking back on my behavior since the day I had met her, I could see now how unsavory I had been. If it hadn't been for crazy Gnomes like Beau and Phelony, I would not have gotten my very own cat-girl. I didn't even care if she was scantily clad or not. No, that was the type of thought the old me would have had. I was trying to be better than that.

So, there I sat one drizzly cold morning in front of the hospital, waiting for my mom. The only other person in sight was the small, tired looking man in a plaid jacket sitting on a nearby bench. I guessed that he was waiting for someone, too, and the only bags he carried were the ones under his eyes. Was he a discharged patient or a visitor? Meep had inspired me to think about other people, to consider their needs and experiences. A mindset that was lacking within my family, one that I was never taught. I had learned so much in college, like how to be a normal person, and now Meep had taught me more. She was so selfless and always thought about helping others. *I want to be like that one day.*

A 1998 station wagon rattled into the parking lot. I stood and waved to Mom. At least she was kinda on time. It surprised me when the tired man also stood. I didn't see another car.

I groaned. Oh no, mom wasn't doing the rideshare thing, was she? That would be just like her, doing anything for money. What lies had she told to get *that* car approved for ridesharing? I bet she hadn't been doing it for long. Maybe this was her first fare, because as soon as anyone left a review, she would be in trouble.

Mom greeted me with a grunt and a toss of her head to the passenger seat, indicating that was where I was expected to sit. Mom's car was mostly clean, with just a few ashes and a crushed cup inside. However, she had a smile and a cheerful greeting for the tired man, apparently named Brian.

I clambered into the front seat, holding the folded-up towel in a pillowcase the nurse had given me to press against my stitches to prevent ripping. I moved the seat back to give myself more leg room. I wasn't a tall guy, but the seat was practically pressed against the dash. Mom yelled at me and called me a "stupid fool" because Brian was sitting behind me. Even though he protested that he had more than enough leg room, Mom continued to berate me until I relented and readjusted my seat. Being scrunched was agony, and I said as much, but Mom just glared at me. Poor, tired Brian offered to switch seats, but Mom told him, "No, my son can figure out how to be a man."

Yes, my family was a warm and cozy lot—a great source of comfort to aid in my recovery. Whatever.

It turned out that Brian was about my age, though he looked much older thanks to those bags under his eyes and the yellowish-gray tint to his complexion. He asked if mom had any bottles of water, but Mom grumbled about not getting enough tips "for uppity shit like that." Afterwards, Brian didn't talk much, other than to request to stop at the nearest gas station. He was probably going to cancel the ride after he was out of the car and had a safe place to hide. How was he taking the smell? Of course, I didn't smell it, but Goblins like me and my mom were notorious for our unpleasant smells. Although, I had no experience with other Goblins, not even my extended family, I presumed that the foul smell was a characteristic shared by all of us.

I sullenly watched him disappear through the doors, knowing what was coming next. Mom must have been expecting the same thing because she turned off her GPS and opened her driver's app. A moment later, she threw it into the floorboard at my feet, rounding on me. "Do you have any idea what this damn trip was costing me? Do you even *care*?"

"Yeah. Sorry I got shot, Mom."

"You didn't get shot, you fucking idiot. You burned yourself doing something stupid."

"Okay."

Mom rolled down her window and lit a cigarette, and the rest of the ride passed in blissful silence as she smoked and fumed. She was building up steam, saving it for later when she and Dad could tag team me together. They were probably going to try to talk me out of college again.

We drove through the few small towns on the outskirts of Hemmons that made Hemmons itself seem like a metropolitan location in comparison, then we crossed the state line into Washington. I pushed my seat back again, seeking relief from the uncomfortable pressure of my bulk against my stitches. I silently dared her to say some shit about it. She gritted her teeth and lit another cigarette instead.

We finally rattled up the short driveway in front of my parent's trailer. It was tidy, with a mowed lawn in an exact six-foot rectangle around the double wide. Mom had several potted plants on the big porch that were painted to look like a giant American flag. The plants were dying, but the white-washed ceramic pots looked nice.

The inside, however, was not tidy. Coming from the sterile environment of the hospital was the only reason the mess stood out to me. Food crumbs, crushed beer and soda cans, and dirty clothes littered every section of the floor. Dad sat on the sagging and torn brown leather sofa watching some daytime news show when we came in. He hissed at us to shut the door in full feral cave Goblin mode. I slowly shuffled inside—it was still painful to move quickly, and I had to climb a few stairs to get up here.

Ignoring him, I limped my way down the hall to the bathroom. I heard him loudly ask how much my mom had made from the rideshare program, but I didn't hear the response as I pushed the door closed.

Facing the grimy mirror, I pulled up my shirt to examine my wound. I removed the gauze, which was only held in place by a small piece of tape and a lot of sticky white antibiotic ointment. I had more ointment and a bottle of big green and blue antibiotics in my pocket. The wound was pink, not red, and not inflamed anymore, although it sure did *feel* as if it were full of flames. I dabbed on more ointment and replaced the gauze. The hospital had given me more but... that still counted as clean, right?

I smiled. Meep had bullied several nurses to help me get these from the pharmacy *before* they had discharged me.

Thinking of her, I pulled my phone out of my other pocket and sent her a text, letting her know I got here safely. *At least physically, if not mentally.*

I looked around, frowning at the thick brown stain I thought was rust around the toilet bowl. I had never thought there was a problem with the way I had lived growing up. As a kid, we had never visited extended family, had never gone to visit friends. Beau was the first real friend I'd ever had, and he was about as messy as I was, anyway. And Chud wasn't exactly attentive to messes, either. I thought this was how everyone lived.

That was until I had walked into Meep's house. It had lots of soft, cozy things, and clean carpet, and it smelled... like her, like warm citrus and cardamom. My very own cat-girl. *I am so fucking lucky.*

Mom made meatloaf and scalloped potatoes for dinner, and if I could have eaten in my room, I would have, but there was nowhere for me to sit and balance my food as I ate. Begrudgingly, I ate with my folks. As I'd suspected, I had just sat down when my dad, an overweight man with thick black hair, started on me. "You cost us a pretty penny. Are you going to pay us back for this?"

"Yeah, sure."

"You told us this college thing wasn't going to cost us anything," Mom said.

"*College* didn't cost you anything. I got shot."

"You keep saying that, but the doctors told us it was a burn. So, what really happened?" Mom asked.

I told them the entire story of the Auditor, the watch, the laser gun, the forest fire, Meep, Beau, Kathleen, Jessie, everyone. I held nothing back. When I was finished, they sat in stunned disbelief. And for a moment, I imagined my parents believed me. And then they started laughing.

Mom got up and got a cold beer for Dad as he drained the last drop out of the can he was currently holding. He crushed the can and tossed it at the trash. He always missed, so I didn't even know why he bothered. And as if on cue, the can bounced off the rim of the can and skittered into the living room. "Ah, so close that time." He sighed deeply and returned his blood-shot eyes to mine. "Aren't you going for some fancy engineering degree or something?"

I blanched. "Yes, civil engineering." I wanted to ask if they believed me, but of course they didn't. I was so frustrated. "You know, Dad, most kids at college have families who celebrate them for being there. There are special honors for being the first in your family that goes. So, what is your problem?"

Mom sat back in her seat and cracked the cold beer for Dad, pushing it towards him. "He got fired again yesterday. What is that, Jon, five jobs in the past six weeks?"

Dad grunted, "Eight."

"Eight jobs. In the past month and a half. And that's pretty average. So, if that is what you have to look forward to, and you damn well know it is, then don't waste your time and the government's money. Don't bother hoping that some fancy piece of paper is going to make people like you more," she said.

"And clearly, you're fucking losing it. You better come off those drugs 'cuz we can't afford therapy and shit," Dad added.

"And you think you have a girlfriend? Doubtful. What was her name?" Mom added again.

"It's Meep," I said gloomily.

"Meep?" Mom cackled.

"That's a fake name, moron."

I pushed out my chair, leaving my dinner mostly untouched. I was supposed to eat with my antibiotics, but I hoped it was not a necessity. I didn't think I would get a lot of food in this house. I limped back to my room and collapsed onto my mattress, thankful that my furniture was at least still here, and they hadn't sold it.

I tried to push their words out of my mind, but they lingered like a haunting echo, ricocheting in my head like a never-ending game of pinball. Dad could never keep a job long. I think he really tried, too. But it was always his hygiene that got him in the end. His coworkers thought he was homeless. Sometimes they even gave him money for a hotel room, which he kept, because of course he did, or else they offered their showers to him to use occasionally. But like me, it didn't matter how often Dad showered, and eventually, those coworkers complained that he wasn't trying. Sometimes they accused him of stealing, which may or may not have actually been true. He gave people living with homelessness a bad name, and half of it wasn't even on purpose.

Those were the people who had raised me. The people who had taught me that nothing I did mattered and nothing I said mattered. They were the ones who had taught me to say what I wanted when I wanted. Meeting Beau had really started to change that. Sure, he wasn't the suavest guy, but he didn't act like *that*.

I gingerly made my way to the bathroom again and took off my gauze to clean my wound and change my dressing like the nurses had shown me. Unfortunately, I stumbled on the uneven plastic tiles that were starting to come up around the edges of the counter and caught myself with my hand before I fell. My bottle of antibiotics clattered to the floor, and the sterile pads I had gotten from the hospital landed directly in the toilet bowl.

I ground my teeth and went back into the living room where I found Dad sitting on the couch watching the nightly news while mom smoked a cigarette at the table. "Can one of you take me to the pharmacy? I need new pads."

Dad scoffed. "What? Turn into a girl at that damn school of yours?"

Mom smiled menacingly as she flicked ashes into her overflowing coffee tin she used as an ashtray. "Just wad up some paper towels, that's what I do sometimes."

"Not too many," Dad yelled. "Those fucking things are expensive!"

"They are gauze pads, and the nurses said I need them to keep my wound clean." After neither of them deigned to respond, I accepted my fate and stalked off as best I could back to my room. I would just do the best I could with what I had.

I had to wait two weeks, apparently, for the doctors to see me again for a follow up and hopefully release me to go back to school. Two weeks of miserable company. I passed the time watching anime and texting Meep and Beau—mostly Meep.

I told her I was okay, and everything was fine. I didn't want her to worry. She had enough to worry about. She said she was sick of pretending to be normal when she knew no one was. And she was finding it harder and harder to care about things like school and work. I wished I was there for her. She needed someone. *Needed me? Nobody ever needed me before.*

Every time I ventured out to get food, or God forbid, tried to socialize with my parents, they only berated me for this or that. For going to college, ironically telling me I would never amount to anything that way. Wasn't it the other way around for normal people?

Meep thought that no one was normal. And maybe she had a point. We were all some type of false-Kin, right? There had to be more Goblins out there, then. Probably suffering the same as my parents. What if there was a Goblin-run business that maybe didn't care if the employees smelled bad? Maybe I could help more than just Goblins. There were people living without homes who couldn't take the showers that we took for granted. I could help them, too. That sounded useful. Meep would be proud of me, right?

I'd be doing this for more than just her. I thought about my parents, about my dad watching the news and being grumpy. I thought about my mom clipping coupons and trolling Craigslist for gigs. My brother, in prison, had been convicted of fraud in three states. I could help them. I could help them all. I could be useful.

As more time passed, and food became harder and harder for me to stomach, let alone obtain, my side burned hotter and hotter. The skin looked pink and puffy. And my clothes became a bit more baggy on me than I was used to. I finally told Meep the truth.

WHAT?!?

She texted back. I didn't know how to respond, so I didn't say anything.

HELLO?!?

Demanding. Was my cat-girl mad at me?

I'm fine, Meep. I found some ibuprofen, and I have my antibiotics. I'll be okay. It just might take me longer to come back.

Can I come pick you up? Bring you stuff? You
let me know the minute I can do anything.

She wasn't mad.

She was worried.

About me.

She was worried about *me*. She had accepted me, and that
thought alone was enough to bring tears to my eyes. The tears I
never shed about anything else. Her acceptance made me cry.

The next morning, Dad burst into my room and woke me up.
"Come on. If you're living here, you need to pull your weight. Get
up."

With bleary eyes, I looked at the clock. 4 am.

"Someone's got to throw these papers. Come on."

I tried to get up, but my head swam, and I collapsed back onto
the bed.

"What's the matter with you? You're pale as a sheet."

I shook my head slowly. I knew he wasn't going to accept me
saying that I thought I needed to go to the hospital. "I need some
water," I croaked. My voice sounded hoarse and scratchy, even to
my own ears.

Blessedly, he did return with a glass of water for me, and as my
clammy hands closed around the glass and brushed his, he stiffened. "Carol!"

My mom shouted back down the hall, "What, Jon?"

"Drop the attitude, bitch. Come here." She entered the room,
mouth pressed into a straight, thin line. "Does he have a fever?"

Mom came close and pressed her icy fingers to my forehead,
and I flinched away. "I suppose so. Guess he should probably stay
here and rest. He can go throw papers with you tomorrow."

They were about to leave when I croaked out, "I need to go to
the hospital." As I suspected, they glanced at each other and left

the room, ignoring me.

My head swam. I felt simultaneously drunk and ill, like I had a hangover. Like the time I had let Chud talk me into chugging an entire six-pack of beer the night before my calculus final. I reached for my phone but only succeeded in knocking it to the floor. I reached to pick it up, leaning over the side of the bed...

Then I woke up on the floor. My sheets were plastered to me with sweat. My phone was a hard lump under my arm. I pulled it in front of me and had a hard time making out the letters. Giving up on crafting a text... I called her.

To her credit she answered so fast. "Jeremy? What's wrong? Are you okay?"

"I need to... hospital..."

She didn't argue. Didn't ask if I was sure. Didn't remind me how much it would cost. "Give me your address." I did and then she said, "That will take me two hours and nine minutes to get to you. You need to call 911."

"No." The high price of an ambulance swam through the fog.

She sighed. "Well, then, I'm on my way."

One hour and forty-five minutes later, she arrived with a vengeance.

I seemed to be fuzzing in and out of consciousness, so my memories played like a flickering bulb. One minute I heard Meep yelling at my mom outside, and the next, she was tugging me into a sitting position. "Jeremy?"

"Meep-Meep," I slurred.

She gave me the smallest, cutest little smile as she said, "I hate that name."

"Meep?" my mom's voice said from somewhere else in the room.

"You're a real live human being?" my dad asked from somewhere else.

"That's a matter of some debate right now. Now, are you going to help me carry him or not?"

"He's fine," my dad said. "Just needs a little rest and some water."

"*Fine?*" Meep dropped my arms, which thudded heavily onto the bed. "Look at him. He looks mostly dead!"

"But mostly dead is a little alive," I said stupidly.

"Help me," she growled above my head.

"My cat-girl... My girlfriend..."

"Help her, Jon, he's delirious."

Meep screeched in exasperation and her mouth closed over mine. She felt cold, and I shivered. She pulled away, and I felt sad.

The next memory I had was being carried between Meep and my dad towards the gray van Meep had driven here.

"How to kidnap a Jeremy... with a cat-girl." I didn't know how much of that actually came out coherently, but that's what I tried to say.

"Shhh," Meep soothed. "I'll get you back to the hospital." Was she smiling? I loved to see her smile. I liked her teeth.

The next thing I remembered was being wheeled flat on my back under fluorescent lights. Meep was nowhere in sight, and I couldn't hear her. A nurse fit a mask over my mouth and nose, and then it went black.

THE END

About the Authors

B.D. Carpenter is a combination of two people.

B was born and raised in Dallas, TX. She spent much of her adult life living in Washington state where she got degrees in Human Services and writing. She has worked extensively as a crisis counselor and brings that experience in to writing deep and relatable characters.

D was born and raised in Michigan where he got a degree in computer science and is currently a software engineer. His love of Sci-fi/ fantasy combined with his technical knowledge and experience show in his deep world building and magical systems that also still make sense.

Together, B.D. married in 2022 and live in Texas with two dogs, two cats, and their dog's cat. Their relationship was built on their love of fantasy and books, and that continues into their writing.